SOME LOVE

Some
Love

PHILIP CALLOW

ALLISON & BUSBY

TO MY DAUGHTER FLEUR
WITH LOVE

An Allison & Busby book
Published in 1991 by
W. H. Allen & Co. PLC
26 Grand Union Centre,
338 Ladbroke Grove,
London W10 5AH.
Copyright © 1991 by Philip Callow
Phototypeset by Input Typesetting Ltd., London
Printed and bound in Great Britain by
Mackays of Chatham PLC, Chatham, Kent

ISBN 085031 947 1

The moral right of the author has been asserted

PART
ONE

1

Johnnie Hunslett sat in the classroom, his arena. He sprawled back on his seat, one leg out stiff in the gangway as if it were artificial. Over to his left was his pal and hero, Trevor Foley. Trevor had his eye on him, so Johnnie laughed across with his silent grimace. The class saw Johnnie Hunslett as a hard case. In fact he was often afraid. He was now. It didn't matter though, as long as your fear didn't show.

Mr Cook, the history teacher, young and irascible, warned the boy for the third time to stop twisting his head round. He was a young man with a scrubby red beard. Johnnie would stare at this beard and lose track of the teacher's words.

'Are you deaf, Hunslett?'

'Me, sir?'

'Yes, you. Any more cheek and you go on a visit. Right?'

'Right, sir.'

He had done it, gone to the brink for Trevor, and for his other friend, Darren Butcher, directly behind him in the back row. Now he tidied himself up with stiff warrior gestures, registering a silent protest that was half-derision. The prickly sensation on his skin warned him that he had come close. His heart pounded, as if about to burst out of his chest.

He began to copy the stuff about the colonisation of America and the Pilgrim Fathers. There was a map to draw. He liked colouring the maps in with crayons, then putting a frame round them and the caption beneath. The rest was boring. Stupid. Everybody in history was dead and therefore no longer mattered. Even Mr Cook thought so. You could hear the boredom in his voice. He just kidded you along, that was his job. He was long-haired, he wore jeans with frayed bottoms. What was history to him?

Johnnie and Trevor and Darren were a gang, in their own eyes at least. Each had his value for the other two. That was why it worked. Anybody could see that Darren Butcher was thick, but his loyalty never wavered. He was game for anything.

Trevor, with his swaggering walk and porcupine hair style, seemed entirely without fear. His father would belt him and so would his big brother. He absorbed it all and came bouncing out of the house as if nothing had happened, his pale eyes never quenched, his twisted grin forever intact. Johnnie, who had no brothers, saw himself joined in fantasy to Trevor in a blood knot, his devotion was so fierce. For him, Trevor Foley could do no wrong. Trevor was ugly like his brother. He had large squashy features and his eyes were dark. He seemed all eyes. He always wore the surprised expression of a frog run over in the road.

Trevor was the biggest, and Johnnie, small for his age, the shortest. He compensated for this by staring at his opponents with concentrated venom and at the same time bunching his fists. 'What's up wi' ya? Wanna bunch o' fives?' he'd snarl. Usually this worked. Being small was bad enough, but he was also skinny. It was a great boon of course having Trevor for a friend. What strengthened him too were the rotten times he had had during the past five years. None of the other kids had experiences to match his. Now, on the rare occasions when he found himself eyeball to eyeball with a foe, his memories fuelled him to such an extent that a boy was liable to turn and run from the vicious hatred distorting his face. It came and went in a matter of seconds.

He had a temper, as they say. Yet his mother had never seen it, nor his sisters. Once his father did. Pat Hunslett was a thin weedy man, who felt masterful only inside his own home, because one of his daughters waited on him and because his wife was always ailing. Johnnie, then eight, had come in from a nearby building site. He played over there. A pitched battle had broken out. Now he was covered in cement dust. His mother took one look at his clothes and began to wail. 'Get in the bathroom, you,' his father said.

Confused, Johnnie did as he was told. In the bathroom his father unbuckled his belt. 'Take them trousers down.'

'No.'

'What?'

Something about his son's pinched face, venomously at bay, caused him to lose his nerve and he began to bluster. He blundered forward and aimed a kick at the boy. 'Go on, out of my bleedin' sight.'

Then Johnnie did an extraordinary thing. He grabbed his father's foot in midair and hung on. His father hopped on the spot, bellowing with rage and surprise.

The boy shot out of the bathroom and out of the house. He crept in again when he knew his father would be round at the pub. His mother had gone to bed. Sue, the older sister, said, 'Dad says he's going to kill you.' She gazed solemnly at him from the kitchen where she stood washing up and clearing away like a little mother.

'If he tries, I won't be here. I'll be off.'

'Where to?'

He looked around at the shabby, littered room behind him. 'Anywhere.'

'Where though?'

She had him. There wasn't anywhere. One day there would be. He'd be off, they wouldn't see him again, not ever. 'Where's me dad's cigs?' he said, and made as if to search behind the grubby cushions and old newspapers on the sofa.

'Hey, you daft fool, he'll kill you!' Sue cried.

'Aw, I'm only kiddin',' he said. He liked to alarm her, it made him feel good. She was bothered about him, he knew that, and so, after a fashion, was Eileen. But now and then, when a sense of loneliness swirled up inside him and he felt bleak, he needed proof.

His mother cared, but she was such a worrier, so what did it mean? She was all mixed up in his mind with worry. If she worried about every mortal thing, was he just one more thing for her to worry about? He pitied her without

9

knowing it. He would stop himself from thinking about her. She was a sad ache in his life, and he could never resolve his confusion about her. Sometimes he hated the way she made him feel: directed a ray of pure hate at her. Doing that was easier. Yet, coming in, the person he most hoped to see was her.

In one sense the running war with his dad was better: he knew exactly where he was. Anyway, it never amounted to anything. His dad was rubbish, he thought. He had a recurring daydream, getting stronger as he grew older, which featured himself and his mother as stars. It glowed there, safe in his head – his secret. When he grew up, his first act as a wage-earner would be to arrive home with his week's pay packet and drop it in his mother's lap. He would watch her face. The shadows would be cleared away as if by magic. He only had to think of this radiant dream for the power and authority to run through his veins in little thrills and pulses. He supplanted his father, brushed him aside like a fly. How would his mother react? By jumping up and giving him a big hug, naturally. He couldn't ever remember getting one. She wasn't what you would call a physical woman.

2

At the time, when he had grabbed hold of his father's foot and hung on, horrifying himself, they were living in a run-down terraced house out at Frecheville. Johnnie had once heard his auntie say to Uncle Steve, on her way out, 'Did you ever see such a dog's breakfast of a place?' That was before Sue took over the cleaning and tidying.

To be a small boy in the suburbs of a huge city like Sheffield meant that you were a visitor when you went to town, just as you would be if you went to London. Johnnie had gone in on a few Saturdays and it was great, diving through subways, getting lost in the Hole in the Road, floating up the dirty escalators from the bus station and into the seething heaps of people, thousands of them. City Hall was gigantic, and so was the Town Hall. Buildings like that made him feel like a midget. 'Does a king live in theer?' he asked his dad, pointing at great fat pillars and long flights of steps.

'No, son.'

'Who does?'

'The mayor. When he's at home, like.'

'Is he at home now?'

'He could be. Making a brew. Shall we have a look?'

'No!' Johnnie cried out in a panic. His father had his foot on the bottom step as if he really meant it. He kept his face straight. Then he laughed. 'Come on, then. We'd be better off in Woolworth's, is that it?'

'Ar, we would!' his boy said, laughing now in sheer relief.

All the noise and bustle went to his head, spun him round. Nobody knew him, none of it had anything to do with him. Being so free was frightening. In the middle of W.H. Smith's one Saturday his father left him alone, promising to come back in ten minutes. 'Will tha be a good lad and wait for me?'

'Wheer you goin'?'

His dad tapped the side of his nose, then slipped away.

Johnnie mooched around, feeling vaguely criminal. He saw a pile of brightly coloured pens and felt an urge to put one in his pocket when no one was looking. Who would miss one pen? The thought made his palms sticky and he licked his lips. He was too scared to touch anything after his thought. Something might jump into his pocket. He wasn't possessed with a desire to own anything, but the very idea of coming away with some token made him part of the crowd, the overheated store, the buying and selling. Suddenly its meaning clicked and he made sense.

Getting back to Frecheville on the bus, he blinked and wondered if he had been dreaming. His own world was small and real. People nodded to him, he went to school there, lived in a poky house that was falling to bits, with identical houses on either side, some in good repair, slick and shiny with bright paint, others as neglected as theirs. Next door on the left for instance was just as scruffy, with a broken window that had been patched with cardboard.

Johnnie knew minute particulars of this world, such as the exact positions of potholes in the road and where the paving slabs had worked loose. Nearby was a tract of rough ground to play on, and in the evenings the deserted building site pulled like a magnet. Some kid would nearly always be snooping around there. Together they would climb scaffolds and heave house bricks into piles of sand which had mysteriously turned into mud. They balanced on the tops of door frames and launched off into space, howling at the sky, breaking their falls with a mattress of cement sacks.

A catastrophe struck the whole household when he was eight. In one stroke the life he knew fell to pieces. It was more terrible and fantastic than anything he could have imagined.

He had come in after school, late as usual. It was a Wednesday. As a rule he would find his mother in the kitchen. Often he tried to wheedle a piece of bread and jam out of her, or dripping, with salt on – that was favourite. 'Can I have a piece?' She would either grumble and give in or say no, wait for your tea.

This time she wasn't there. She didn't seem to be in the house at all. He bawled 'Mam?' a few times, and then was on his way out again, clambering downstairs, finishing the last three stairs in one jump. He thought he heard a sound at the back door.

It was his mother. The first sight of her horrified him, yet he had no idea why that should be. What was it? His mother was a small, subdued woman, rather pallid, with a sad expression in her large brown eyes. These were the eyes that would plead with him, and with him the whole world, to stop worrying her. When he first went off to school she stood on the front step, which they never used, and watched him go. He could feel that haunted gaze following him. He wanted to run back, young as he was, and tell her it was all right, he wasn't afraid. But he was, and his mother could see through him to his secret with that haunted look of hers.

She wasn't haunted or worried now, she was bursting with something, an elation, as if hugging some terrific secret of her own. She always kept herself neat and tidy and now her hair was wild, a hairpin falling out. It fell at his feet. He gaped at her. She smiled and smiled, not just her mouth but her whole face, as if some inner mirth had begun to overflow in her, unstoppable, taking her over. It ran out over everything and she couldn't stop it. Instead she stood there and let it happen.

'Mam, what is it, Mam?'

She leaned back against the door, not speaking. Then Johnnie noticed a truly awful thing. It was mid-November, a cold dank afternoon. His mother had no shoes or stockings on. Struck dumb, he stared at her bare feet, at her toes, at her bunions which he hadn't seen before. While he stood gaping, suddenly she spun round, like a little girl in the playground at school. She shot out of the back door again. A burning shame rooted him to the floor as he pictured his mother, who always kept to herself, scampering down the entry and into the open street in full view of everybody.

13

A friendly neighbour, a burly capable woman, brought her in after a few minutes. 'Johnnie,' she said, with his mother smiling away madly, her hand in the strange woman's hand, 'I want you to go straight round to the doctor and tell them to send somebody quick, it's an emergency. Do you hear what I'm saying? Go on then, love. Quick as you can, duck, there's a good lad.'

His mother had gone dancing down the street clapping her hands before they caught her. Johnnie couldn't bear to look. Feeling utterly abandoned, he began to cry. His mother was whispering something to him in great excitement, caught up in her terrible unnatural happiness. She waved him closer with such urgent gestures that he had to go, passing by on his errand. 'Don't, Mam,' he mumbled, blinded, not knowing what she said. Other strangers had come in, one a woman his mother particularly disliked. He recognised her hard greedy face, her sharp nose as she pressed forward avidly and called his mother Marilyn, asking if there was anything she could do. The boy bent his head to his mother. The beefy woman kept her hand on his mother's shoulders, pinning her to the kitchen chair. 'Johnnie,' Marilyn whispered to her son, 'let's go to the pictures. Shall we get a taxi?'

'Hurry up, love,' the strange woman said. 'Your mother's poorly, you see.'

'Listen to her,' the sharp beady woman crowed, sounding almost pleased. Johnnie hated her.

When he got back his sisters were in. Eileen had been crying – she was always the cry-baby. Her stained face was frightened. Sue, staring angrily at everyone, had her arm round her. Johnnie saw the ambulance drive off, and later in the street passing a knot of women by the corner shop he thought he heard his father's name mentioned.

Sue, a serious girl determined to act well and be the mother, broke the news to their father when he came home from work. He was a machinist, always smelling of something sour and sharp that he called 'suds', the cutting oil he used on his lathe. His nails were clogged with greasy dirt. Hearing the bad news his tired irritable face darkened. He jumped up from the kitchen table and

14

banged against things as if he couldn't see properly. 'Christ Almighty, not again!' he yelled, and kicked out at the table leg. The cat flew through the door as if on a spring, a streak of ginger fur. 'Not again!' he groaned, over and over. No one understood what he meant. Had their mother been ill before they were born? He sat down again to be fed, and Sue carried in his dinner. On his feet he had seemed big and frightening and out of control, arms and legs exploding. Now he seemed to wilt, to shrink, and when he spoke to Sue it was passively, almost like a child himself who was bewildered by the chaos of life and wanted to be led by the hand. 'Now what do we do?' he moaned, half to himself. 'Bleedin' Christ, why me?'

'I wish you wouldn't swear, Dad,' Sue said, prim in her new role. Already she had taken complete charge of the kitchen. She poured his tea. Watching her, Johnnie felt safe.

'Sorry,' their father muttered. Later on, reading the *Star*, he dropped off to sleep as he usually did. His mouth fell open and he started to snore.

On Saturday they travelled out to the hospital together: a sullen father, clean and shaved, in a white nylon shirt and acid green tie, his children staying close, with Sue undeniably in charge. They rode into Sheffield on one bus, then waited in a High Street shelter in cold blowing rain for another. Sue nagged at them all in a way that Johnnie liked. His father looked peculiar in a collar and tie, he thought. He wasn't speaking, but Sue kept at him.

'Dad, that shirt's too big.'

'What is?'

'Look at the cuffs, they're too long, look where they come to. Daft, they are.'

'Any road, here's the bus.'

'Is that the only tie you've got?'

'Give over.'

'Is it, Dad?'

'I got lots.'

'I bet they're horrible an' all.'

15

The rain blew sideways, into the open shelter. They huddled close.

'I'm cold, my hair's getting wet!' Eileen wailed.

'Change places with me, stand here,' Sue ordered. 'Baby.'

'Shurrup, you. You're so bossy.'

It was afternoon. Restless crowds surged everywhere. Johnnie eyed the massive cream and brown doubledeckers as they went clambering uphill. They kept coming. He counted them to pass the time. One, to his amazement, was driven by a young woman. The monster stopped, the young woman opened the cab door and jumped down. He couldn't get over how slender she was in her dark blue.

Johnnie was in a daze, lost, when they got out. It was in the country somewhere, which was like saying nowhere. They tramped up a long crunchy drive. The low buildings in the distance came nearer. It was curious how the father, so confident in his own house, seemed cowed by his surroundings. He asked an officious porter to direct him, and Johnnie heard the strangely servile voice come out of his father.

'Straight on till you get past that bed of rhododendrons, see? Bear right, and you'll see a sign for Moortop.'

'Thanks, much obliged.'

Entering, they passed through a glassed-in lobby or veranda which had chairs and tables and a few magazines. It was empty but for one woman, round-shouldered, who sat at a table weeping uncontrollably, her head in her hands. This picture of naked misery tore into Johnnie and he would never forget it. From this day he would tend to see women as suffering and defeated creatures, broken by life and put on exhibition for the world to gaze at, even when they seemed very different. They represented the inexplicable: they were at the mercy of cruel forces and if you clung to them it would be your fate too. A few years later, when he did a bit of baby-sitting for Tina Belcher to earn some money, and opened her Van Gogh book without permission, there under his hand was an old man sitting on a stool whose attitude of despair was exactly that of the woman he saw now. The old man's fists were bunched against his ears, as hers were. The drawing was even called 'Despair'. It should have been a woman, Johnnie thought immediately. As a precocious teenager he would pause and shiver on the brink of the darkness of women, both drawn and repulsed, in a secret part of himself afraid for his mind.

Marilyn Hunslett sat in the Day Room. 'There's Marilyn, look,' a nurse said. She smiled and disappeared.

Only women were in there, two others: a large truculent-seeming person with a soft floury face and dark rings under her eyes, and a frail and gaunt refined-looking lady who kept twisting compulsively at her wedding ring. Johnnie, a small figure hunching himself up, felt torn in his stomach. He wanted to do two things at once: run up to his mother and make her well, coax her to come home out of this horrible place, and he wanted to go instantly into reverse, back out and charge off through the swing doors, out of the glassy horror, until he was in the open again and alone and loose in the streets where he lived. His sister Sue, growing stronger with every minute, shepherded him and Eileen forward and it was no good, he had to go. There was a blubbering orphan self inside him which he despised and he feared it might betray him in public. What was his mother doing? Couldn't she speak? What had they done to her in this place? Faces in here looked so ugly. That was it, they worked at you till you were ugly and trapped, hating yourself and each other because everyone had been made the same.

They stood in a dumb circle around Marilyn, and Pat blurted out too loud, in a rough cheerful voice, 'How are you then, sweetheart?'

The children stared at their shoes, bitterly ashamed. Another nurse came up behind them, startling Johnnie and making him jump. 'Pull up some chairs, I should. There's no charge.'

He was shocked to hear the nurse laugh, yet her warm motherly tones filled him with a desperate longing for his mother. He stood missing her as he had never done at home, safe with his sisters. There he could at least

17

remember her how she was. Not now, not here. He was faced with a brutal truth. She had left him, left them all without warning. Why?

She was staring listlessly across the room at nothing, at the blank wall opposite. Grief entered him like a knife. He had lost her, maybe for ever. He saw moisture run out of one of her eyes and down her cheek.

3

They went every Saturday on that long journey to see her. Once she was quite chirpy, brighter than her normal self in fact, so much so that Johnnie could hardly believe it was his own mother. He sat trying to catch a glimpse of someone who had got lost behind a mask. It chilled him, failing totally like this to make contact with someone so familiar who had weirdly changed. He wanted her restored to him, but not like this. Why couldn't she be the same as before? He wouldn't mind about the sad ache, which seemed nothing now. He realized he had been happy with her just as she was. He wanted everything back exactly as it had been. He was used to his dad. His sisters were pests sometimes with all their dresses and stuff, they washed too much and had lots of baths and made a fuss about stupid things like face flannels when he mixed his up with theirs, but really he liked them and they encouraged him to feel strong.

'See that woman over there?' their mother whispered. They were in the Day Room, clustered around. Their dad had gone off looking for a toilet. 'She keeps us awake at night in the dormitory, sometimes she has little fits, epilepsy or something, poor thing, all the same she's a damn nuisance, chuntering and moaning away so that you can't sleep. Know what I did the other night? I yelled out, "Lorna, for God's sake shut up!" Yes, *me* – and she did! How about that?'

The third Saturday afternoon they set out without their father. He gave them bus fares, even extra pocket money, and told them to tell Marilyn he was sorry but he couldn't make it, something had come up.

'Why can't you?' Sue demanded, standing over him powerfully like a grown woman. She even had her hands on her hips.

'I can't, not this week,' he said. He was in the corner

19

of the sofa, his corner, with its greasy upholstery where his head and hands rubbed. He kept opening and shutting the pages of the *Star*. Sue was worked up, angry, her eyes spitting.

'Tell me why,' she insisted. Eileen was pretending not to watch.

Finally the man at bay lost his temper. He screwed up the newspaper in a great bundle and threw it at Sue. 'Because I'm soddin' well not, all right?' he bawled, like a big kid, and scrambling up he made to take hold of her. His face was dark and so was his neck.

She stood her ground. 'If you touch me I'll scream, I will, I'll scream the place down.'

'I'll touch you, I'll touch you, Miss!' he mouthed, but he didn't.

'It's disgusting, that's what I think,' she said finally, and left the room, taking her brother and sister out with her. She slammed the door.

'Why won't he come?' Eileen asked.

'How should I know? One of his mates is coming round I expect. Or he's going to the football. How should I know? I hate him sometimes, he's disgusting.'

Johnnie was secretly glad. With his father absent he felt himself to be the focus of his mother's attention, that is if she was well enough. Now and then she looked sadly and intimately at him, and he was penetrated in the old anxious manner. He didn't count his sisters, not being in competition with them. They were involved with his father, for all the friction, in a way he sensed and dimly understood, dismissing it with contempt.

Pat Hunslett had stopped going to work. Sue hated that, coming in from school and finding her kitchen – she saw it now as hers – in a filthy state. There would be the remains of a meal glued to a plate, newspapers littering the table, a beer can rolling on the floor, the bowl in the sink messy. The slovenly morose man said nothing to anyone, watching the sport on television, crashing in late at night, long after they were all in bed, as if every night was Saturday night. His eldest daughter saw his unhappiness and the dejected slump of his shoulders pained her. She cooked for him resentfully because he did not confide in her, feeling obscurely let down in her pride.

One day, in front of the others, she questioned him. He wouldn't meet her eyes. 'What?' he kept saying, shouting. 'What?'

'You heard me,' she said. Her brother and sister held their breath. 'Why shouldn't we know? Don't we live here?'

'Know what, know what? Ask your teacher, he'll tell you. That's what he's paid for.'

'Dad, that's stupid. Rubbish, that is.'

'Shut up, I'm getting indigestion here. These carrots are half-cooked, did you know that, Miss know-all?'

'Never mind the carrots.'

He was glaring madly at her now. White-faced, she stared him down. He stabbed at his lamb chop with his fork as though it was alive. Johnnie, on the sidelines and beginning to enjoy the fray, choked back a laugh.

'There's nowt to tell,' he said finally.

'Have you got the sack?'

'You watch your lip. I'm good at my job, I am.'

'Tell us, then.'

'What difference does it make?'

She hung on like a terrier. 'My friend Iris asked me why you didn't go to work.'

'So that's it. Bloody hell.'

'Dad!' she warned.

'Tell her the firm went bust. Which it did.'

'What does that mean?'

'Bust, broke, down the plug. Gone to the wall. Finished. Kaput. Iris can ask her dad, he'll know.'

'She hasn't got a dad,' Sue said, mollified. All at once she was sorry for her father, glad he was there to argue with, toying with his food, with no wife, no job. The poor man. She would take care of him too, like Johnnie and Eileen. She could do it. 'Shall I take this?' she said, and reached for his plate. 'The carrots should have been all right. Mine were.'

'Never mind, love,' he said, 'I'm not very hungry.'

21

'That's because you drink too much,' she said severely.

'Oh is that it?' he said ironically, grinning.

'You don't want to be an alcoholic.'

He burst out laughing, not unkindly. 'Sue, you're a scream.'

'I mean it.'

'Fat chance, on my money.'

'Are we hard up now?'

'What do you think?'

'Should we all be going out to the hospital every week? Isn't that expensive? Last time it was a waste. Mam was ill again.'

'That's true,' he said vaguely. He sighed, all his self-pity in the sound.

'We could take it in turns.'

'Why not?' He had lost interest.

Marilyn had had a relapse. They found her in a closed ward, among broken, grotesque women, some of them such pitiful cases that Johnnie, shocked and upset, afraid that he was going to be soppy instead of a big boy, refused to go again for a month. It was useless. The mother he knew had died; that was how it seemed. What he saw was a mere husk, a ghost. 'She'll get better, she *will*,' Sue told him fiercely. It was her task to instil faith, as well as to soothe Johnnie's anguish.

'Leave me alone, will ya,' he shouted, running off out. A wild grief possessed him.

Coming into the house now, he always felt better if Sue was there. She had become his mother. Late at night, if he couldn't sleep and came down for a glass of water, wandering around, he would sometimes see his father on the sofa in front of the TV, his beer cans lined up on the coffee table, a cigar in cellophane. Pat seldom acknowledged his son. Once Johnnie came into the room and Eileen was on his father's lap, the TV screen ablaze with noise and action. Johnnie saw the hand with clogged nails and hairy knuckles stroking Eileen's bare thigh in a funny lingering movement. Johnnie had seen plenty of films, he guessed what it meant. His dad was rubbish, he decided finally, climbing the stairs to bed.

*

22

Pat Hunslett sank rapidly into debt. He ran up an overdraft at the bank. Letters from the bank manager would leave him in a bad temper for days. The phone was taken out. One day the gas men came to cut off the supply. Sue was in the house by herself. 'Can't you leave it till I see me dad?' she pleaded. 'Our mother's ill, you see. I think he must have the bill in his pocket. I heard him say he was going to pay it, only the other day he did.'

'Afraid not, love,' the man in charge said. 'Orders, like.'

'I'm in the middle of cooking the meal!' she cried, furious with them and her father and everything, the stupidity of the world.

Blows fell in swift succession. Some busybody down the street had been in touch with the authorities. A social worker called one evening, a young fellow in a zipped cord jacket, wearing steel-rimmed glasses. His manner was easy and casual. Eileen noticed his chain bracelet. Pat was missing, so the official, with his rather sweet milky grin, addressed his remarks to the biggest girl. 'Terrible memory,' he said, grinning. 'Better jot down a few bits and pieces here.' In his notebook was the information: 'Anonymous caller, female. Alleges father frequently seen drunk. Possible neglect, ill-treatment. Investigate during pub hours.'

He noticed at once the one-bar fire blazing away, in front of the unlit gas panel. It was a ferociously cold night in February. Dirty ribs of congealed snow from a fall over a week ago still lay frozen in side streets.

'No gas?' he asked mildly.

Coming in through the kitchen he had already seen the Baby Belling on a table near the gas cooker. Pat had fetched it from his brother over at Walkley. It was rusty and primitive, but worked after a fashion. There was even a tiny oven, and a tin indicator you could push over with your finger. Johnnie was intrigued with it. As for Sue, she muttered as viciously as any housewife, struggling with the 'useless thing' in a rising rage. 'Oh it's so slow,' she would cry out in frustration, slapping at the enamel oven sides, desperately shifting saucepans to try to make them fit on the single flaking hotplate, a lifeless slab of rusty iron.

'Are you from the gas people?' she said hopefully. 'Who did you say you were?'

'The Council,' he said.

'What for?'

'Oh, we're doing a survey.'

In his notebook he had scribbled, 'Allowed entry – no parental supervision.'

'It's my dad you want,' Sue said firmly. 'He's not in at the moment.'

'No, right. By the way, where is Mr Hunslett?'

'Gone shopping.'

'You mean in town?'

'Not at night,' she said scornfully. He was nice really, whoever he was, but her mother had told her often enough not to tell their business to strangers. A thought entered her head. 'Do you have women doing surveys as well?'

'Certainly,' he said, and looked pleased. 'Why, did you fancy a job?'

'I'm at school,' she said gravely.

'Of course. When you leave.'

Suddenly she clammed up. 'Don't know.'

Johnnie came bursting in, and stopped short, staring at the intruder and then dropping his gaze in an access of shyness. In one hand he had a paper bag of sweets, a chocolate flake and a walnut whip, and his other clutched the neck of a Pepsi bottle.

'Been shopping, young man?' the social worker said. He was all smiles and openness, you trusted him. A new face was nice.

'Yes.'

'At the corner shop?'

'Yes.'

'Is your dad round there at the moment?'

Sue was glaring at her brother for some reason, her face red, as Johnnie answered, 'No, he's gone t'Crown.'

The man added a note, 'No visible bruises or abrasions. Living room and kitchen clean. Children decently

24

clothed.' Then he got up to go. 'Thanks very much,' he said to Sue at the door. 'I'll try to catch up with your father another time. Perhaps we'd better make an appointment with him.'

Stiff with hostility, Sue shut the door on him without a word, then turned the key. She waited for the man's footsteps to die away before she shouted in to her brother, who was licking the delicious crumbs from his milk flake packet, 'You're daft, you are, our Johnnie! What did you want to open your great gob for?'

'I never,' she heard him say, not attending to her. He was watching a television programme, some American series he had that moment switched on, a power struggle utterly beyond his comprehension. Only the tensions held him and for some reason he liked it. He liked the incredibly luxurious apartments and the clothes, the drinks poured from decanters. The whole glossy show hypnotised him; it exuded power. He would wait for the build-up, to do with money or a woman, the fat cars streaking away and then the inevitable violent climax.

Sue left him alone. A foreboding, which she tried to stifle, warned her that some new calamity was approaching, rolling along and getting bigger, more and more unstoppable. She wandered around picking up newspapers. Why did her father need so many? Apart from the sports pages, she had seen him running his finger down the small print of the classified ads before tossing the paper down in disgust. If there was only someone she could talk to about her fears, someone who would reassure her, maybe tell her to stop imagining things – but there was no one. Living in shadows made the days drab, like having a room which you never managed to get clean. She had a craving for sun, an urge to throw open windows. She made a firm decision to make her father talk, tell her things. She was old enough, he should trust her. It was unfair of him and stupid to keep her in the dark. The same instinct warning her of an impending disaster told her that her father would do anything rather than face the truth of their situation. He had various remarks for avoiding your questions. If cornered, there was always his authority, a sheer wall, with a voice at the top of it saying NO. She should be doing her homework, she had plenty. All her energy these days was being absorbed in fretfulness. Responsibilities were fine if it was made clear what you had to do. Then you felt important and necessary.

She heard a bang on the door and marched to see who it was. Her face had a grim suspicious look and she stuck out her bottom lip in a way that always made Eileen laugh. Opening the door she said rudely, 'Yes?' before she could see properly. The dark brick passage was unlit, smelling of frost and cats.

It was Gerry, one of her father's friends. She stood back and he came in as far as the cooker, a bluff, clownish man with powerful shoulders, always twinkling with half-suppressed laughter as if just being alive was a joke. A drinking pal, her mother would say. When he spoke to the girls he usually touched his ginger moustache with his fingertips, like a sign. Baggy trousers hung from his belly. 'Is Pat in?' he asked rapidly. 'I've got a bit of news for him.' His friendly body filled up the space. He smelled of night.

'No, he's not.'

'Ar, well. Any idea where he might be?' He seemed a little bemused by her stern front.

'Probably at the Crown.'

'Ar, right.' He turned to go.

'Will you tell him a Council man's been?' she called after him on an impulse. All at once she felt spiteful. Why shouldn't her father be stirred up and bothered? Men thought everything was amusing, a joke. Well, it wasn't.

'Right you are, love,' she heard Gerry answer, and by his voice she guessed he was vague and preoccupied. She expected him to forget.

The next thing she knew, the house was up for sale, a post displaying the name of the agent nailed to the front wall. Pat Hunslett had heard of a council flat, his name was down and he was eligible for it. It was the only way he could see of clearing his debts, his mortgage arrears, the outstanding gas and electricity bills, the hire purchase instalments. Demands came in almost daily, and he just drank himself into oblivion to escape the system, as he called it among his mates, supping his bitter and making truculent noises, airing his resentments in sympathetic company. Though he would notice how smug their politics sounded to him now. They still had their jobs, they weren't experiencing his stinking luck. Words were cheap, they came easy when you had a regular wage packet. He wanted to tell them that, but held his tongue. What the hell, he would have been equally complacent in their place.

At one time he would enjoy getting drunk. Alcohol expanded him, the narrow-gutted timorous reality of his days dissolved, fell away, and a glow of cameraderie that he felt to be his true element took hold of him. Now he drank simply to escape, and his manner turned ugly and rancorous. Old drinking pals slipped off home to their cosy hearths, thinking he didn't notice. 'Bastards,' he swore after them under his breath. In the mornings the hangovers poleaxed him. Long after the children had gone off to school, supervised by Sue, he crawled out, sometimes too sick and desperate to face the day. They were used to it, and anyway it was better than his shambling, scowling presence. Soon it made sense to booze in the middle of the day as well as evenings, though he had never before been a hard drinker. Whatever it meant, it was an answer his body demanded at certain hours, then was grateful for. All he could afford was beer. Even so they were running out of household items. Toilet rolls, soap, toothpaste – as they dwindled the girls indignantly protested. Mainly it was Eileen who squawked the loudest. One Saturday morning she slammed out of the bathroom and squealed, 'No toilet paper, no toilet paper!' in a tantrum on the landing. 'Plenty of newspaper, use that,' her father shouted. It was just a remark. 'I'm not using newspaper!' she howled down the stairs, outraged.

'Why not?' he sneered. 'I did when I was your age.'

'I don't care, who cares about that, this is the twentieth century, Dad!' she wailed.

'Is that a fact?' he said, heavily sarcastic, laughing at her hysteria. Even Sue was trying to stifle a giggle. But it was not funny. These days her father's teasing was partly malignant, and under the surface were harsh facts. At the sink they had run out of washing-up liquid. How could you keep a household going on no money? Pat was muttering something idiotic – as he sent Johnnie to the shop for a few essentials – about wiping yourself on the tail of your shirt as he once did. Sue pursed her lips. When her father was coarse she became her mother, he was hateful in her sight.

4

The upshot of it was devastating and final. It happened swiftly, without warning, though of course Pat must have known. As with everything vital, he had kept this to himself. But what could he have said? The Council moved in one Monday evening and took his bewildered children into care. 'It's only temporary, don't you fret, I'll be out to see you at the weekend,' he said in a low craven voice, exactly as he had sounded at the hospital. Whenever he was faced with officialdom he seemed to cave in. It was horrible to see him crumble so abjectly. Johnnie was ashamed, then began to breathe easier when they turned the corner. He thought at first it might be an adventure, like a surprise holiday. He loved surprises. At home it was pretty lousy, his dad always in a filthy temper about something, and the cloud always over them that Johnnie had begun to dread, not knowing each time they approached the hospital how his mother would be. This might change the whole pattern magically, mysteriously, like turning the pages of an illustrated book. It was a bombshell, a total surprise. If only his silly sister would stop blubbering. That was the trouble with girls, they showed you up. He didn't count Sue, who was more resolute than anyone he had known. She had gone strangely quiet. Johnnie took a quick look at her and was horrified to see that she was crying without making a sound, like his mother at the hospital that first time. This threw him into a panic. So what was happening was terrible after all. Something broke horribly into fragments inside him. In his shocked state he turned against her. Not Sue – she shouldn't cry!

One shock followed another. He hadn't dreamt that they would be split up, his two sisters torn out of his life. Before he had a chance to protest, to say goodbye or ask where they would be, that was it, they were gone. Why hadn't Sue uttered a word to him? He depended on her absolutely as a guide through life now his mother was absent. Could it be that she didn't know either? At the back of his mind, while a part of him rejoiced to be escaping from his father's drab world, he had been telling himself that everything would be fine if he stayed close to Sue. She would take care of him. Now she had vanished and a nightmare place of strange surroundings, strange voices and faces closed around him. 'It's not fair on her, it's not fair,' he said over and over to himself in a whisper, rocking his body to and fro in time to the words.

They had crossed the city and plunged up hilly streets and across junctions teeming with traffic into districts which bore no resemblance to the cramped, easily comprehended web of streets where he had grown up. Trembling with fear he was taken into a large building where everything looked heavy and sad. He allowed them to lead him up a flight of steps and through a succession of big shabby rooms, the lower walls painted an uniform olive green, scratched and gouged in places, with chipped skirting boards. They went up to the first floor and entered an area in which he caught the smell of urine and thought of babies, and saw one or two toddlers, one little girl with a length of dirty frayed rope which she trailed behind her for a toy.

He was led down a long corridor and entered a dormitory of twenty narrow beds, all neatly made. 'Come down for supper as soon as you like, all right, son? Think you can find your way?'

He nodded dumbly at the man, who planted a huge hand on his head and roughed up his hair. Another boy was in the room. 'This is Sam. He wants his supper an' all, I bet. Let's ask him. Want your supper, Sam?'

'Aw, stuff it,' the boy said. He sat on his bed and didn't even look up.

'That means yes,' the tall man said placidly. 'He's got a funny way of expressing himself. Anyhow, he'll take you down I expect.'

He went clumping out over the stained boards. He

seemed kindly, but Johnnie wanted nothing to do with him, or any of them. He wanted his sisters, he even wanted his father. At the centre of his body was a hole, an aching for what he had remembered, how it had been. Nothing would have been more welcome at this moment than the sight of his father, surly and complaining or else slumped in a corner of the sofa with his paper. This place was dark and threatening in a way he couldn't grasp, but he sensed it, not the anonymous people but something else, seeping from the walls and ceilings. Why did they call it a Home? It was nothing like a home. It put him in mind of the hospital, only without nurses. There was even a disinfectant smell.

The other boy spoke up. Now the man had gone he no longer used a belligerent tone. 'You wanna go down now?'

'Suppose so.'

'What are you called?'

'Johnnie.'

'It ain't bad here. Not bad at all. I bin in worse places.' He was ten or eleven. A squint he had made him look tough. Johnnie saw him as a veteran of this new frightening life, and felt glad he was not alone.

'Where is it, this place?' he said.

'How d'you mean?'

'Here, where I am. What's it called?'

'Ain't nobody told you that? What a load of wankers!'

Johnnie felt ridiculous, a baby. He blushed, feeling even more stupid and small. This tough kid, Sam, would make a good ally, he thought. He ought to keep in with him. 'They might have done, I forget,' he said foolishly.

But it could be true. He was so shaken and sick, he had stopped listening to anybody, hiding away inside himself. Already he had lost track of time. It was like a bad dream, only when he blinked and told himself to wake up it refused to go away. He was reminded of a prison he had seen once on a film, transfixed by the endless doors slamming one after another like steel traps, feeling the suffocating confinement in his own chest. He even glanced up at the windows of the dormitory to see if they had bars. No, nothing like that. They were just very high up. You couldn't have seen out without a ladder. Sam saw him peering.

'This is Highup Hall.'

'Oh.'

'You believe me, honest?'

'What?'

'No, listen, I'll tell you what this place is called, shall I?'

'All right.'

'Undercliffe. Heard of that?'

'No.'

'Wanna know what district?'

Johnnie nodded, playing along with this boy who was having such a good time being a know-all. It was a power game, he was used to it at school. You went through the ritual, it was a test, and then the older boy let you off. He might even stick up for you if you were lucky.

'Stannington,' Sam said. 'That's where this dump is.' He stuck out his chest. 'Ever heard of it?'

'No.'

'You have now.' Sam gave a horse laugh, throwing back his head theatrically. 'I'll tell you plenty later. Kids run away from here, know that? If you don't know where Stannington is, how would you know which way to run when you got out?' He stared. 'I ran off, twice.' Then he said to Johnnie abruptly, 'You ten?'

'Yes,' Johnnie lied.

'I'm eleven. What school you at?'

Johnnie told him.

'Never heard of it. Waste of time, school. Can't do with all that crap.'

'I thought I heard a bell,' Johnnie said.

Sam leapt up from his bed and took hold of the new boy's arm officiously. 'Last bell for supper – that's what they call it. Leavings from dinner, stuff like that. Come on if you're coming. What's your name again? Johnnie?'

'Yes.'

'Ever pinch anything, Johnnie?'

'No.'

They went down the stairs full pelt, joined by one or two others.

'I have,' Sam panted. 'Never got caught, neither. Easy if you know how. I'll tell you later, it's a trick somebody showed me, okay?'

Johnnie nodded his eagerness to be initiated. Being singled out by Sam was surely a stroke of luck. Whatever Sam had done, he wouldn't let on. Sam must have sussed him out, guessing he could keep a secret. Immediately he felt better, slightly hopeful, glancing round the long communal table at the other inmates. It was a refectory table, huge and black, the biggest he'd seen. You sat on either side on wobby hard benches that were covered in scars and dug-out initials. Eating some left-over potatoes and cabbage warmed up in a frying pan – bubble-and-squeak his mother called it – and helping himself bashfully to the sliced bread spilling out of the wrapper, he gulped down the greasy food to be like the others, to belong. It was what his instinct told him he must do from now on in order to survive. He was a quick, bright, impressionable boy, and his natural liveliness began to respond by sheer instinct to these very different conditions, with no girls watching over him. He was in a loveless and competitive male world.

He got through the first week, bewildered to find himself transferred from his old school to the one every boy under eleven at Undercliffe attended. At the weekend he watched visitors arrive, not many. The doors of the main entrance hypnotised him as he hung around there, wanting his sisters to appear out of the blue, even hoping to see his dad. It was a fantasy but it took hold of him. By Sunday his homesickness was worse, and when a tall kid of about his own age called Davey started slinging his raincoat to a pal in the dormitory he went for him, not giving a damn for his size, he was so wretched. His misery soaked down through him, into his arms and fists and he didn't care, nothing mattered, he almost wanted to get hurt.

'Gi' o'er! Gi' us that, it's mine!'

'Thar 'as to get it first.'

Why had he been dumped here, what had he done? Angry and scared, he ducked his head like a goat and flung himself at the bony kid, whirling his arms. Davey was chicken – he threw the raincoat on the floor and shot out, whooping as if it was all a laugh. But Johnnie knew he had won.

5

Another week passed. Then on Monday evening, swamped by another wave of homesickness and unable to bear the thought of one more weekend, Johnnie ran away.

He had thought it out. His first impulse had been to go straight as a bullet to Frecheville, to the street of his desires, where he belonged and was happy. Then he remembered that the house was up for sale, perhaps sold by now. And he couldn't deny that it was his dad who had allowed them to bring him here. He headed instead for his father's young brother, Steve, who lived with his wife Lilian at Walkley.

Getting into town was easy, so easy it amazed him. He ran a good distance along the road away from Undercliffe before he dared to stand at a bus stop, waiting there tensely with a banging heart for the hullabaloo to break out. An old woman came by and he asked her the way. She laughed, all gums and cackles, throwing back her head as if delighted.

'Wrong side, hee hee!'

'Pardon?'

'Other side. Git over t'other side!'

'I want the town please.'

'Wrong side!'

He went red as his mistake dawned, dodging over the road in a gap in the traffic.

A bus lumbered up. He got on. With his pocket money he paid for a ride to Division Street, then transferred to a 95. It was very dark. A bitingly cold March wind was blowing. Now that he had his bearings he was able to stop trembling. He watched every movement from the corners of his eyes like a cat. Nobody paid the slightest attention to him. Being a small kid, he realized gratefully, was the nearest thing to being invisible.

35

On a bench seat near the doors, so that he could leap out into the night if challenged at one of the stops, he peered out at shop fronts he thought he recognized as they trundled powerfully along West Street. He saw himself doing things, as if in a film he was watching. Over one shop he saw Hartley Seed, in big letters, a funny name he remembered. They drew up at the lights after passing the army recruiting centre, an old dirty block daubed with faded anti-war slogans – TAKE THE TOYS AWAY FROM THE BOYS – ARMS ARE FOR LOVING – LITTLE BOYS GO HOME. He hung on to the next seat as they swung sharply and began to climb a steep gradient, past a women's hospital, Jessop's, and saw on a factory wall another slogan, one he failed to understand: IF YOU'VE SEEN ONE NUCLEAR WAR YOU'VE SEEN THEM ALL.

Catching sight of the university signboards for various departments he knew he was nearly there. An enormous roundabout swung them in a circle. The bus laboured again, up a hill that kept twisting them round serpentine bends, and he saw a neat park, a boating lake, children's swings, before they were enclosed by lots of tatty streets and cheap shops, all tilting upwards like the bus. He got off when the driver shouted 'Commonside', recognizing the crumbling brick of the men's urinal.

He was sure this was it, though in the dark everything looked changed, threatening. A large pub, the Hallamshire, even though it was lit up he remembered it. Near here was where his uncle and aunt lived, and he saw it again in his mind's eye, on a high point overlooking a deep cluttered valley, an industrial wasteland that had been weirdly colonised in higgledy-piggledy fashion, veined with sharply descending streets of working men's terraces running into raw new estates, here and there an incongruous high-rise poking up. Beyond that again were the grimy sheds and railway yards and gaunt stacks of a superseded epoch. At night the whole sprawl of ashy landscape shimmered in the dark with thousands of pretty lights.

The wind ripped across the ridge and the lights seemed

to crackle and shiver as Johnnie ran along on the level, past the blowy gaps. He soon found the little house, in a terrace of four stone-built dwellings. He dived through the ginnel to the rear, standing with his back to that dizzy view. His heart was thumping as he banged on the kitchen door.

He was sure this was it. The lighted window was covered by the pale yellow slats of a bamboo blind, not curtains. He had thought it funny, but it had impressed him. Once his Uncle Steve let him yank on the cords and it rolled up dryly, one side higher than the other.

On his last visit, his aunt was 'expecting'. Lilian had smiled at him with her thick lips, tight-bellied. Afterwards he heard Eileen whispering to Sue about babies, asking things.

'Who is it?' he heard his aunt call out now very suspiciously, without opening the door.

'It's me,' he piped.

'Who's "me"? How am I supposed to know who "me" is?' The voice sounded querulous and cold, not like Auntie Lilian at all.

'Johnnie,' he called, shuddering there in the vast windy dark. Behind him the awesome falling land was like a gigantic crater on the moon. He glanced back once over his shoulder, suddenly menaced and precarious on the desolate exposed lip.

'Hang on a minute,' the voice said crossly.

He heard bolts being drawn, keys turned, his aunt jabbering away to herself as if she was engaged in an argument. The door opened and she stood in the light, staring over his head comically and round the doorway. 'Is it just you?'

'Yes.'

'Good gracious,' she said, pop-eyed. 'Come in, then.'

He stepped into the beautifully warm, dazzlingly bright and clean interior.

'God, it's cold out there,' she muttered, shooting bolts and turning the key again.

He was always surprised at how young she looked in comparison to his mother. He stood waiting submissively on the new Chinese matting, holding an oilskin shopping bag in which he had his pyjamas, shirt and pants, a toothbrush, a comb, a pair of socks. The belt of his raincoat was twisted. This was the first thing Lilian noticed. She had to stop herself from straightening it. 'Now then, young Johnnie, what's going on?' she said. 'And at this time of night, eh?'

'I've run off,' he said. 'Now they'll be after me.' And perhaps because of the words with their admission, and the soft female aura of his young aunt – even though her face was closed and cold, suspicious as a teacher's – he burst into tears in front of her.

It was the best thing he could have done. Perhaps in a part of himself he was aware of it, at any rate enough to let it happen. Lilian, a sentimental woman, always ready to weep over the child in herself, sat him down at the table while she put the kettle on. 'Never mind, that'll do now, you'll start me off in a minute,' she said, beginning to sniff. 'Just tell me what this is all about.'

Johnnie stammered out his story. Lilian gave him hot chocolate in a heavy stone mug which had an olive green saucer to match. As he gulped it down, telling her bits about the Home, it was already unreal to him and distant, all that. Oh, he liked this house, the bright colours, the warmth, the clean feel of it, as if everything had been carried in that day from a shop and unwrapped, gleaming new. The kitchen opened on to a little side porch, and the back yard was divided from either side by wooden picket fences, ending in a stone wall low enough to sit on and then the hypnotic view, with only the roofs of houses visible.

'Where's Uncle Steve?' he asked meekly, ingratiating himself.

'Oh, at his judo class,' she said, with what he thought was a sneer in her voice. 'Look here, Johnnie, are you telling me the truth?'

'Yes.'

'You haven't done anything wicked?'

'No.'

She chuckled knowingly, in that insinuating way adults

have. 'Oh well, I suppose I'll have to believe you. What's in that bag you've got?'

'My things.'

She hooted with laughter, startling him. 'Who d'you think you are, Huckleberry Finn?'

'Who?'

'Finish off that drink,' she ordered abruptly. 'Do they give you enough to eat in that place, what's it called?'

'Undercliffe.'

'You're hungry I suppose?'

'A bit,' he said slyly. He was thinking that the more things he did here, fitting in and behaving nicely, the longer they would let him stay.

'What boy isn't,' she muttered, half to herself, 'or man either.' She said, louder, laughing crudely, 'You're all alike. All kids. Men or boys, it's all the same.'

'Pardon?'

'I've got some fruit cake, home-made. Would you like a piece of that? Yes?'

'Yes, please.'

She took his strangely heavy mug away, and wiped the yellow varnished wood with a cloth, yet he hadn't spilled a drop and the table was spotless so far as he could see, with woven cane place mats. Everything looked pale and fresh. The kitchen chairs had rush seats, the walls were covered in woodchip paper and painted a matt white. Johnnie's eyes were drawn to the spice rack, a recent acquisition, something he hadn't seen before anywhere – rows of small labelled bottles, the shelves edged with navy beading, so nice and trim and so orderly. What kind of life must go on here, how different! What astounded him most was the sense of order and control, every trace of dirt eased away and all roughness vanquished to usher in this totally unfamiliar regime.

Lilian came up behind him with a slab of cake and a knife, on an olive green stone plate like the mug and saucer. She trailed her arm over his shoulder, touched his cheek. 'Thank you,' he said, a model of good behaviour.

'Good lad. Aren't you a good lad.'

'I weren't in trouble, Auntie. I never run off because I was in trouble.'

'You're homesick, is that it?'

'Our house is sold up. I think it is.'

'Poor little mite.'

She always fussed over him when he came. Even if it was a bit false to be petted as if he was a puppy, he enjoyed it. It was because of this that he had made a bee-line for her. Although she fussed, unlike his mother she never fretted. Under her sentiment he sensed a cold indifference to him as a person. He represented something she wanted to handle, a growing, dependent thing, to whom she would be everything. 'Am I pretty?' he had heard her ask Uncle Steve once in a petulant wheedling voice. Johnnie thought her large rather goggling eyes were nice, and her piles of abundant blonde hair. She had beautiful soft skin on her face and neck. He was always fascinated by her croaky babyish voice, which had an indolent quality, though her mind was sharp and quick. Until she became pregnant she was a secretary. There was a subterranean contest, joined years ago, between her and her husband, a garage mechanic. She would chivvy him from time to time for his lack of ambition. Again this had gone on since before they were married. He was dark, with thick hair around his ears and down on his forehead. He would stretch out his long legs and gaze around restlessly at his Lilian-scented home, looking caged, answering only when forced. They had been married for two years and he had lost interest in her. She was all on one note, and smarter than him, critical of him. It screwed up his nerves.

'Let's go in the front,' Lilian said, leading the way.

Johnnie followed her into the cramped front sitting room. Johnnie had been hoping for this. But when he got there he wished he was in the kitchen again. Without understanding why he felt it was more genuine and cheerful in there. This room, with its flounced curtains, was like Lilian – it was putting on an act. Going in, he bumped against her, and she clutched at him in fun, only it was serious too. He smelled the shampoo in her soft loose hair as she pressed him to her. He was unused to physical contact, and her warm pulpy figure was a wonder. She laughed girlishly and it reminded him of Eileen, the funny rising shriek, but different. There was something lazy and bland and foolish about her which freed him. He was not under any compulsion to care about her.

A gas fire burned away with a soft insistent heat. Lilian turned it up. Instead of sitting on the settee or on one of the armchairs, waiting immaculately with its antimacassars, she lowered herself down awkwardly on the sheepskin rug and put a cushion behind her back. This amazed him. He didn't know adults sat on floors. It shocked him a little. Her legs were spread apart, her skirt rode up, and she let him glimpse whatever he liked, sighing contentedly. Who was he, anyway – a kid of eight or nine? In her home she did as she pleased. Steve was out having a good time; he should have been back before this. Had he sneaked off again for a quick drink with one of his mates? That was fine, but he should be honest about it. Men were dishonest, they were kids. 'This is nice,' she said indulgently, and seemed to sink into a reverie, forgetting her nephew altogether.

Johnnie was perched on a cold leather pouffe. Unsure, he smiled across at her politely. She wasn't looking. The warmth enveloped him, crept over him. He gave himself up to his sensations, exhausted by the day's events, his miraculous escape, wanting to lie down in a bed and be tucked up by Lilian in this seductive house, his troubles laughed at, banished, soothed away by kind hands.

He woke up with a jolt, hearing someone – it must be Uncle Steve – blunder in and the back door crash once, twice. The catch was faulty. Again he sat alert and nervous with his newly awakened terrors, a hollow-eyed runaway kid ready to spring up and catapult himself into space.

'Is that you, darling?' Lilian called, in an oozy, sly voice. She sounded helpless and in need of protection but anyone could see that wasn't so. Johnnie stared at her, puzzled, at the thick smiling lips. She looked transformed, like a little girl expecting a present.

'No, it's the gas man,' Steve said, entering the room. Then he caught sight of Johnnie. 'Hallo, what's all this about, then?' His nephew gaped at him, confused by his new appearance. What had altered? He had grown a full gushing moustache which drooped around his mouth at the corners. His face was set obstinately, another difference. Johnnie was used to a friendly uncle, eager and boyish, who did what his aunt said.

Lilian said coyly, 'Listen, Steve, you know where Johnnie is . . . '

Steve refused to come in any further. He began backing out, glaring from side to side belligerently. 'What the hell's wrong?' he said.

'Oh, stop it, come and sit here, come in properly for God's sake, I want to tell you something.' Lilian patted the sofa beside her, staring peevishly at her husband.

'No. I don't want anything to do with it.'

'Steve, stop being so stupid and listen to me.'

'No. If it's trouble, count me out. We can't afford to get mixed up in it.'

Lilian lost her temper. 'Stop that! Will you give me credit for a little intelligence? And please come over here and sit down in a proper manner, Steve Hunslett – I'm getting a crick in my damn neck trying to talk to you.'

He came in then and plonked himself down at her side, looking sullen but submissive, her geyes jumpy. He refused to look at his nephew. 'I'm listening, go on,' he grumbled.

'Darling, I've been lonely,' Lilian said. From her position on the carpet she pushed her hand up his trouser leg, gripping his ankle. Steve twisted his body, to discourage her. 'Where have you been, sweetheart?'

'You know where I've been,' he said uncomfortably. 'My class.'

'Did you go for a drink after?'

'Just one, with Freddy. I left him there.'

'He lives in that pub.'

'Not true.' Snuffling out a laugh. 'Slight exaggeration.'

42

'I don't like him.'

'Freddy's all right.'

'Aren't you going to kiss me? I need a little kiss and a cuddle.'

He bent over her obediently, leaning down to her mouth. Johnnie, who disliked him now, was glad to see him bossed about. Lilian suddenly jerked away and slapped at Steve's head as if swotting a fly. 'That's more than one! I hate that beer smell, it's disgusting. You know how it upsets me now I'm in this condition and you still do it, and don't consider me in the slightest do you, you selfish pig!'

'Lilian, do you mind? We're not exactly alone here.'

'Stop changing the subject! How many have you had?'

'Two.'

'Liar!'

'Two,' he said wearily, 'and a half.'

After a long furious minute, Lilian told him in a cold logical voice, her secretary's voice, to go upstairs and make up the bed in the spare room for Johnnie. 'Then he can go to bed, and I can talk to you. Right?'

'Yes, all right,' he said, jumping up. He seemed pleased to escape. 'Hey, I'm starving, is something in the oven?'

'Lasagne.'

'Great, great.'

'I want the bed making up first, Steve.'

Johnnie heard him running upstairs, unconfined. A little later he came back and sat on the settee again. 'All done.' He put an arm round his wife's neck. Lilian was gazing into the gas fire. A handsome black cat strolled into the room and leapt on to Steve's lap. He lowered his head to it, murmuring, saying how gorgeous it was, addressing it directly like a person and stroking it with long subtle strokes over its head and down its supple back, depressing its flat skull. This crooning intimacy was too much for Lilian, who burst out all at once in a passionate cry, 'I hate that cat!'

'Smokey's beautiful. You're beautiful, aren't you? Anybody can see that.'

'I'm your wife, you should be doing that to me! I hate it, moulting all over the carpet in here. Get it out, go on.'

'You're not moulting, are you?' Steve said. 'Not in the winter, never.' He carried the cat out in his arms, cradling it.

There was another lame silence, and then Johnnie's aunt said, in a changed, responsible adult's voice, 'Off you go to bed, love. D'you remember where it is?'

He said he did. He thought he had better give his aunt a kiss, to keep in with her, and because of the tantrum about the cat. He felt sorry for her, wanting attention like him. She was neglected. Perhaps that was a good sign and meant he would be allowed to stay – after all they shared the same predicament. But when he kissed her cheek she ignored him, slumped there on the floor like something no one had any use for. Her dress was pretty, an Indian cotton in reds and browns, an intricate pattern, with smocking over the bodice, yet she had allowed herself to look bedraggled. He thought she might be going to cry, so he slipped thankfully out of the room. He was so tired, he swayed as he walked.

6

The next evening they took him in their smart red Renault over to Frecheville. Steve seemed to have changed back to his old self, laughing and talking nonsense, that is when he and Lilian weren't bickering over the route. He even spoke to Johnnie as if he was fond of him. 'You okay back there?' he called over his shoulder as they sped through the streets, sickeningly fast and efficient. Johnnie managed to nod, the skin of his face so tight he felt it was about to split. Why couldn't they have kept him a bit longer? As they shot across intersections and swung smoothly into the roundabouts, he wished – as he often did when he was on an outing – that they would take a wrong turn and get lost, plunge into the depths of the country and be swallowed up by lanes which shrank to mere tracks and then petered out altogether. 'You can't win 'em all,' Steve was shouting. 'Don't worry, it may never happen. Hey, Johnnie, we'll come and see you, how about that?'

'That was too close!' Lilian suddenly gasped. 'Steve, for God's sake, will you stop turning round and watch what you're doing?'

Steve only smirked. As soon as he was wedged behind the wheel of a car he seemed to go a little wild, slipping free of Lilian's influence as he felt the power in his hands, under the soles of his feet. His eyes gleamed and a hardness came over him, he leaned forward from the waist like a gunner. She hated him when he was driving. Every movement he made seemed to be aimed maliciously at her. She drove, too, but being a mechanic he handled the car with a kind of insolent carelessness. This had thrilled her once, when they had first started going out together. It was a display of prowess, no less. Once she called round for him at the garage and he was rearranging the forecourt, leaping in and out of the cars and parking them like an inspired lunatic, at crazy speeds, all for her benefit.

In no time they were drawing up outside the house at the bottom of the street with its 'For Sale' notice still displayed. On the cement patch outside the unused front door was the usual overflowing dustbin, and a heap of plastic bags, one split open and spilling its rubbish. Johnnie got out, biting his bottom lip. Let his dad try to belt him – let him just try! He'd be off down the street like a rocket, they'd never catch him. A bitter resistance made him strut cockily as though he didn't care, with stiff knees, his back rigid.

Pat was waiting at the entry door to let them into the kitchen. He had shaved hastily. Now he was dabbing at a cut on the side of his jaw with a grimy-looking towel. Lilian went in looking severe, like an official, and Steve, still high on the exhiliration of the drive, said with a broad grin, 'We understand this character is related to you.'

Lilian shot her brother-in-law a baleful look. 'Hello, Pat.'

'I'll put the kettle on,' Pat said, grunting it out, not meeting Lilian's eye. She was all right to look at, an inviting body, but as a personality she got on his nerves with her solemnity. 'Come on, son,' he said to Johnnie, 'let's hear your side of it.'

Lilian began to gabble at high speed. 'How did you know we were coming, I don't get it, who could have known we had him?'

Pat shrugged. All he knew was that they had already been round from Undercliffe making enquiries. 'So have the police,' he said grimly.

'Good God!' Lilian shrieked.

'What did I tell you?' Steve said.

'Them bastards I could do without,' Pat said.

Johnnie stood where he was, defiant. Nobody suggested he should take his coat off and sit down, and he didn't want to, not here. He hated it here now. This was where he had been betrayed. Lilian glanced everywhere surreptitiously while Pat's back was turned, wrinkling her nose in distaste. What a tip, what a stinking slum! She vowed to herself that these Hunslett tendencies would never overcome her. She had noticed already in her husband a tendency to let things slide. More than once, lying in bed with the burden of Steve's dead weight on her, smelling his mechanic's smell after he had come too soon and then dropped off to sleep, dozing against her shoulder and dribbling at the mouth, his hard bones digging in, she had felt the dangerous downward drag of him. But it wouldn't happen, she would resist, reverse the pull. As a couple, soon to be a family, they were going to rise. And he would learn to like it, she told herself with savage relish. She saw it as her task to change him, make him better, more appreciative of the fine things. But Jesus, look at this shit-heap! She took note of details, coarsely exulting. There was always a whiff of leaking gas from that filthy cooker, and she could smell it now, even with the supply cut off. Poor Marilyn up at Maltby came into her mind and it made her shudder, and move closer to Steve. She took his arm and cuddled it. She imagined herself living here, battling with dirt and losing, going mad.

Johnnie thought he would be sorry to see his aunt and uncle go, but he wasn't. He was glad. They had no time for him. He would have liked more of Lilian's squashy body, which was like the sensation of eating chocolates, your mouth full of syrup, but there was no denying that her love for him was faked. Otherwise she would have done something, found a way to hang on to him. As for Steve, he did what she said. Now she rushed up and smothered her nephew, gave him a wet smacking kiss from which he recoiled, while he stood mutely with his arms dangling. 'Be a good boy now for your dad, Johnnie, you hear me?'

He refused to answer, or look. The door banged.

His father made him sit down and then produced the remains of a huge pork pie. 'All right?' he kept saying. 'All right?' Johnnie had expected a belting, but he saw at once that this wasn't going to happen. He wasn't hungry, but it was nice sitting down with his dad, so he pretended.

Anyway, there wasn't much. 'Hang on,' his father said, and he heard him scrabbling round in the kitchen.

He came back with a squashed tomato, which he cut carefully in two. 'Want a glass of milk?' he asked. Johnnie nodded. His father opened a can of beer, and his son waited for the loud crack as he yanked at the ring and tore off the tag. He liked to hear it.

His father sat munching and swallowing and not saying anything, and after a decent interval Johnnie took a chance – not that he had any real hopes, because his father gave off a hopelessness, in his eyes a shifty, beaten expression – and asked, 'Can't I stay here, Dad?'

'Afraid not, son.'

'Why can't I?'

'It's not up to me. It's them.'

'Why is it?'

'I'm not arguing with you.'

'I wouldn't be any trouble, honest.'

'Nothing to do with that.'

Johnnie knew it was no good. It was simply that he had to try. If it had been a real possibility his sisters would have been here. In Lilian's beautiful little spare room, so white, with a plumped-up pillow, a flowered duvet on the bed and his own table lamp, he had dropped off to sleep already wrapped in a fantasy of Sue and Eileen opening the door to him, overjoyed to see him again. In the morning, opening his eyes, the first thing to meet his gaze was the framed Renoir print of a radiant little girl with almond eyes, the colours melting with family happiness.

He had another question, but he hesitated, unwilling to make the atmosphere worse. He allowed some minutes to trickle away, and then asked, 'Are you taking me back in, Dad?'

'No,' his father said. After this he wouldn't say anything.

Two social workers arrived next morning in a Mini. This time Johnnie could see where they were taking him, and as they drew up he saw the large board outside, 'Undercliffe Children's Home'.

He was taken into an office off the foyer, and a bull-faced, bald man with glasses, obviously someone important, asked him quite gently if he was unhappy and if so, why, was he being bullied? He wrote on a form, then told Johnnie to carry on. Johnnie admired the black fountain pen he used, its gold nib and heavy gold clip. He was fascinated too by the man's hands, his nails, clean and cared for, exuding confidence. As he talked they lay quietly on the white paper and seemed to invite admiration.

That afternoon he was messing about downstairs and spotted Sam Wickens, who tore across to him. 'You fucked off, you did.'

'I know.'

'What's up then?'

'I was fed up of it.'

'Did you want your mam?'

'She ain't there, she's poorly. You shut it, you!'

'They caught you quick.'

'They never.'

'Where'd you hide?'

'Nowhere. I was at my auntie's.'

'They find you there?'

'No. My uncle, he took me home.'

'Then what happened?'

'They come for me.'

'You silly wanker, 'course they did. Got any money?' he asked, all in the same breath.

'Why?'

His father had given him fifty pence, and Lilian had slipped three ten pence pieces into his hand as she was kissing him, as if she didn't want Uncle Steve to find out.

'I'm out of cigs,' Sam said. 'You got any money or not?'

Johnnie handed over the three tens. 'Have this if you want.'

Sam turned the coins over in his hand, flipped one and caught it, then ran off without a word. Afterwards he came back and told Johnnie that he had been to see a boy

who had Benson and Hedges to sell. 'They're cheap, see.'
He showed Johnnie the gold packet sealed in cellophane,
then stuffed it out of sight hastily as one of the assistants,
a woman, came down the corridor. 'Did you steal it from
your old man?' he whispered hoarsely.

'What?'

'The money, you stupid berk.'

'Yes,' Johnnie lied.

When Sam gave him a long hard look, and then,
convinced, said, 'Clever kid, ain't yah,' he was too choked
and dizzy with pride to answer. Suddenly he was ready
to believe that the whole miserable escapade had been a
triumph of bravery and initiative, that he had come away
with the spoils of victory in his pocket.

In bed, as the realization that he was back hit him, he
sobbed bitterly, muffling the sounds under the
institutional sheet and blanket. He had little sense of a
future. As far as he could tell, this was his world, probably
for ever.

Going off to school next day, trooping down the wide
featureless street with a gang of spindly boys from his
dormitory, the feel of the open space expanded him and
he felt better in spite of himself. Surprised, he acted like
the others, kicking gleefully at the heaps of dirty slush
with wellingtons provided by the Home, splashing
through every puddle he could find.

Sam Wickens went to the big secondary modern a few
streets away, so Johnnie had no contact with him until
after school. One day the older boy came up to him
looking nasty, with his shock of black hair and flaring
nostrils. He stood over Johnnie, fuming. 'Who do they
think they are? All they do is slag you off, the shower of
twats!'

'Who?'

'School. Teachers. It's so fucking boring. It's just balls.
Complete bollocks, it is.' He lowered his head and
whispered urgently, 'I'm going down town tomorrow –
wanna come?'

'Where to?'

'Anywhere. Tell you what, I'll show you how to ride

the handrail on the escalators down at Pond Street. Bus station, right? You wanna see me, I can go like the clappers. You comin' or not?'

Johnnie thought about it. The lure of his friend, primed with discontent, his eyes gleaming angrily, was irresistible to him. He nodded. 'I wouldn't mind.'

'You're frightened I bet. Little squirt like you.'

'Am I heck!'

'See if you can cadge any cigs.'

'Wheer from? Why?'

'So you can gi' 'em me.' He went off tittering.

They met outside in the street by arrangement after breakfast, ran across the road together and caught the first bus that came. It was easy. Down at the bus station Sam led his friend into the cafeteria, while crowds of people heading for work milled around, clogging the passageways and queuing for transport.

No sooner had they sat down on the moulded grey chairs than a woman came up to their table, slopping away with a wet dishcloth. She was middle-aged, with a paunch and great brawny arms. 'You boys ought to be at school, know that? I hope you ain't being naughty.'

'Nah,' Sam said, curling his lip and shooting a glance at his protégé. 'We're on an outing, see.'

'Where to?'

'Dunno. Ask the teacher.'

'I can't see one.'

'No, he hasn't come yet.'

'Well, you can't sit here unless you have something. This is for customers, here.'

'Yeah, we want tea.'

'It's up at the counter.'

'So it is.'

'And less of your lip.'

Sam gave her two fingers behind her back, acting big for his friend. The woman at the counter saw. 'If you don't behave, out you go,' she said sourly.

'What's up?'

'Don't be so cheeky.'

51

'Two teas and a packet of gingers,' Sam said, in such a loud injured tone that Johnnie wanted to laugh out loud.

When it was quieter they made for the escalators which lifted you straight out of the busy terminal to the pedestrian bridge, a world of concrete parapets and graffiti and vantage points, of blowing litter, newsagents, the smell of chips, of meat, down below a bird's-eye view of the buses and roads, the Sheaf Public Baths, the markets, and on the skyline opposite enormous grey ramparts of high-rise flats with their rows of balconies and coloured curtains and hung washing.

'Here, cop hold of this,' Sam said.

Johnnie found a roll of mints in his hand. They were just passing a kiosk jammed with papers, magazines, confectionery.

'What's this?'

'It fell off, like. I just caught it, didn' I?'

His laugh was at the same time a sneer of contempt. Johnnie, who hadn't seen a thing, marvelled at his daring and expertise.

He was too scared to attempt what Sam did next, balancing on the moving handrail in a crouching position and accelerating past old ladies as they descended with their shopping, backs turned, giving gasps of fright and nearly dying of heart attacks. He zoomed down at breakneck speed while Johnnie followed as fast as he could, vowing that one day he'd manage it too. Sam didn't jeer at him. After all he was the star, and swaggering now with Johnnie's adulation.

Johnnie spent the whole day following his friend and protector around like a shadow, always in a state of excitement and tension that was half fear. They got back to the Home just as school was over, circled the streets and went in wide-eyed, slyly congratulating one another. Sam owned a watch. He organized their every move like a true commander.

Johnnie played truant for the rest of that week, compelled by the sense of a strange ritual he was following, together with a blind loyalty. On Saturday he broke free, initiated. He walked around feeling superior, tougher than other kids of his age. On Sunday, listless and miserable again, he was astounded to see the figure of his father plodding towards him with an odd constrained smile and that fatalistic walk he recognized at once, leaning forward slightly as though the air was something solid which had to be shoved through blindly. Johnnie thought first, in a flash of panic, that it was terrible news about his mother. In fact his father never mentioned her.

'So this is it, eh?' he said, staring round vaguely.

'Visitors allus sit in there, Dad.' Johnnie pointed at a side door.

'What for?'

'Dunno.'

They sat in the visitors' room, which had a carpet. Then Johnnie showed his father round, as they were encouraged to do, not forgetting the lawn at the rear, soiled with ribs of old snow, and the walled garden and shrubs and flower beds. 'Hey, this isn't bad, not bad at all,' his father said at one point, to the boy's satisfaction.

Because Pat had asked him about school he went back, in trouble with the teacher for not bringing a note to explain his absence. Another weekend arrived, and more homesickness gathered to drown him. This time it was unendurable. He ran off in the direction of Frecheville, with a little speech prepared for an excuse. His legs were strong with purpose, his heart pumped violently, his lungs sucked in air, all in the service of one burning desire which had taken him over completely and seemed to be thrusting him from behind, urging him to go still faster.

He had to see his mother. He thought that if he didn't succeed in seeing her he would howl, disgracing himself in front of everyone. Only the night before he had dreamt that she was dead, burned to ashes in a fire. The flames roaring were alive in his mind even now. He got off the bus and careered round the corner of Mona Street, no longer frightened of what his father might say.

It was Saturday night. Next door was blazing with lights. It was on the corner, the only house which boasted a garage. They had no car, but Jason, the teenage son, kept his Suzuki in there, and also used the lean-to construction as a den for himself and his mates. They were inside now, playing heavy rock records full blast. Johnnie hammered in a sudden frenzy on the door of his father's house – he couldn't think of it any more as his home. The instant it opened, he blurted out, 'Is me mam dead? Is she, Dad?'

His father stared down at him, red-faced, without uttering a word. He took a deep breath, grasped his son's raincoat in a handful and pulled him inside with it. Not until the door was shut did he say, his chest rising and falling, 'Not you again. Bloody hell-fire, what are you on with this time?'

'I want to see me mam.'

'You want to see your mam,' Pat mocked. He was making a huge effort to control himself. 'Just like that. Don't talk so daft! Son, you're heading straight for trouble the way you're acting up. How long do you think they're going to put up with your silly capers, eh?'

'It don't matter if I come here to see me mam.'

'Who says so? Does it heck not matter!'

'I thought you could take me tomorrow.'

'And who said I was going?'

'Nobody.' Johnnie hung his head. So his mother was alive. It was just a nightmare he had had.

'Who is it, Pat?' he heard a voice call from the sitting room. 'Who's there?'

A strange heavy woman came out. She smiled foolishly, a smile without meaning, and put her hand to a wing of reddish hair falling over her forehead. She was younger than his mother, yet looked harder. There was something familiar about her – she was like any one of a dozen women he had seen around here in his childhood. She said, her voice friendly, 'Are you Johnnie, then?' When he nodded, unable to speak, she said, 'Cat got your tongue?' He guessed she would say that. She turned back into the living room and he saw that she had no stockings on and her slip was showing, hanging in a slant well below her skirt. The flesh of her legs was pasty.

On Sunday afternoon he was on his way back again. He sat sullenly with his father on the bus into town,

54

rubbing a hand repeatedly over his stubbly hair as he pleaded once more to be taken to his mother. He asked now without expecting a result. The frantic need within him had subsided. Still, it warmed and comforted him to ask, and to hear again his father's grudging promise. 'I'll come for you in a week or two, in the proper manner, understand?' he said, with an ugly movement of his head, his eyes unseeing. 'Now will you shut up about it. We're taking you to Undercliffe. What am I going to tell them about you this time, eh? Concentrate on that.'

7

A month passed, then another. He played truant again
with Sam Wickens, and was warned by the headmaster
and also by the master in charge of Undercliffe, Mr
Robbins. This was the bald, soft-spoken man in the
private office.

He was taken to see his mother, twice. She was greatly
improved, chatting to inmates as they walked about,
better than he had ever seen her. It was wonderful to
think he had regained her, and to hear her speaking freely
about old times.

'I'll be coming home soon, Johnnie.'

'When?'

'Soon. And so will you, love.'

'When will I?'

'The minute I do. Don't you fret. We'll soon have you
back, and Sue and Eileen as well.'

'When though?'

'When the doctor says. So stop pestering your poor
dad.'

She was looking into his face, really seeing him. She
kissed him when he left.

At Undercliffe one day, told to gather his belongings
together, he leapt at once to the wrong conclusion,
ramming dirty shirts and underpants into the small
suitcase his father had given him and tearing down to the
vestibule. Then he had to wait for ages, fretting.

He was taken to a Children's Admission Unit, a drab
echoing building with stone flags everywhere. Again he
was in a part of the city that was unknown to him. After
three days he was called in to an interview room. A
woman social worker, smiling stiffly, then resting a hand
on his shoulder as she stood over him, explained that a
lady was coming in who may want him to go and live
with her and her family. Before he could think what to

say, a well-dressed woman, the picture of self-assurance, entered the room and sat down by the desk.

'This is John Hunslett,' the social worker said. Johnnie had brushed his hair that morning in a new style in imitation of Sam Wickens. Now they were apart he hero-worshipped him more fervently than ever. He had stuck his head under the tap and then found a nail brush, jabbing it into his too-short hair impatiently. He looked permanently startled.

The woman beamed at the boy, at his small peaked face, wary and lost and nervous. She exclaimed, 'Oh my, isn't he small, poor little soul!'

Peggy Tomkin was a widow in her forties. What hypnotized Johnnie in those first moments were the shining happy grey-green eyes which never left his face for an instant, and the nice clothes she wore, the correct speech. Also the fact that this overwhelming lady had put in a request for him before she had even seen him. What a thing for a stranger to do!

'Would you like to live with me, Johnnie?'

'What for, Miss?'

The woman's hand flew to her mouth; she giggled. 'Because I'd be very pleased.'

Johnnie said, twisting his neck to see the social worker, 'I'm goin' home soon.'

'Yes you are,' the lady said. 'Until you do you can live with me, can't you?'

Johnnie turned again to the social worker, who was nodding yes and smiling at him.

'Have you got a dog?' he asked the strange lady.

Again the woman's hand flew to her mouth, and this time she let out a peal of amazed laughter. 'How on earth did you know that? Who told you that?'

'Nobody, Miss.'

'Then you're very clever. My name is Mrs Tomkin. Peggy.'

'Yes, Mrs.'

Outside, Mrs Tomkin settled the boy in her car, a black sleek affair, much larger than Steve's. Moving through the streets was like gliding on silk, black silk, like a film or a dream, purring along. She had sat him beside her after depositing his scratched suitcase on the rear seat. She did this gingerly, with a little pat. 'Let's see, how old are you, young man?' She wanted to hear him say it.

'Nine, Mrs.'

'Are you really, John?'

'Johnnie. I'm Johnnie.'

'I see. If that's what you prefer, Johnnie it is.'

He nodded, gazing out as they sped along. He felt safe beside this confident, scented woman, relishing the sight of her gloved hands on the wheel, resting there so lightly, guiding them through the heavy traffic, cars and vans and lorries zipping past in the other direction like missiles.

'Do you like cars?'

'Yes.'

'That's good.'

'Is this one streamlined?'

'Is it – what? Oh well, yes, I think I know what you mean. Yes I'm sure it is. Aren't you clever to think that!'

'It looks it.'

'Does it really?'

'Curved, like.'

'I see.'

He listened hard for the engine as they drove on. All he could detect was a faint throbbing, a pulsing up through the soles of his shoes. He tried to relax and take his ease, but didn't know how. If Sam Wickens could see him now he'd do his nut! And this lady was posh – her long stretched smile, the way her head turned in curiosity, her finicky hands. She gave the impression of someone choosing a path, someone with the freedom to choose. Her total difference to him and to people like his mother struck him in a single impression.

Sitting there, a wave of bitter rage shook him. Why had he been misled, why did they let him think he was going home to his mother, the only woman he wanted? He sat still, viciously hating this stupid dressy woman who thought she could step into his mother's place. The spasm passed, ended like a fit and he was left unchanged, empty, wondering what was coming next. Mrs Tomkin hummed quietly to herself.

They drove out in the direction of Derbyshire until they reached Millhouses and a length of flat park, laid out by the wide road and backing on to a swift-flowing stream full of green slimy rocks. Beyond that was the railway line. They were slowing down.

Mrs Tomkin's house looked prosperous, big and solid, of pale clean stone, with generous windows and a deep imposing porch overflowing with plants on ledges, each plant on its saucer. 'I want you to meet my boarders,' the woman said, strangely breathless. 'Let's see, what time is it? Oh yes, they'll be in now.'

They passed through the house and into a two-storey annexe built on at the rear, jutting out towards the rockeries and trellis arches. Everything became shabby and sour-smelling, the stair carpet worn through on every step, wallpaper stained and peeling. Upstairs, Mrs Tomkin led the boy into a largish square room that was nearly bare. Outside it was getting dark.

An unshaded bulb hung down. Mrs Tomkin switched it on. 'Let's have some light, shall we, dears?' she cried.

Two men were sitting on a cheap settee which had torn, dusty upholstery. There was a junky armchair with a coloured boy of fifteen or so squatting in it, his legs drawn up, the corrugated soles of his trainers showing. An enormous colour television, sunk down on one side, was transmitting a fuzzy lurid picture containing too much red, the faces looming out diseased and blotchy, on fire.

The man nearest the door said hallo in a warm sentimental brogue. 'Now who might this be?' he asked, like a too-friendly drunk. Mrs Tomkin perched on a hard chair and told them that Johnnie had come to join the household, and to be nice to him. 'As I know you will be,' she rushed on, 'because we're a happy family here, and so fortunate to be enjoying the love of Our Lord.'

A young man with black curly hair in the far corner of the settee, huddled there like someone condemned or ill, his thin body lifeless, stared at nothing. The ingratiating older man, whose shirt was missing a collar, began to talk

59

garrulously about himself. 'I'm Terry, you can call me that. I come from Dublin, Ireland, I wonder if you know where that is, a little feller like you? Over the water, a long way off. One day I'll be seeing it again, oh yes, when I've got myself straightened out. I've got problems, which you're too young to understand, never mind, bless you, lad. This kind lady has brought me into her house and with her helping hand I'll be just fine. Things aren't so bad, and getting better by the day. Listen Johnnie, I've got a boy not much older than you, what d'you think of that? He's in Ireland with his dear old gran –'

'Yes,' Mrs Tomkin said rapidly, 'we have so much to be thankful for, don't we, all of us.' She turned to Johnnie and steered him towards the door. 'Now come and meet my daughter, her name's Janice.'

'And a beautiful name, a favourite of mine,' Terry babbled. 'Maureen is another.'

'We know, we know,' Mrs Tomkin said. She led Johnnie out on to the landing. Then she dropped her voice to say, 'Terry, poor man, he's got what's called a drink problem. I took him in because he was desperate, and now I'm glad. Rewarded.' Talking to him as if to an adult, she went on, 'I have three boarders, and one to come – at least I think he's coming this evening from wherever he's been living. Ted, yes. I was told he was very unhappy, and I said yes, send the poor man, although really I'm full up. My boarders are all unemployed, I only take those in need. I give them breakfast, nothing else. They have their own kitchen which they share. Only men I take, it avoids problems that way.'

It was a mystery that she should spill out these details to him. Like all the other mysteries, he accepted it. They returned to the spacious house proper, with its solid dark furniture and thick beige carpets, flounced net curtains in creamy swathes at all the windows. A young black and white sheepdog ran out from another room and began jumping up at him. 'Down, darling,' Mrs Tomkin said in a sharp voice. The animal took no notice.

'What's his name?' Johnnie asked.

'Ben. Bad Ben.'

The dog leapt up again and he caught hold of it, placing its front paws on his chest. Johnnie rumpled its ears and it barked joyfully into his face, bright-eyed, its wet tongue slithering between its teeth. 'Good lad. You're a right good un!'

'Noisy dog,' Mrs Tomkin said. She hurried off somewhere and Johnnie was left alone.

The rooms he peered into were all surprisingly disorderly. A girl was sitting in one, crossly looking up from the bay window where she sat, frowning at him. Johnnie stared at her. She had her mother's rather blank good looks, but her eyes were small and not pleasant. She was about the age of his sister, Sue. Just for a second he thought she had materialized by magic, come to fetch him home.

Mrs Tomkin came back. She introduced him. 'This is my daughter, Janice.'

'Oh lord, not another one,' the girl sneered.

'That's not very nice. This is a Christian family, as I've explained to Johnnie, and everyone who lives here belongs to it, we have no exceptions, you know that perfectly well.'

The girl heaved a sigh. 'Mummy, do you mind – I'm trying to do my homework.'

'I can't see any. Where?'

'This, this.' Janice kicked at a book down by her feet.

'How much do you have?'

'Too much. Loads.'

'That's no excuse for bad manners,' her mother said, in a tone which told you she had said it a hundred times already. 'Come along, dear,' she said to Johnnie, 'I'll show you your little room, nice and snug and all to yourself. It's an attic, I haven't quite finished clearing it out yet.'

'Not that crummy place,' Janice cried. 'It's foul, it's got rotten broken chairs and spiders.'

'I'm sure Johnnie will help me clear it up, won't you dear?'

'I wouldn't put our dog in it,' Janice muttered. Her mother didn't seem to hear.

Climbing the stairs, she said. 'You'll like Lionel, he's a

61

lovely open boy. This is a happy house, as you'll soon discover.' Lionel was the Jamaican youth in the annexe, expelled from school and out of a job. 'He's been bad, under the influence of bad company. He adores it here. I've only had to get rid of one person, one failure, a drug addict. My daughter comes first, and that's what I told him. And I'm responsible for others, weak unfortunates who depend on me for shelter.'

Johnnie no longer paid any attention to the woman, who clearly didn't need his answers and who was creepy and perhaps mad, he thought, but not in a way you could explain to anybody. Mad and crafty, or acting a part, he couldn't decide. Confronted by the clutter and dirt in the tiny attic, she merely said, 'I haven't been here for a while. I'll get one of the men to come up here, a strong willing person,' and turned away with a bored expression.

A little later, she was saying, she would give him his pocket money from social services and deduct fifteen pence towards soap and toothpaste. 'Everything is so expensive now, unless I balance my budget I'm in trouble. Then where would we all be? That's right, isn't it? Do you know what a budget is? Of course you don't, not yet. But I have to.'

A thought struck her and she halted on the stairs, halfway down. 'Donald, you saw Donald, he's very depressed and doesn't say anything as a rule.'

Johnnie couldn't wait to get back to the dog. As if reading his thoughts, Mrs Tomkin halted on the stairs again. 'Would you like to take Ben out into the garden?'

'I would, Mrs.'

'Will you be happy here d'you think?'

'Yes thank you, Mrs.'

At the bottom of the stairs, he said, 'Can I tek 'im out for a walk on a lead, your Ben?'

'Oh, I expect so. Only not today.'

By Johnnie's standards the district was a wealthy one: precise lawns, roses, wide empty side roads and no blowing litter, flowering cherry trees bursting into blossom, lots of space and light. The house backed on to public wooded land that extended as far as he could see, rising gently as it receded. A sign with a pointing finger said 'Bridle Path'. To him it was an enchanted domain, with paths winding through and the hoofprints of horses.

One Saturday he was out with Ben. Well away from the house, he unfastened the leash. The dog ran around in a circle, sniffing at every blade of grass under its nose. Yelping happily it flopped on its back and squirmed its spine.

This was the day he saw his first horse and rider close up. The glossy flanks of the great stately animal, powerfully working, were so near that he could have reached out and touched. A girl in a hard round hat, pale as an apparition, nodded gravely down at him as she passed.

8

He was moved to another school, Abbeydale Road Juniors, at the seedy edges of the city bordering on Heeley, a rough area. The surroundings were of a familiar kind: strong-smelling pubs, cheap stores and little cut-price super-markets jumbled together, second-hand furniture on the pavement, the usual chippies and newsagents and a bookie; a fancy unisex salon, Gino's, derelict houses with smashed windows, a junk shop packed with reconditioned TV sets, a sex shop, Adults Only. Slummy side streets ran a short distance to a line of railings or were blocked off by small nondescript factories. Asians trailed by, Indian women in silver and rose saris, wearing nose studs, who always walked along unhurriedly. Johnnie was lost again, not knowing where he was, a stranger to everyone.

One day Mrs Tomkin handed him a letter. 'For Master John Hunslett – could that be you?' She smiled coyly and went away.

The lined notepaper was carefully addressed and dated, as his sister had been taught at school:

Dear Johnnie,
    This is me, Susan. I hope you are well. I think of you a lot, and so does Eileen. They have given us your address, is it a nice house where you are staying? We are back with Dad now, who says you will be as well if you behave yourself and stop running away and mitching school and that. Our mam is coming out of hospital soon we think. I am very well. The house was sold up and we are in this council flat, third floor, here is the address. It is all new and very nice indeed. I am only afraid of the lift. If we can we will come and visit you this weekend. What is the lady like? Keep smiling. This is a long letter for me.
                    Love, Sue.

Sue came as she promised on Saturday, but she was alone. She stood ringing the bell, awed by the leafy suburb, standing very tensely in her red winter coat. Her effort not to be intimidated gave her whole figure a resolution beyond her years.

She and Eileen had been fostered, but nothing like this. It had been in a dump over in Pittsmoor, at the bottom of a terrifically steep hill called Sydney Street. That was after they had spent a desolate week in the Admission Unit. The Sydney Street place was the weirdest house she had ever been in, squeezed into a narrow space and on different levels. The layout of the building was all wrong, makeshift. The girls found it hard to work out. Mrs Davies, the foster mother, would notice Sue's bewildered expression and say, 'Now what have you lost?'

'My room.'

'Oh dear, now you're in trouble. Where did you leave it?'

Sue laughed. 'I can't remember.'

To get to the kitchen from the street you went up a flight of stairs and twisted round, to go to bed you descended into the cellar, or where the cellar would have been in an ordinary house. Inside, everything was dilapidated, woodwork painted the same washed-out green. Two doors further down the street ended in rubble and a tip left by the builders, on the level ground which they were still making into a raw estate with unfinished roads, the drain gratings poking up. Beyond this wasteland was a high-rise tower, one only, perched at the edge of nothing and soaring aimlessly upwards, like a mistake. Lit at night, it achieved a fragility which Sue perceived as beauty, except that the weight and crazy isolation of it scared her. If she was out she tended to look elsewhere, away from that direction. It had a stricken air, and made her at times deeply uneasy. Now and then she saw a stray old man or a woman with a pushchair moving in or out at the base of it.

The house where they lived had a funny atmosphere, as if it was brooding, but nothing to do with them. They were dealt with, given meals, and then ignored. 'Come and get it,' the woman called when it was time to eat. She was big, morose, dark, always standing in the kitchen or at the ironing board, with no words for her husband or for anyone. The household was permanently chaotic. Who cared? A baby girl toddled about and fell over, a crazy puppy was leaping out of its skin with life, squealing like a pig when it was stepped on. There was an ugly obese cat, grown too fat to escape through the cat door, hissing with bad temper. A boy of six had a cardboard box containing gerbils which he carried from room to room. The mother always seemed about to make some baleful remark, but when she did speak it wasn't anything worth saying. Somebody in the street said she was Jewish.

Martin Davies, the absentee father, came and went. He called out to his wife, 'Joanna, I'm off for a bit.' Usually there was no response. Once Sue heard her mutter to herself. 'You've been off for years.' Eileen whispered to her sister that Mr Davies must be the ugliest man in the world, 'like a gorilla', and Sue agreed. Yet she liked him.

They had only the vaguest idea of what he did, which was teaching part-time in a college. A battered, hulking man, he took the mad pup out on a lead. After five minutes he would bring the dog back and be off to the pub. Upstairs he had a cramped room, the smallest in the house, called a study, where he holed up at weekends. Once he caught Sue cautiously peering in. He called to her. There were paperbacks everywhere, slipping off chairs, heaped in confusion along badly-fixed shelves. On a wall was pinned a huge blow-up portrait of a man whose lean bald head and slanting eyes proclaimed that he was foreign – and something else. It was a compressed head, all bones, aimed like a fist.

Martin saw the girl staring. 'Seen him before?'

'I'm not sure.'

'Have a guess.'

She shook her head.

'Lenin, that is. Have they told you about him at school?'

'I don't think so.'

'They might get round to it. Wouldn't bank on it, mind.' His speech was slurred. He was blundering about,

66

dropping papers, grinning at her with his rotten teeth. He gurgled something, coughing and spluttering.

'Pardon?'

'Why, what have you done?'

Ash fell from his cigarette. Tommy burst in to say the dinner was ready.

Sue waited. She heard a noise behind the door. A woman's high voice cried, 'Wait a minute.' The door swung open importantly and a black and white sheepdog ran out. It leapt over the low wall to her right and disappeared into the overgrown garden next door. 'Oh Ben, that's naughty!' the excited, fluffy woman said. She hitched up her skirt and scrambled on to the wall. A girl came out. 'Mummy, what on earth are you doing up there?'

The woman reappeared, flushed and pleased, shooing the dog in front of her. 'It's all right,' she told Sue intimately, 'there's nobody living there at the moment. Have you come to see Johnnie?'

'Yes.'

'How nice for him. He's here somewhere I know.'

'Is that a new coat?' Janice asked the visitor rudely.

'Not really.'

'Where did you get it?'

'Etam.'

'That's a cheap shop,' the girl said.

'I know.'

Johnnie sidled up, and Sue wanted to give him a hug, he looked so sheepish and sad. Instead she said boldly, 'Are you going to show me where you sleep?'

'All right.'

'Yes, you take her up, dear. This is your home, you go where you please, don't you.' Mrs Tomkin was all smiles. She left them alone, and Sue said, 'It's awful big, this house.'

'Why're you whisperin'?'

'I don't know.'

'I hate it now.'

'I don't like that girl – what's her name?'

'Janice.'

'She's horrible. The lady seems fine. Does she always talk like that?'

'She's a nutter.'

'Johnnie!''

'This place is full of nutters.'

'Why, who else lives here?'

'Lodgers.'

'Where are they, then? Are you making it up?'

'Course not.'

She twisted the clasp of her shiny black handbag and gave him a paper bag. 'Look what I've brought you.' He opened it sullenly without answering, fishing out the Mars bar and a tube of Smarties. 'Now what d'you say?'

'Thanks.'

'Johnnie, listen, you'll be out of here soon, back home with me and Eileen.'

'When though?'

'Soon, they say. Are you going to school properly?'

'Course I am.'

'I hope so. Shall we go down again now? Are we getting any tea?'

'Dunno.'

Downstairs, Sue jumped as the doorbell rang. Mrs Tomkin appeared. 'Who can that be? My, aren't we busy with callers today.'

A man who must have been forty, his black hair nearly gone, with brilliant points dancing about in his eyes, stood on the threshold. He cried out at once in a strange passion, 'I got lost, I did, Mrs Tom-kin! I took the wrong turn!' He had a white chubby face and the excitability of a child. When he caught sight of Sue he backed away, grinning and afraid.

'Never mind, Danny, you're here now,' Mrs Tomkin said. She took his arm firmly. 'We'll go and find Janice, shall we?'

'Janice knows. She likes Danny.'

'We all like you. I thought you were coming last night to see us?'

'No, I couldn't, I couldn't,' the man gabbled. 'Some

boys played a trick on me, see. Shut me in a phone box, held the door to.'

'That wasn't very nice. Well, you're here now.'

'I got lost though, Mrs Tom-kin!'

Left to themselves again, Johnnie and Sue looked at each other. 'See what I mean?' Johnnie hissed. 'Nutters.'

'Poor man,' Sue said gravely. 'Don't say that word, it's cruel. He's what they call retarded.' She stood there, an untouched, skimpily-fleshed girl of fifteen, shaken by her encounter. She had been afraid she might be touched or blundered into by the child-man with his fear all loose, flying chaotically into his eyes and making them shine madly. Why was he so eager, in such a rush? His shiny wet mouth was too loose, slushing away at his words. Aware of her disgust, yet with pity for the man's helplessness working in her, she wanted to keep her feelings of repugnance a secret from herself. He was too naked, he ought to be covered up, she thought wildly, in confusion. His stubby nail-bitten fingers gave her the shudders. 'I'll have to go in a minute,' she told her brother, her voice upset.

'Why has your voice gone funny?'

'It hasn't!'

'When are you coming back?'

'Next week perhaps. Now you be good and go to school. You are going, aren't you?'

'If I feel like it.'

'Johnnie!'

'I was only kiddin'. It just came out.'

'I can never tell with you.'

On the way home she was preoccupied with something else, a violent scene she had witnessed earlier on the top deck of the 24 bus. A fight had broken out on the back seats between two teenage girls. A noisy pack, girls of around her own age, had taken over the rear seats with their squawking, raucous shrieks and catcalls. Suddenly the fight erupted. A skinny blonde and a bristly-haired girl who was small and dark threw themselves at each other as if they meant to kill. 'You take that back, dirty bitch!' the small one raged. 'Say that again, once more, go on, bleedin' little bitch you are!' The blonde girl swore and lashed out with her bag, staggering on her high heels. Caught off balance by the surprise attack her accuser fell back, dragging the taller girl on top of her. They struggled madly in a heap, legs entangled. Then a hefty fellow in an anorak had jumped up and was trying to prise them apart. He fell over himself briefly, got up again and was saying in a patient, shocked voice, holding the two girls away from him, 'Hey, fuckin' 'ell ladies, cut it out. Hey, they'll throw you off in a sec.'

Sue was twisted round in her seat and saw everything, her heart pounding with a strange excitement at her closeness to danger. The raw spurting hatred had a meaning for her; she exulted in it without understanding why. At the same time it made her feel sick. The blonde girl left the gang and shouted back some final abuse, getting off. 'I'll get you, see if I don't,' the scrawny little one screamed after her. 'You wait, I'll get you good.' Then the bus reached the Heeley stop and the other girls piled down the stairs and gathered in a flock on the pavement. Sue craned to see. She couldn't take her eyes off them. They were bunched on the corner and from where she sat, peering down, their thin shoulders were terribly similar. They glanced anywhere but at each other and yet were undeniably a group. Suddenly, as if controlled, they took off together, down the slope to the left and past some open grassy banks towards the railway bridge, twittering and fluttering. Their tight skirts and pointed shoes made it look as if they had been copying each other.

9

Johnnie went right through to July on his best behaviour. Often he was tempted to play truant. School bored him, and he thought he might bump into Sam Wickens or someone else he knew from Undercliffe if he roamed the streets. He kept reminding himself of Sue and the things she had said. If they had him marked down as 'unruly', that was the word, he wouldn't get back home so early, maybe not until Christmas. His stomach sickened at the thought.

Sue had warned him solemnly, 'No theft, Johnnie.' The word was foreign to him.

'What's that?'

She thought he was acting stupid. Then she saw he wasn't. 'Theft, you know. Thieving. Taking things.'

'What things?'

'Things that don't belong to you.'

Who could have told such a lie about him? No one had accused him directly, or gone through his pockets. Who had been spreading a rumour like that?

He was puzzled too by his sister's remark that it was entirely up to his father now, who had taken out a Voluntary Care Order on him. All he had to do, she explained, was cancel the order and take responsibility for his son. 'But he won't if you're unruly,' Sue told him.

'Who says I am?'

'I'm just telling you.'

'I'm not, anyhow.'

'Good.'

Anyway, she was only repeating what she had heard. He would be running around in the playground and it came into his mind, 'unruly'.

August came. On a muggy, airless day he was taken by Mr Stanley, a social worker he had met before, to

Providence Park flats, part of the immense estate he had seen only from the outside, looking across to the skyline from the concrete shopping balcony above the bus station. He was fascinated to think that this was where he would now live. On his own he would have been petrified. It was like entering a prison. Unshaven men in grubby vests squatted against smeared walls. They went up a common staircase, the tiles reminding him of all the subways he had run through. From one interior where the door was flung wide open he smelled cats and mildew. On another walkway, open to the sky like a long bridge, there was a stench of urine. He saw the graffiti, several smashed windows, a derelict flat cluttered with junk, a mongrel scrabbling in a corner. Then, at number 82, going inside, it was another world. He was home. The square room, clean and nice-smelling, gleamed with light.

His sisters had told him to expect his mother. She came up and embraced him shyly without a word. He was thrown into bewilderment, deeply embarrassed because she never did such things, and Mr Stanley was present with his papers, saying something official which no one heeded.

Marilyn Hunslett said, 'Johnnie.' She tried not to feel cut off from this boy, silent and contained like a man, who seemed unaccountably altered, freezing her with his difference. She wanted to rock him in her arms but he was already too old, he would have hated her. 'You all right, Mam?' he stammered, not knowing what to say, worried by her. For him nothing had changed. A sadness about her made him lose heart, and now there was something else, a haunted look coming and going, as if a shape she couldn't quite see but dreaded was standing behind her. She lived in shadows. Now she made an effort and emerged, smiling nervously at him, hoping Mr Stanley would go soon. 'Aren't we lucky?' she said to Johnnie, to everybody, not properly focussed. 'This has just been redecorated. I like primrose, nice and fresh. It's the balcony I don't like. I want you to stay away from there, all of you.'

She also went on about the lifts, how dangerous they

were – not that the girls needed telling. 'It's not just the stink,' Eileen told Johnnie sagely. 'You can get pounced on.'

She was now thirteen, wary with a knowledge shot through with contradictions, saying something dire with a deadpan face and then grinning cheekily, wide-eyed and curious, as if to say: that's the way it is! In the same breath she mentioned blithely that she had joined the Stop Smoking sessions at school, as they sat round on Johnnie's first evening at home.

It was a steamy night. Johnnie listened, a little alarmed – though he wasn't going to show it – by all the strange sounds, clattering footsteps out on the walkway, the odd blood-curdling screech. His mother's face was dreamy, vacant.

'Where's me dad?' Johnnie asked, then fell silent when he saw Sue frowning and shaking her head.

His mother mopped at her forehead with a tissue. If she smiled across at them it was obviously an act of propitiation, a plea to be ignored. One of the girls, usually Eileen with her tactlessness, would forget and press her too insistently with some question, driving her to turn at bay. In her eyes would be a desperate, frantic look. The idle chatter would die down. Her peculiar, unexplained intensity frightened them.

Eileen wailed once to her sister, in the semi-privacy of their room, 'Why can't we have an ordinary mother like everybody else?' Sue, who refused to admit to any unease, told her angrily to shut her mouth. It did no good talking like that, and their mother had been through enough, she shouldn't be hurt by cruel words. How much could be heard through these plasterboard walls?

Sometimes the fear was contagious. Usually the girls were saved by selfishness, by curiosity, a hunger for new contacts. Their mother's shadowy being was like a question hanging in the air which didn't concern them, a troubling irrelevance. Nothing would alter it, so why bother? In her callous moments Eileen saw her mother's brooding introspection as something which went with the flat. Any time you wanted to get rid of it, you opened the door and went out. She had learned at school the lesson about restrictions, that they were there to be dodged.

Johnnie felt an aggression in his younger sister which was new to him. 'I didn't know you smoked,' he said. 'Stupid, that is.' He wasn't averse to a drag himself, but he was a boy, it was different.

'Yeh, you do it, like,' Eileen said, flicking glances towards her docile mother, at her melancholy downcast face. 'Nearly everybody does to start with. You think it makes you cool, but it just makes you smell awful.'

Sue said nothing. By her expression she was unconvinced. When her mother went into the kitchen she answered Johnnie's questions about her father's disappearance in a low discreet voice.

'Where's he gone, our dad?'

'London, I think Mam said. That way.'

Eileen was stroking at the paper sleeve of her new Dire Straits single, bought that day. 'This is great, this,' she crooned to herself. No one paid any attention to her.

'What's he gone to London for?' Johnnie persisted. He was vaguely relieved. He liked the female atmosphere, which reassured and cossetted him, even though it got on his nerves after a few hours. What he appreciated most was the absence of tension, and feeling wanted, soothed by the care given to small things, the feminine attention to details which at the same time irritated his skin after a while. Sue didn't seem inclined to answer him. He asked again.

'Oh, looking for work,' Sue said evasively, so that he didn't believe her. Not that it mattered. He thought no more about it.

Suddenly he felt drained, dog-tired, after absorbing such a mass of first impressions. The charged reunion with his mother had exhausted him too; perhaps that most of all. Marilyn, always telepathic where her son was concerned, said, 'Johnnie, it's past your bedtime, you know that?' He put up no resistance.

The two girls shared one small room. He was in a corner of his parents' bedroom. There, facing him, was the dominating double bed he had last seen at Frecheville.

74

Lying in the strange room alone he tossed about briefly, stifled by the heat. A ferocious cat fight woke him up. Then in the small hours he jerked awake to find himself in a panic attack, seized by the terrifying wild premonition that his mother would be danced off again into irrationality by a force erupting from nowhere – a repeat of that black Wednesday when everything he thought was permanent had been blasted, razed to the ground. All his miseries could be traced back to that day. Before that it had been paradise. He sobbed into the pillow, wanting his mother to come, but she was oblivious. He could hear her snoring on the other side of the room.

10

His premonition was both right and wrong. His mother fell ill in the new year, with winter upon them again and the darkness locking them in early each night. But it wasn't like the first time. Anyway, he didn't witness it. Nothing happens in the same way twice.

One day his mother simply wasn't there. The teacher broke the news to him at school. He took the boy to one side, fumbling awkwardly over his words. 'John, now listen carefully, and don't be upset by what I'm about to say . . . You won't be going home tonight. A Mr Stanley will meet you after school, he'll explain the situation to you better than I can, okay? Sorry to have to tell you like this. Off you go, lad . . . '

He heard the full story later. When he went out to the hospital at Maltby it was confirmed by what he saw. His mother had her left leg in plaster. One morning she had gone downstairs to visit young Mrs Blecher, a friend, on the second floor. She knocked on the door, heard a voice call out and went in. The living room window gaped open. Tina Blecher had been entertaining a few friends the night before and now she was freshening the air. A cold wind flapped the curtains.

Marilyn had gone down in a desperate state, unable to bear herself, full of a black water which kept rising, rising. She entered her friend's flat and ran straight for the window. A chair stood there. She climbed up and in one movement she was on the sill and out. Tina Blecher screamed. Marilyn lay sprawled on the ground among cans and scraps of torn paper, her leg broken. At the hospital she was subjected to ECT, lying anaesthetized on the rubber sheet with her plastered leg.

Another series of bad experiences began for Johnnie; another Home, more foster parents in districts he didn't know existed. Tougher than before, he coped better this time. Again he lost contact with his sisters.

His mother came home. On the eve of his twelfth birthday they were once more reunited as a family, again in Providence Park but allocated a different flat. They were on the second floor of the same block. And now no one bothered to dress up the truth about their father, who had abandoned them. No one expected to see him again.

'The rotten bugger,' Johnnie said to Sue.

'Shut it. Just don't let Mam hear you talk like that.'

They weren't even supposed to mention him in front of their mother. It worked her up and she was liable to lose control of her nerves again, they were told.

Sue was talking all the time now of finding a place of her own and moving out. She had left school and worked for National Travel. Around midnight she came in flushed from discos, or stayed overnight with friends because of the danger of getting into the block late. At times she drew close to Eileen and they seemed good pals, then a furious row would break out and Sue would storm through the door saying she'd go mad if she didn't soon have a room of her own. 'Get one, then!' Marilyn would shout, trembling all over. 'Bloody well get out and shut up about it, and good riddance!' Then mother and daughter would make it up, clinging to each other like wreckage, blubbering, as Johnnie called it.

Sue's face was changing subtly, her intelligent eyes more secretive and inward. She dolled herself up, bought make-up which she locked away in a casket, wearing the key around her neck like a charm, threaded on a thong of leather. She applied her eyeliner expertly, even curled her lashes, creating a mask for herself, sinful-looking, yet chaste as a doll. Bland and clever, her exterior was becoming impenetrable, a cold shell inside which she lived for herself alone, not confiding in anyone, not trusting others too much.

For different reasons, Johnnie also kept things to himself. He had learned to avoid telling the whole truth. Blurting everything out could get you straight into trouble. No one in his family knew the full story about him any more, how he had run away from one foster mother, for instance – he hated her, that plump shiny face! – and slept rough for a week, until the police picked him up. In a yard behind a construction site at Broomhill he built a little shelter out of doors that he propped one against the other, lining his refuge with polythene sacks. He spent two nights there, then found his hut demolished when he sneaked back at the end of the second weary day. Cold and hungry, he slept in a partly wrecked car left up an alley. Each morning he stole milk from doorsteps. In Sheaf Market he flitted past the fruit stalls with apples in his pockets. At Tesco's he got away with biscuits and crisp packets under his coat, his face tense, pushing up close to a woman shopper at the checkout to give the impression they were together.

On his fourth day he met an older boy who was on the run from his stepfather.

'What's your name then?'

'Johnnie. What's yourn?'

'Martin.'

That evening they raided a cash-and-carry warehouse on a trading estate, lobbing a brick through a window and shinning up a drainpipe. They filled a plastic bag with Park Drive cartons, stashing the loot in a nearby park. Johnnie was on his way there the next day when the policeman nabbed him. Shocked, he said no to every question: No, don't know. He was taken back to the social services office in town while they decided what to do with him. He was now a problem. They found a Home with strict discipline. He lasted a month, then cut and ran again. Once more, they warned, and it would be a Community Home for him – this was their euphemism for an approved school. 'Do you understand what we're saying, boy?'

'Yes, sir.'

'You don't want to end up in prison when you're older, do you?'

'No, sir.'

'Well, you think about it. How old are you?'

'Twelve, sir.'

'Old enough to know better.'

Silence. Johnnie made for the door.

'Now where are you going?'

'Out, sir.'

'I'll tell you when.'

'Yes, sir.'

'Are you listening? Is anything going in? Anything at all?'

'Lots, sir.'

'Go on, get out of here.'

Then one day a member of staff marched up and told him to pack his things.

'What for?'

'Just do it, Hunslett.'

A social worker waited outside with a car, not Mr Stanley but a bright-eyed young fellow wearing jeans and trainers and a leather jacket.

'Where am I going, Mister?' Johnnie asked as they drove off.

The man, with his clean, frank features, hair curling on his collar, was like his Uncle Steve, only nicer. 'I've got a surprise for you, John. We're going home to your mother. How does that grab you, eh?'

'All right, ta.'

'My name's Adrian by the way.'

'Yeh, right.'

As they drove up the approach road to the huge estate, the social worker said quietly, 'Try not to mess it up, there's a good lad. Your mother's been through a lot, so I believe.'

'I know she has.'

So he was home again.

Adrian Bagley was a voluntary worker, and unlike any official Johnnie had encountered. He would call round on the off chance, no arrangement. It was obvious that his mother liked him. She went pink, dashed away to make tea, talked in a new fast, rather scatty outpouring, on and on about nothing at all, until Johnnie itched and wriggled uncomfortably, wanting her to stop. Adrian just laughed and joked, from time to time scratching his head boyishly in the wry gesture that seemed part of his character. Eileen liked him too. Once she dived into her room and then sauntered out after a decent interval wearing her brand new white ra-ra skirt and flimsy pale blue top. She sat ogling, her manner so odd and offhand that she soon had Johnnie longing to aim a kick at her. What a show-off! She was pretty now, endlessly brushing her long fair hair. Johnnie would see that wooden hairbrush with nylon bristles appear in her hand and yell, 'Not again! How many times is that today?'

'You can shurrup,' Eileen would snap, or 'Who pulled your trunk?' Once she said, 'Up yours,' and her mother heard. She threw her out of the flat and slammed the door. 'Come back when you've washed out your mouth!' she screamed after her.

At first Johnnie was convinced that Adrian's calls were for the benefit of his mother. The man listened patiently, nodding, asking if it was all right to smoke his pipe, while Marilyn poured out her troubles, at first haltingly, then in a flood, helplessly talking, pausing only to apologize for unloading her worries on a total stranger. 'You carry on,' he told her. 'Get it off your chest. I'm a very good listener.'

She mentioned the Valium, her crying jags, pains in her stomach, the times she had lain awake in the small hours, horrified by a mounting fear of never being able to sleep again.

'Never?' he asked softly.

'Yes, never! Can you understand that, have you ever felt that?'

She watched him, in the grip of a compulsion to talk that was stronger than sex, altogether more important, wondering if she should be ashamed of herself. Did he see her as lonely and pathetic, whirling round and round inside her own head, endlessly thwarted? Had he met dozens, hundreds like her on his rounds? He must have done. As she talked on, her eyes pleaded for him to regard her as special, as Marilyn Hunslett, not confused with anyone else, while her half smile came and went, as if she were mocking them both for taking such drivel seriously. 'It's all a waste of time, anyway,' she said aloud, angrily, almost glaring at him in accusation.

'I don't agree,' Adrian murmured firmly. He sat back and waited. A wave of irritation and mistrust stopped her, and her eyes became less friendly. How did he have so much time? He was so young, what experience could he have? His motives were unclear to her. She lost confidence in him.

'It's just words,' she muttered in disgust, clearing away the cups and saucers.

'You don't really believe that.'

'Don't I?'

'No.'

Whatever he was doing, sitting there scribbling or picking his way over to the window to glance out, he gave the impression that he was ready to leave off, to listen again without a murmur of complaint when her mood swung her into another confessional. His endless receptivity and his view of himself as a person able to coax people into confiding in him, made his good intentions seem a little cloying and complacent. Marilyn fell silent: the mad urge to turn herself inside out left her. She saw in front of her this rather self-satisfied young man who only irritated her. He looked unmarked by life. She said she had to go out shopping in a few minutes. He took the hint and left.

But he was very stubborn, and convinced by himself. In a couple of days he was back, fixing up an outing for Johnnie to see Sheffield Wednesday play at home. 'If you like football, that is,' he said, kidding, winking at Marilyn.

'I do, yeh.'

'Are we on then?'

'I'll say. Thanks, Adrian.'

His mother warned him not to be cheeky, poking at him in reproach, but Adrian gleamed with delight, assuring her that it was how he liked to be addressed. He went off triumphant. 'Never mind what he says,' Johnnie's mother lectured him, 'I don't like to hear it. It's rude. Call him Mr Bagley, you hear?'

'He don't want me to.'

Marilyn lashed out at her son's head. He ducked nimbly out of reach. 'Do as you're told!' It was a losing battle with boys. Tell them one thing and they did the opposite. Girls were sensible, boys just silly. Without a man around to keep order, what was the use? She opened her mouth to say more, then shut it again. Johnnie had escaped.

So why bother? Why not give up, forget, take each day as it came, like the other women around here? Like her friend Tina Belcher did. Or did she? Marilyn liked her for her easy temperament and her warm nature, opening the door to her smiling. Her eyes would register surprise, then light up with genuine pleasure. Hair always in a tangle.

Marilyn would feel an impulse to sit her down and comb out that unruly-looking head, to groom it, and in so doing draw closer to her. 'I'll put the kettle on,' Tina always said. Marilyn stopped wondering then if she was making a nuisance of herself. Sometimes she experienced a pang of memory, recognizing as if in a mirror a former self, far back, when she was hardly ever angry or tired. One thing about the hospital, it was a rest. Often she disliked herself, spending time futilely with this pleasant young woman. Yet she was drawn to her for some reason.

Tina's direct gaze, and a certain concision about her speech, seemed to help Marilyn clarify her own thoughts. She felt refreshed, less tormented in spirit, without knowing why. She asked herself what lay behind that friendly, rather sluttish exterior. What was the catch? No one, in her experience, had life totally sorted out. She would wait for some mention of a problem, a little resentful at being kept in the dark.

Tina had a small daughter, a toddler, an impish tomboy of three who ran about entirely naked on summer days. Another smiler. Marilyn had no objection to the child's nakedness, though without exactly approving of it. Once she went down to the estate shop with Tina, and Jan came, still naked, wearing a pair of sandals and nothing else, running ahead of them and up to the counter for her ice cream. Marilyn noticed the woman's face as she handed over the cornet, and that was her feeling too. Out in the open a child should be covered; she and Tina parted company there. But she kept her opinion to herself.

Johnnie ran out and she was alone again. It often happened these days. Eileen would go down to the youthie – that was her name for it. As for Sue, she might be anywhere. Marilyn saw little of her. Next door's ITN news penetrated the wall.

She saw her family as respectable, and her grip on it slipping. Johnnie was quarrelsome and he defied her now with ease – look at that wedge haircut! Instead of asking her permission he went ahead and did things, then came in primed and spoiling for a fight. One word of reproach and he was rearing up, so touchy. She felt her energy to be insufficient; she needed help. What could she do? No use depending on Sue now for any backing. The girl couldn't be blamed – it was the age she'd reached. Marilyn saw how other mothers' children behaved, those friends of Sue, feverishly tearing around, and counted herself lucky. Essentially Sue was a good girl, still thoughtful. Now, though, there was something extravagant in her passion for change. She had to make her own way, strike sparks of excitement from those hard walls, experiment. Marilyn saw that and accepted it. If only she could stop worrying. It was such a jungle out there, prowlers were loose, traffic surging over crossings in brutal rushes. You heard frightful stories.

11

At thirteen, Johnnie was either daydreaming continuously in a steady stream, flowing and uncooperative, or else a boy with a definite goal lined up in his sights. He felt on the threshold of things, as if he had virtually got there, come through plenty of punishment and shown he could take it and survive. He imagined roles for himself, thought now and then of Sam Wickens and was either inspired to dreams of generalship or overcome by restless moods. School was only tolerated for his mother's sake. When it was too boring for words he tuned out, got cuffed for innumerable lapses of attention, and none of it really mattered.

'Wake up, Hunslett.'

'Sir, I am awake.'

'Prove it.'

'How can I, sir?'

'What did I just say?'

'I stopped listening for a minute, sir.' The class laughed. Smack! 'Ouch, that hurt!'

'So you are awake, Hunslett?'

'I must be, sir.'

'Leave the jokes to me, all right?'

'Sorry, sir.'

Out in the streets was interesting, where he was totally concentrated, his limbs moving slickly with perfect coordination, but how could you tell a teacher that? No one could see that he had two distinct lives, one outer and one inner. He liked now to act a dual role, as both the surrogate man about the house and as one of the lads. Nothing infuriated him more than to have one confused with the other. He'd be acting responsibily, gruffly, and his mother would begin laying into him on the subject of his outdoor, inviolable self, throwing one of her fits, until he was reduced to an idiotic muddle inside himself. 'Aw, stuff this!' he bawled at them all in this house of females, lumping the females screeching at him into one. He flung out of the place and hurled his small body down flights of stairs, hoping to get bruised or have a violent collision with a wall. His fists punched at air. Slouching at a corner, breathing hard, he fingered the knife none of them knew about up there, a stumpy dagger in a leather sheath.

He wanted to grow up, literally to put on more inches, a foot and a half – that was his secret, shameful wish. One day he was going to cut a path clear out of this mess, this shit! Already his fantasies were drawn up before his eyes, within touching distance – the Suzuki 250, a pair of Doctor Martens', some shiny leather gear. He skipped out past the gaping hole of the lift and noticed fresh graffiti, then the burnt strip of cooking foil fluttering by the first gate. He sneered and went on. Somebody had snorted up a 'Chinese'. On the grapevine only the other day the word had come round that a girl pusher had been badly beaten up behind the garages. He took pride in knowing these things. Out in the open he shivered in the biting air; he was inadequately dressed on purpose. He went hunching along in a hurry, hands dug in his pockets.

At his friend Trevor Foley's house over at Crookes he squatted in a back room upstairs which was always in a shambles, listening to records from a collection that belonged to Trevor's big brother.

'Where is he?' he asked idly.

'Who, Neil? Off with some bird. A new one. You should see her, she's weird.'

'Why, what's up wi' her?'

'She never says owt. Stares at yer. I think she died and nobody noticed.'

Trevor had a giant can of coke and a packet of spearmint gum. Johnnie sat sprawled at his ease on Neil's bed, against the wall. Rock music had never meant much to him before. It was something to do while they had a smoke, before going down town to play the space invaders. Now its brash impudent choruses were beginning to reach him, giving him a sense of his own intermittent truculence and extending an invitation to him personally.

'This is great, this.' He sat pressing his knobbly knuckles against his teeth and ignored the lyrics, letting the rough tide of sound break over him, urging it on as if he was already astride that Suzuki, blasting across lights with the power between his legs. The music with its hooligan yell charged him up, like the impatient roar from the terraces at a match, bustling and loud like the streets, the town, telling him over the heads of adults that he belonged. Lads, lads! It was like hearing his name called over and over: Johnnie, Johnnie, Johnnie . . . The simple, audacious message ignited him and he burned in it, a real thing, flamey. Vivid and quick inside, he sprawled in a heap as if only half alive and chewed the wad of gum Trevor had passed over, gazing dopily at the ceiling, his face gone blank. He looked bored, disengaged, cold. The monotonous chomping of his jaw made him appear moronic.

He would go swimming at Sheaf Baths with Trevor. Coming out he felt great, tingling and yet softened all through, his limbs moving lazily. At one end of the baths was a wall made entirely of plate glass. People hurrying past for trains and buses glanced in at the big pool and the boards, swimmers diving and splashing, fooling around, the pale wet bodies in another dimension, removed from the street and yet mysteriously solid. At the core of him was anger, so many days and years made up of anger, transmuted at times within him to a curious melancholy pleasure; but this vision set in front of him, that he dipped into, that dissolved his sorrow with invisible fingers, was another kind of satisfaction, flashing into him like joy. Johnnie liked to look in at the swimmers when there was snow on the ground. Pausing there in the darkening, soiled world gave him an odd sensation, a porridge of dirty slush under his feet and the doubledeckers swinging into their grey aisles. He would look in bleakly and forget, time slowing down in mysterious currents, seeing the unhampered movements of bathers by the lighted blue water. He hung in the balance, hesitating.

It was a Saturday morning in early spring. Trevor called for him at Providence Park, as the baths were close at hand. The windows and balconies of the flats looked down on it, high above Pond Street. Johnnie had been up for some time and was urgent with the need to move, get going. It could have been the spring sunshine, beginning to filter into the living room at this hour. Hearing Trevor's knock he sprang up and was out in a flash with his rolled towel. He wore swimming trunks ·under his jeans, all ready.

They ran along the walkway, jostling and laughing, trying to leg each other over. Johnnie felt giddy, slightly sick with anticipation. The light inspired him. Coming towards them was a youngish woman who looked vague, preoccupied. Unseeing, she drew level. Johnnie wanted to be acknowledged in front of his friend, so he called out, 'Hallo.'

She glanced up with a start. His rush of confidence spent, he couldn't look into her face directly.

'Oh it's you, Johnnie. Off somewhere nice?'

'Swimming.'

'Good. I think it's going to be a fine day.'

'It is, yeh,' he said meaninglessly. Grown-ups said these things. What was it to him, the weather?

'How's your mother?'

Another dopey question, but he answered politely, 'Okay, thanks.' That was what you said.

'Wish I was,' she said, smiled at him and at Trevor, and went on.

Johnnie hopped down the stairs in a series of fast leaps with Trevor, puzzling over her remark. Then he sank into his own thoughts and forgot her, until Trevor said, 'Who was she, that woman? What's her name?'

'Mrs Big Tits.'

'Don't you know?'

'Course I do, knob 'ed. That's Tina. Me mam's friend.'

He spoke now with Trevor as an equal, by unspoken

agreement. His friend granted this privilege with the easy magnanimity of a superior. Johnnie was happy with this.

Waiting outside the train station for the stream of traffic to ease, Trevor took Johnnie by the arm and swung him back against the stone wall with a thump. They both laughed. 'Look, quick!' Johnnie yelled. He was pointing. They raced through the gap as one, speeding cars and a towering juggernaut bearing down on them.

'That was close!' Johnnie gasped, alight with pleasure at his own speed and cunning.

'Too close, you dick 'ed.' Trevor threw a punch at him and Johnnie side-stepped.

They ran up the bath steps together.

PART
TWO

12

Tina Blecher closed the door quietly behind her. Jan had dropped off to sleep unexpectedly, achieving a perfection which still astonished and touched her mother – the chubby face like a closed flower. It was so sudden, like a light extinguished by a switch. Where had the terrific energy gone? What was it, this rapt blissful state?

She had put her in the cot and then nipped down quickly to the estate shop for a packet of cigarettes and some Tampons. Hearing nothing from the bedroom she stood where she was, a thief in her own flat, hearing the sound of her own breathing. So now what? The incessant demands of her child on her had ceased, she was released into a freedom which only irritated her, making no sense. An obstinacy prevented her from sitting down, from picking up the book she had been attempting to read on and off for a week.

Thoughts ran rapidly through her mind, all of them ironic. Here she was feeling foolish, angry with herself because her day was all supply and demand. When the process cut off she had no meaning, she was useless. When Jan dropped off like this, it meant a longer evening for her and that was bad news. She went to the window and saw nothing, her gaze inward. She tore blindly at the black pack of Players, as if her fingers insisted on working for their own purposes. Inside she felt like the packet, black, skidding on shiny surfaces and hard edges which then transferred themselves out of her body, a couple of feet away at least, prodded by her nerves. Why didn't this packet open? A feeling of utter clumsiness outraged her. And her coordination was faulty. This morning she had reached for the brimming ashtray to empty it and the next thing it had flown crazily in the air, a shower of cigarettes and ash and burnt matches raining down on the carpet. Such clumsiness! And so idiotic, so unjust. All at once she saw herself in an ugly light, as a dead loss, let down by a body she hated for its dragging, inept bulk. A stranger in her own flesh, she could have easily opened the skin with something cruel and drawn blood, gouged at it like an enemy. Instead, tears spurted out of her. Jan had clapped her hands when the ashtray exploded in mid air, wanting a repeat performance. Then she fell instantly asleep, and wasn't even woken by the roaring of the clumsy old hoover.

No, another voice told her – no, it wasn't any of that. She stopped whining inwardly and accusing herself, it made no sense. The row with Nick last night was the obvious thing to concentrate on. A perverse, intent look settled on her face as she ran the scene through like a film, acting both parts with great fluency and a nice touch, directing the action with precision, even floating around on the periphery to provide an audience, for registering the nuances of dialogue and atmosphere. She daydreamed her way to the climax, fitting the pieces together exactly, allowing the irony of what she was doing to filter through to her, so that she smiled critically to herself. Behind her, the dead Hoover with its tools and dusty flex cluttered the floor space. She forgot that and everything else. This was crucial: at a certain point she had made a statement of great importance. What was it? A vital realization, to do with the direction her life was taking, eluded her. She went back obsessively to the very beginning.

She lit a cigarette and took a deep drag. Jan cried out in her sleep, a single sharp cry of fear. Tina lost track of where she was in her reverie, lost the whole point of what she was doing. She saw Nick's infuriating white grin cancelling her out, negating her. The bastard!

13

Nick Rudkin was an ex-art student who came from Rawmarsh. He got by on odd jobs, the dole, a few hours a week instructing a painting class at the Walkley Institute, and he saw everything he did as temporary in some sense. That was how he liked to keep things. He took pride in having a definite view of himself, though there was self-mockery involved in this. A lot of his time was spent talking in cafés and pubs with friends. Some of these friends he allowed Tina to meet, others he kept separate. One of his characteristics, a sort of deliberate narcissism, was a taste for analyzing himself, making a joke of what he did, what he was, where he came from. His father was a miner, invalided out after an injury. Nick had a youthful belligerence which he masked with humour, a pugnacity he acknowledged by saying you could encounter it any day of the week in a Rawmarsh pub. He was quick-witted, difficult to pin down. You couldn't say for certain whether he was loyal to his background or contemptuous of it. His position fluctuated in any case; he danced around things. He was against a too serious approach to life and would delight in pointing out accidental surrealistic effects. His white staring face, with black-fringed eyes and a sweep of shiny black hair, was still round and boyish. He wore a silver ring in his left ear lobe. He seemed to live in the same Fair Isle jersey and sand-coloured jeans.

They had lived together for the past two years. This caused him to shake his head and scoff when he thought of it. He wouldn't have imagined himself capable of such domesticity; it wasn't how he saw himself. Still, it was temporary. He had drifted into it.

Tina was a good sort, she was fine. The sex was good. Staying on was easy, and he was intrigued with his own success at fitting in, adjusting to a separated woman with a baby. How protean his nature was! He wondered what else he might be capable of, given the opportunity.

At first he had been stirred to get a sketchbook and fill it with drawings of the baby, but the impulse died on him. A baby was so fluid, almost a contradiction of art. Tina had modelled naked for him a few times, in the beginning: not now. Lately she seemed to have the devil in her. Last night, for instance – what the hell was that all about? Oh, he could see how precarious her mood was. For some reason this only provoked him. She would wear that fixed unsmiling look which was not interested in indulging him. His charm fell to the ground; he was stung by her indifference. As always he retaliated by aiming his grin at her, trying to make her feel foolish for not seeing the funny side, taking things so damned seriously. Nothing matters that much. But she struck out at him, at that shiny grin which refused to fade.

'What are you, anyway, that's so clever?' she said.

He flinched, and tightened his face against her, still laughing silently. In a way he couldn't help it. He saw she was dangerous, but something drew him to the edge. His legs moved, he blundered forward as if he was being tugged.

'Me?'

'You don't give me anything,' she said.

'No?'

''What are you? Nick Rudkin – who's he when he's around? Do you hear what I'm saying? You aren't real to me any more, you aren't there.'

'Where am I?' he mocked, with his air of amused condescension.

'How should I know? You tell me.'

He followed her into the kitchen, where she turned her back on him.

'Is that it?' he asked. 'Don't I even get the right to reply?'

'Go on, reply.'

'To your face,' he said. 'Not to your bloody backside.'

She swung round, so violently that he flinched. 'Say something that's not funny,' she said. 'Just for a change.'

'All right, I will.'

Suddenly she laughed in his face. 'Come on, what have you got to say?'

He said slowly, 'I don't understand your questions. They aren't making any sense. I don't know where they're coming from. I never do. I doubt if you do either.'

'You aren't a real person. You have no idea who you are or what you want.'

'What I want?'

He grinned, but now out of his torment, crumbling before her and yet fastened to her mouth, her eyes, the words landing on him like little stinging slaps that he found absurd and at the same time painfully insulting. She moved again, back to the living room, and he trailed after her, gluing himself to her as if addicted. His grin remained, but his eyes watched her cravenly. He longed to be dismissed even more drastically, to be told with even more hurtful precision what he was. What could she see? What was wrong with him anyway? And what did he amount to? His eyes raged, then pleaded with her. If only she would go on, deeper.

'What I want?' she mimicked. 'What I want? Stop answering a question with a question. Say something for yourself.'

She sat down. Now he was standing over her in the unconscious stance of an attacker, his lithe body bunched against her. She was the enemy he lived with, ate with. They were pals, he thought bitterly, his self-pity prompting him, while another part of himself – where his sex lived – which had no use for sentiment whatsoever, told him what a lie that was. She wished for his downfall. Hated him.

Seeing him braced there, Tina could have howled aloud with misery. It was like her husband all over again. Yet she saw Nick's automatic antagonism without surprise as a barrier that would always confront her. She had gone as far as she would ever go. He wasn't special at all. His generosity and openness was part of his chameleon-like nature. It was merely another thing he did to amuse himself. He was like her father, like any man who felt trapped and threatened. What had she seen in him? Even

95

now, with his limbs tensely cramped, defensive, ugly to her, his considerable charm affected her. But she saw that whatever it was that charmed her had gone sulky, beaten a retreat back to his dreamy adolescence where encounters had been all in the mirror and questions were never asked.

He sat himself down facing her, simply because he was standing there without meaning, like a post in a field. She had tipped him off balance by a treacherous act. He felt a flash of hate for her, relishing it. His eyes narrowed and he leaned at her, to have it out. That was what she was after, wasn't it? He said in a mean, resentful voice, 'It isn't me at all, it's you. What's biting you?' He was bony-faced and shocking, so hateful to her that she could not bear to look.

She picked up her book. She was actually reading. Enraged, he shouted at her in a broadened accent, 'You started this, Tina! You got bored and thought you'd stir things up, to hell with anybody else, Tina's bored, and now you've had enough, you've lost interest. You! It's all you!'

Tina closed the book over her finger, so as not to lose her place. This flagrant insolence caused Nick to gobble with rage. Any second now he'd pounce, smash the book from her hands, send it flying across the room. Then the hate would be out in the open and declared. She said coolly, 'Did you speak?'

They sat staring at each other. She was motionless like a snake, and he felt sick with fear, as if he stared into a bottomless well and was about to pitch into it, unable to help himself. 'Come on,' he said, 'tell me. What's biting you?'

'Apart from you, this place,' she said. Her cold malevolence horrified him and he felt on the point of being maimed for life, with every illusion torn from him. What had he done to deserve it?

'Apart from me, what's wrong with it?'

She gave an odd grunt, like a cough, of sheer disgust. 'I'm bringing up a child here,' she said. 'Or haven't you noticed?'

'Well, yes, I can see the snags, obviously. It's a bit risky, yes. I've been in worse, but you've got Jan to think about,

I know that. Why come here in the first place?' he ended wildly.

If he told the truth he didn't dislike it here, not for himself. In fact the element of risk was not pronounced enough for him. An image of himself prowling around in a dangerous world enlivened him; it had a certain romance. As a student he had shared a council flat with two others on an estate over towards Rotherham that was altogether rougher than this. Things happened there that stimulated him, fired his desire to work. And funny goings-on, with the surrealistic ingredients he relished, so that he escaped the muted aquarium life that was England to him. Once, coming in after midnight, he surprised two prostitutes who lived a few doors further down on the ground floor; they were loading up a handcart with their belongings for a moonlight flit. On top of the heap of junk was a large framed picture of a naked woman in an explicit pose – part of the tools of the trade. Overjoyed, Nick rushed in to tell his friends. It became one of his favourite anecdotes.

Now Tina explained – with a slow and carefully enunciated speech that maddened him, making him want to leap up and grab her by the throat – that as a single parent she had little choice, it was here or nothing.

'Well, look around,' he said. 'Then just move.'

'I see.'

'Naturally I'll help.'

'Thanks, but no thanks.'

'No, I forgot, I'm not real.' Then it flew out of his mouth before he could stop it: 'You're screwy, did anyone ever tell you that?'

'Oh, they told me. It doesn't take long for them to tell you that. Their explanation for everything.'

'That's a cheap trick,' he cried, 'lumping me with others. I'm me. Talk to me, address me.'

Tina fell silent. 'It doesn't matter,' she said finally.

'Don't you get any help from Arnie?'

Arnie Blecher was her husband, a white South African she had first met in London when she was a nurse. By the time she was pregnant they were already estranged.

The birth of their child failed to reconcile them and Arnie walked out. He had been threatening to return home for months. In some respects their final scene had been similar to this. The mention of Arnie's name still wounded her. 'No. I've told you already, he's disappeared. Anyway, I don't want any.'

'But you're entitled. It's his kid as well as yours.'

'Is that so?'

Her dry tone goaded him to insist, to probe further. 'Has he ever paid?'

Flushing angrily, she said, 'It's none of your business. It's got nothing to do with you.'

'Nothing has.'

She saw him winding himself up, and said wearily, 'I prefer to get it from the State, no strings.'

'Can't they trace him? Make him cough up?'

She said with indifferent contempt, 'You haven't got a clue. Men never have.'

He floundered before her miserably, his self-esteem in tatters. He was five or six years her junior. At moments like this she saw someone younger still, a bouncy teenager who needed to be handled carefully, plenty of verve to sweep you along but no resources in a crisis. She was out of patience with his youth, his touchy pride. Suddenly she felt truly alone. And so sick of herself, stewing around, fluctuating wildly from one day to the next. Arnie at his best would have been able to steady her; an old stick-in-the-mud, but she would never have been tempted into these operatic scenes with him. He would simply have shrugged phlegmatically, put on his coat and walked out. He was what he was, take it or leave it. In the end she drove him away, after years of casting about for an emotional, intense partner who would take her inner life seriously. Round and round, and now here she was gnawing at the same bone. Nick let her down in the same way; he only seemed different. Essentially he wasn't interested in her, he didn't want to know. He made demands, endless demands, no different really from a child, from Jan.

Then she swung on herself, sitting balefully in the mess

she had made. What a foul bitch! She felt distorted, a disgusting misshapen object, a mistake, bleeding there on the carpet with her lousy complaints and blaming him. Nick saw her face, furious with itself, an imp of fury glaring from it. He came face to face with another person. The Tina he remembered came and went, appealing to him for recognition like a drowning person. It broke his heart to see her.

'Hey,' he said gently, in a croak of love. She was strung tense as a wire, her eyes begging and warning him.

'You know what?'

'What?'

'I think I'm going to scream.'

'Scream, then,' he said.

He spoke toughly, but it was the last thing he wanted. He should have gone over to her. Why didn't he? His throat worked. What he had felt a moment ago as pity curdled. As he watched he thought he was going out of his mind, seeing her terror of what she might do. Then the horrible string snapped, he was free. He got up. Just as he reached her she put her hands to her face and cried out, pressing fists into her eyes.

She didn't relax against him but stayed rigid, as if about to curl up in a helpless convulsion. He was afraid, making himself stay against his will. She was always outwardly calm, never crying in his presence. She wasn't crying now. The demon in her, if he could have seen it, was non-human, hideous, a clear threat to his logicality – to whatever it meant to be a man. Her forearms were hard against his chest like the palings of a fence. He thought in despair, 'I'm not meant to get any closer!'

'Come on,' he muttered, in a hoarse, shaky whisper that sounded distraught, that upset him to hear, persuading him that he did care, not sure of his intentions, whether he was trying to comfort her or himself. 'Hey, come on,' he croaked. 'What's this, eh?'

She stood shivering and frozen in the warm room, stuck fast. He stroked repeatedly down her shoulders and arms as if to thaw her. Nothing seemed to work, so he gripped her, sinking in his fingers, filling his hands with sweater.

More than anything he felt giddy, his lungs or his heart wildly fluttering. To avoid stumbling backwards and losing his balance he hung on to her. Tina's eyes were shut, her face closed. Up through his hands ran the sensation that it was now the aftermath of the crisis, and he lost his fear of the demon or whatever it was, imagining it as a storm of specks, formless and without power, slowly diffusing in her blood and sinking away. Now she lowered her arms and he got his sceptical body to work, moving her sideways to an armchair and pressing her down into it.

'How about a cup of coffee?'

'No,' she said. She stared blankly at him.

'No?'

'What's wrong with me?'

'Who said there's anything wrong with you?'

She only said, after a long silence, 'I've got to think. Sort it out.'

Fearing the obscurity of this, chagrined to find himself unwanted, he blurted out, 'Give it a rest, Tina. You think too much. Actions are better. What's there to think?'

Really, he did not object to his own introspection, which worked for him, he thought, in his favour, rather than against him, undermining him. Faced with hers, an instinct warned him to oppose it. Wasn't it unhealthy, like shutting yourself in a room without light or clean air? At the core of his disapproval was a suspicion that he was gradually, inch by inch, being eliminated from her life. The thoughts she generated were entirely for her own dark ends. That was it, they were full of darkness. For all he knew they may be suicidal. Suicide and death flowed around, mixed up with the earth, engulfing, stuffing your mouth, sometimes giving birth to you, so that you sprang up again all sappy and green, only to be scythed down. Tina was all this, she was *it*; a blood ceremony. His thoughts swung him outwards, hers bogged her down in a mash of black stuff too repulsive to be contemplated. Then it was over and she would laugh, surpassing him in brightness. It came and went in her, while he was stuck in his sameness, predictable. What kind of magic did she have, emerging clean and fresh from that dark awful muck?

Tina fixed him with her level, serious, more ordinary stare. He breathed freely, grateful to be recognized. He waited humbly for her to find a use for him, a cunning voice inside him telling him that this was wise. To his dismay Tina began speaking his fears and thoughts, entering his head, which he wanted to clutch – it was so uncanny. He listened in agitation as she told him with a strange dreamy detachment about herself and Arnie, and the time when she locked herself in the bathroom and tried to cut her wrists.

'What?'

'It was pathetic, all I could find were those disposable razors, refills. No good at all – the plastic part guards the blade too well. I sawed away at my skin, my wrists and up my arms, just nicking the skin everywhere, only making myself raw. I remember seeing the blood and being interested. Just gawping at the criss-cross marks oozing my blood. Arnie was hammering on the door. Then he smashed the bolt and got in. He went for me.'

'Why did you do it?'

She said in a dopey, stupified voice, 'I can't even remember.'

He slipped across to her, putting out his hand. 'Poor kid.'

'I don't think you'd better touch me.'

'What's wrong?'

'I'm in a funny state.'

'Are you cold?'

'No.'

'Tell me what I can do.'

'Nothing. Go for a walk.'

'After a story like that? I'm not leaving you, I can't.'

'Don't be so stupid. Don't you understand, I need to think.'

He shook his head, frightened. His fear chained him to her. Demoralized again, he pleaded with her. Seeing that he couldn't help himself she relented, pitying him, sighing with discouragement. She had barely enough energy to speak. She pitied him more than herself. He was out of his depth with her.

14

Next morning it was another day. He was glad to jump out of the plump sweaty bed, to escape her soft flesh. He had lain awake on his back beside her for an hour as if lifeless, as if he was in a warm bath, sluggish with his own damp eroticism.

Dressing, thrusting off the night, he jerked on his clothes in sharp, hard gestures, indifferent to the materials. His movements in the kitchen were brutal and rudimentary. The energetic clashing woke her up.

He brought her a cup of coffee, doing good, restored to his normal flippant self. The cheeky earring shone. His slightly protruding teeth, attractive to her, chipped away with that habitual white jaunty grin. 'See you later!' he shouted from the door, then crashing out. What did it mean, when you thought about it? No more than shaking off a bad dream. The sky outside was tantalizingly veiled, with a springtime fragility which impelled him to break into a sprint.

He had plenty to give her; he felt a swift beauty in his limbs, his walk, like a rare gift he would reveal when the moment was right. He walked along with a pleased, seizing stride, stood impatiently poised on the kerb waiting for the traffic to dwindle and part, hurrying across with Tina's exclamations in his ears. He felt sure-footed, practised. She would appreciate him all over again.

In the flat, Tina was changing Jan, who wriggled in silent protest like a fish until she got a slap. He's a condescending little sod, all things considered, Tina thought. And then, perhaps influenced by the light, she laughed.

In the midst of her laughter she wanted to cry, tears of vexation pressing out of her eyes. But she was too angry to give way to it. Four or five days of this, she might have said, and I'll be myself again, free of these crazy swings and loops. A man would say so – sure of who he was. Men, they knew nothing, nothing! Yet how could he be expected to grasp that she was no longer Tina Blecher but a no-name without a memory, spilling ashtrays, knocking into the furniture a woman called Tina had left there, a woman unrelated to her, who would never be fired at night by obscene blood-curdling dreams, who was orderly and reasonable and a patient mother? Her child – hers? – ran about heedlessly behind her and called to her in a shrill little voice and she paid no attention, taking two ferocious steps to the window and halting there, a crackle of terrific energy detonating deep inside her, forcing her eyes wide.

She stared madly down. An overweight, torpid woman she knew only by sight waddled out from the entrance beneath her and made for the street, across the meaningless vacancy of the asphalt. She wore a hat like a Chelsea bun, coiled round and topped by a furry knob. The light touched her cheap shopping bag and it became sleekly luxurious, a wanton object.

The beetle-like gait of the woman below caused Tina to bring her hand up sharply to her mouth. About to laugh hysterically, she suppressed it. She went and sat down, looking about, letting her gaze drift over each item in turn, in a rising panic when she failed to find names to attach to them. Her daughter, who usually said 'Tina', and only 'Mummy' when she felt threatened, came pushing against Tina's knees and tried to haul herself up beside her mother. In a deliberate attempt to prevent this, Tina had sunk down in the armchair rather than the settee. It hadn't worked.

'Go away, please. Play with your dolls.'
'No.'
'Teddy, where's Teddy?'
'Mummy, lift me.'
'I'm not well enough.'
'You *are* well.'
'I don't feel it.'
Their conversation was at times, to anyone listening,

103

almost like that of two adults. Tina refused to speak baby-talk. Her child had begun to address her with growing familiarity as an equal, with an odd pedantry to her speech which Tina herself didn't possess. The intimacy she justified by saying that as a single parent it was better this way, more natural. Not everyone agreed with her.

'Tina, are you happy?'

'No.'

'What's happy?'

'A nice feeling.'

'Is it a nice feeling, Tina?'

'I've just said so.'

'It is,' the little girl said solemnly, her head tipped to one side. 'Yes it is, isn't it Tina?'

'I said yes.'

'Am I happy?'

'Most of the time.'

'Now, am I?'

'Yes.' Losing control suddenly she shouted up at the ceiling, 'Yes, yes!'

After that, she got up and began walking round the room in as wide a circle as she could manage, on and on, at first in a desperate attempt to calm herself, stepping over toys, shoes, until she was hypnotized. She went rambling compulsively along an invisible track on the carpet like an unhinged person, deriving a sullen comfort from the zombie-like action of her legs, and increasingly afraid, as she forced herself round and round, of what she might do.

Tired out, she went into the bedroom and lay down. Jan snuggled up against her on the wide bed, fidgeting, no longer asking questions because she hoped to stay there a long time against the solid warm wall of her mother.

Tina woke with a jolt out of violent dreams. She lay as if stunned, heavy with sex and power. A swarthy thickset man had trapped her in a corner at the point of a knife. When he backed away, she pursued him, a more predatory hunter than he had been. Then she was him. A timid fluttery knocking that she thought at first was the beat of her heart, became amplified in the dream until it alerted her to where she was, on the bed in her own skin. She could taste her own sour mouth, but felt sane again. She went to open the door to Marilyn Hunslett. No one else knocked so apologetically.

The whey-faced, haunted woman came in, her eyes downcast. 'Sorry to be a nuisance,' she mumbled.

She was eternally sorry, forever in the wrong. Once Tina had been driven to say to her, 'Look, Marilyn, stop being sorry! You know something? Even your knock sounds sorry. I knew it was you. It's a bad thing to keep saying. Sorry, sorry. Sorry for breathing. Sorry I exist. I was the same once.'

'Were you?'

'Not any more.'

'Oh well,' her new friend had said, embarrassed, unable to look at Tina directly.

Tina had been in a strong frame of mind that day. Her blunt squarish face was always open, receptive, but Marilyn faltered before her, sensing something relentless in the other's mood. Tina's heavy breasts seemed aimed at her. She was not to be argued with. Tina had said, 'I think I'll ration you to one sorry a week. How about that? Say something else instead, Marilyn, I should. Fuck it all, eh? Say that.' She burst out laughing at the older woman's expression. Her breasts shook.

Marilyn smiled wanly, a little shocked. Though she had heard plenty of language, she came down hard on Johnnie if he let that word slip out in front of the girls. And Tina didn't seem the type. Still, she was younger, her world was different. She had one or two funny-looking pictures up on the wall. It wouldn't do for everyone to be the same. Sometimes, hearing Tina's free laugh, she would wonder what she was doing there. Apart from motherhood, did they have anything in common? This rackety dump they were stuck in was to blame – you were glad to make a friend of anyone. 'Sucking your thumb are you, darlin',' she said to the little girl, in a bright coaxing voice. Babies and toddlers gave her a pang, though how she had ever found the energy to cope she couldn't imagine. But she wished hers were at that malleable, sweet age.

Tina was explaining that she had been asleep and that was why she looked such a fright. It was true, she looked wrecked, plunging her hands through her hair and making it even worse. Her skirt was twisted.

'Let me clear some of this junk off the settee. Here, sit down. I called at your place this morning. Well nearly. I saw Johnnie on his way out. Did he say?'

As if she hadn't heard, Marilyn said, 'I hope you weren't doing anything.'

'Only lying down. I must have dozed off.'

They sat facing each other. Jan ran from one to the other until she overcame her fear of the visitor. Then the child began to persecute her, dragging toys into the room, upending a cardboard box, running to fetch her big rainbow-coloured beach ball. She was filling Marilyn's lap with bricks, farm animals, soft toys, more and more objects, squealing with pleasure. Her mother told her to stop it.

'Are these all mine?' Marilyn said mournfully. 'Can I have all these?'

Jan threw a red brick at her, chortling. Marilyn shielded her face.

'I said stop it,' Tina ordered.

The low menace in her voice startled Marilyn. In her place she would have screeched like a parrot. God, how had she ever handled little ones? Tina sat glaring balefully. Something is wrong, Marilyn thought, and got ready to leave, weakly needing an excuse. Usually she left Tina's feeling brighter, even hopeful. It won't work this time, she thought. If Tina was unhappy, she still managed to look strong, Marilyn reflected. She stayed drearily where she was. Strong characters were very difficult to leave. They cast a spell on her. They spoke and acted in a way that convinced her they were in possession of a secret, some clue she had missed, that she was too fearful to see for herself.

She waited, though she had lost faith in Tina's secret. All she saw now was a smeary woman gripped in a dilemma like herself, locked in this enormous cage of flats, barricaded on rowdy nights, cowering and rodent-like as herself, only younger, stronger. In a vindictive corner of her mind she rejoiced. The discovery that Tina too was miserable set a mean voice crowing inside her. So they were the same.

Marilyn said at last, reluctantly, 'It's Johnnie.'
'What is?'
'I hadn't better say in front of . . . '
Tina jumped up. 'Jan, let's see if we, can find you an ice-lolly in the fridge, shall we?'
'I can do it, I can do it!' the child cried, rushing out.
'Eat it in there, darling,' Tina called. She grinned wryly at her friend. 'Worth a try.'
'I'm worried about him,' Marilyn said.
Tina waited with a fretting impatience for the woman to unburden herself. She saw a woman who would always be sorry, hopelessly discontented with herself for being sorry. Yet she could see another side to her that she would like to reach, to help out into the room and make welcome. This other self waved feebly, obscured. At times Tina felt sickened, as if by something grey and squashy, struggling helplessly on its back with legs waving.
Mostly she was able to be relaxed and gentle, in ironical contact with her friend. It's Marilyn Hunslett, that's her, that's how she is, she would tell herself without condescension, glad to be approached by this sad woman who was exasperating but who always came back. It took her mind off her own predicament. Afterwards, shaking her head, she was able to treat the fix she was in with a measure of contempt. Changes were imminent – the sensations in her body told her so. She wished she could transmit some of this certainty to poor Marilyn. Then on other days nothing made sense, only the fact of Marilyn and her woe. Tina would live her life as if she was doomed to it.
Today, strung up as she was, Tina felt with a sudden hard resolve that she would be out of here soon, but not Marilyn. She felt she had a duty to be kind to this woman.

Also there was a degree of superstition in her attitude. She tended to think that Marilyn, grubbing away in fear and never lucky, was in some mysterious fashion helping to give her the chance she needed. Maybe there was a sense in which a woman like this with a jinx on her forced others, such as Tina, to make their move. She sat fatalistically, in an unnatural position, her body refusing to cooperate with her, thinking without cruelty of Marilyn as an unconscious sacrifice. She even believed – in her feelings, not in her thoughts – that when someone died, then you were propelled forward that much harder, greedy to live.

'Why, is Johnnie sick?' she asked. 'What am I saying, I'm not with it, what's the matter with me – I saw him only this morning, off for a swim.'

'That's right. Trevor came for him.'

'So why are you worried? Tell me, Marilyn. Stop making me nervous.' It wasn't the friendliest of openings. Why, when she wanted to tear the place apart, the room, the flat, the whole gruesome building, had she opened the door to this befuddled woman?

'He's not sick,' Marilyn said stupidly, peering over like a blurred drunk with her worried lined forehead. Tina remembered that she was on medication, subjected to heavy doses of valium, seconal, what was it?

'Tell me what.'

'I think he's been glue-sniffin', Tina.' As she let the confession out she became nervous, glancing over at the door.

Tina took a firm line. 'Now what makes you say that?'

'I think so, yes. Think he has . . . '

'Why, who told you?'

'Nobody. Well, a boy our Eileen knows said something . . . said that –'

'Said what?'

'About Johnnie and that . . . '

The woman's ignorance, and that sheep-like submission to her own fate, made Tina want to shake her. Instead she herself shook, inside, in a weird irrational rage, hearing the very sort of female passivity she feared might be lurking at the bottom of her own will to betray her. She said harshly, like a doctor who has seen it all, who dismisses supposition and demands hard evidence, 'What are the signs?'

'Signs?'

'Yes, are there any signs?'

'There could be, I suppose . . . '

'No, listen. Is he acting in a funny way at all?'

'I hardly see him these days,' Marilyn muttered bitterly, head down.

'When you do. What are his eyes like? Any different?'

'I don't know.'

'That's the give-away, the eyes. The same with any other drug. Same with drink. It's a drug, Marilyn – you have to watch for the signs. Never mind what some kid or other tells your Eileen, that could be a load of old rubbish, just worry for nothing. Marilyn, now listen. That kid of yours looked as right as rain to me when I saw him this morning.'

Marilyn was eyeing her friend strangely, with a curious fixity. 'Only I wondered . . . ' she said. Jan sat propped at rest against her legs, glassy-eyed, sucking her thumb.

'Go on,' Tina said, almost through her teeth, she was so out of patience.

'If, maybe, well, if perhaps you could . . . sort of have a word with him, Tina. Next time you see him. He never tells me anything these days. He says nothing to nobody, just keeps to himself. Clears out, and I never set eyes on him till bedtime. No dad to answer to, that's what it is. Sometimes when we've had a shouting match he stays out all night, at Trevor's I suppose, and tells me after.'

'I didn't know.'

'He's been playing truant again, Tina.'

'I didn't know that either.'

Marilyn was nodding, nodding. Tears ran down her face.

After a long furious moment Tina said quietly, 'If I see him I'll have a word.' She was torn between pity and anger, put on the spot like this. And after all, it was a simple enough favour. 'I *will* try, I promise.'

'Thanks very much. It's just that I can't stop worrying.'

'What makes you think he'll talk to me? Or listen, even? Marilyn, he hardly knows me.'

'Oh, he might. I can't say anything to him, he only screams at me or says something disgusting.'

'He's at that age.'

'Who else can I ask? He might see you as diff'rent. Well, you are. Younger, like.'

Tina laughed. 'Oh thanks. If I bump into him, I'll try.'

'Sorry –'

'There you go again!' Tina exclaimed, startled and alarmed by her own shrillness. Normally she would have been amused. This time she had to restrain herself from doing something violent. Stupid, silly cow!

'He should have a room of his own now, not sharing with me. Not a lad of thirteen. When Sue goes I can move Eileen in with me. Then Johnnie can have a room to himself. He might be more settled then perhaps. Eileen won't like it though,' she finished worriedly.

'Sue's going? I didn't know she was about to fly off,' Tina said, oddly touched and surprised.

'She hasn't got any plans, but you can tell, can't you? Any day now, that's what I think. She's got ants in her pants, that one.'

'Is that what she's got, oh dear!' Tina couldn't help laughing a wild cracked laugh at the expression, while her friend frowned and coloured up and looked even more despondent.

15

Marilyn, not for the first time, admired Tina's speaking voice. It was clear and never slovenly, even when she was in her present state, jumping with nerves. That kind of speech set a good example. She wished Tina would come round to her flat more often, so that Eileen picked it up, influenced by hearing proper speech. Pat when he was around had been a bad influence, indifferent to his children's manners. Marilyn did her best, but always felt she was losing. Only the other day she heard Eileen say her Geography homework wasn't due in 'while Thursday'.

'Is that what they teach you at school?'

'No, course not.'

'Does your teacher let you say that?'

'Which one?' Eileen said, sneering, a clever snap to her voice.

'I'll smack your face, madam. You take care – you think you're too big but watch out.'

'Now what have I said?' Eileen cried, flinging down her pen and scrambling to her feet, pink with temper. 'I'm never right, am I!'

'Turn that television off, that's another thing. How can you watch rubbish and do your homework?'

'Easy,' the girl said. She squatted down again on the carpet.

'Not properly. Nobody can do two things at once.'

'I can.'

Tina found it natural to identify with Sue. In her place she would have been off even sooner. She left home herself when she was sixteen, to escape her stepmother and two stepbrothers, brawling noisy brats, years younger than her. It was hell. After her parents split up she had had to share a room with two babies. She loved her father, then as soon as she began experimenting in puberty he

111

accused her endlessly, with jealous blazing eyes, of being whorish. She moved into a desolate bedsitter and he helped her with money, sometimes flinging it at her across the café table in a torment. Once he struck her across the face so heavily in a car park that her jaw was dislocated. When he broke down and wept before her she was torn horribly, despising and loving him.

Marilyn opened her mouth and closed it again.

'Yes?'

'I was thinking of Sue,' Marilyn said. 'At least when she's gone I'll have one less on my mind.'

'Don't say she's a problem as well?'

'She's getting money from somewhere, a lot. I'd like to know where.'

'Isn't she still working at that travel place?'

'Not any more. They cut down. She was the last one in. So whose money is it, Tina? She clams up when I ask her. She's another one. I tell you. Who'd have kids, eh?'

Voicing these fears, she made up her mind to have it out once and for all with Sue. Probably she'd be wasting her time, but who else was there to make the attempt? She thought bitterly for a moment of Pat's evasions, his back-sliding. If he did come back, just drifted in at the door and stood there, what would she feel like? It was the lack of someone with whom she could talk about these things preying on her mind that she missed most of all. Pat wasn't so bad. There were plenty worse than him around. With him drooping there before her in her imagination, down on his luck, mutely asking to come back to her, his wife, she shivered with longing. He knew more about her than her own mother. He had seen the kids grow up from fretting babies, everything. She weakened, whimpering in her body. Yes, she'd take him back, give him another chance, why not? He belonged here with her. Life had a way of backing her against a wall. She needed someone. In her mind she tried to fit together a jigsaw puzzle, with Pat's face as the missing piece.

Marilyn suddenly said, 'No, Tina, forget what I said.'

'Where are we now? Forget what?'

'About Johnnie. I always do it, put people to a lot of trouble and it's not fair, not to you. Anyway it's a daft idea, what am I thinking of?'

'I said I'd try. I mean it.'

'Don't you bother yourself.'

'Are you going to be sorry you asked me, is that it?'

Marilyn flushed. She got up. 'I'd better be getting back I suppose.'

'I was about to put the kettle on.'

'Thanks, Tina, no, I must go down town for a few bits before Eileen comes in.'

Entering her own jumbled, stale flat, Marilyn saw a pair of red high-heeled shoes, the heels worn down, flung in a corner by Sue. At the thought of demanding the truth from her daughter, a girl as tall now as herself, bewilderingly dressed like an alien in the current street style – suddenly it struck her that it was all too late. The problem defeated her utterly. In any case, who had bothered to warn or advise her when she was of that age? If they had, would she have listened? Kids these days were more knowledgeable than their parents.

She stood in the kitchen, scrawling out a shopping list on a torn scrap of wrapping paper. In one sense Sue had already rejected her – that was her gut feeling. She seemed ready and willing to dump her family, a first stage in that process which would lead her inexorably to some kind of permanent replacement, maybe a family of her own, or another way of life entirely. These days, who could tell? Meanwhile, let her get on with it! She'd find out soon enough how hard it was out there, and how cold. Certainly the last thing she had imagined was that Sue, with her thoughtful traits, would one day be making her cruel, secret preparations.

Sometimes, if she told the truth, she didn't give a damn about Sue any more. The leggy girl sniffed disdainfully at her food, wouldn't look her in the eye and paraded in and out with that affected stalking walk. What a pain she was!

Her thoughts circled monotonously around. If Sue was

113

having money given her, how was that different from those teenage girls who went from these flats on the heights and got themselves picked up by the police for soliciting under the city abbatoir walls? For money. To get money. She came as close as she dared to thinking it, her own daughter in unthinkable circumstances, then took fright and swerved away in her mind. She refused to believe for a second that Sue could be such a fool. She wasn't remotely like one of those loose little bitches. But how was it different? Marilyn would think guiltily of her eldest child as a stranger, a coldly inscrutable one, following her urban path with the instincts of a city nomad, weaving incomprehensible patterns out of spite to fool her mother. Whereas Johnnie was always transparent to her, no matter what he did.

Most of her anxiety these days came to rest on Johnnie. He was still hers, he had time for her. He might look like a tough from the streets but his hard stare was different, directed out at the world, not at her. It was simply maleness, he had to do it. Because he was small for his age she continued to see him with a protective, yearning eye, aching maternally for his sake.

She traipsed down to the arcade of shops in Pond Street, perched on their concrete shelf overhanging the bus station. Toiling back up the steep approach road to Providence Park, she entered her block through the same doorless opening from habit, sensing rather than seeing the mountainous wall poised over her head, escaping thankfully into the dingy stairwell and feeling the tons of weight lift from her at once.

It was as if she lost her bearings for a terrifying instant. She paused, catching her breath as she always did. The scaled-down dimensions and the sudden enclosure invariably soothed her; she could comprehend again who she was.

16

Johnnie, heading downhill from the flats in a shower of rain, saw his sister Eileen climbing towards him. She was engrossed in conversation with someone and hadn't seen him. He took particular note of her, critically, like a father. She went sidling by on the other side with a school friend. That walk told him everything, long before they drew level and he was able to see her cupped hand behind her back and the cigarette hidden in it.

He was on the point of jeering, shouting out to ask her what she'd got there. No, he would yell sardonically, 'Got a light?' He did neither. The cruel urge subsided in him. And she was nice to him as a rule, he remembered. He felt sorry for her, having to act shiftily; he wasn't going to make it worse for her. The rain suddenly lashed down, and he glanced over his shoulder to see if he was still unnoticed, then briefly up at the sheer cliff of concrete, staining and going black as the water soaked in. This sinister effect, and the rain clouds dragging past in grey tatters behind the estate, made a shiver pass through him. He felt desolate, and went down the hill hugging the sensation to himself, satisfied to have the melancholy pride in what he was somehow sanctioned and confirmed in him.

It was a Friday. He had skipped school, then gone home at the right time so as not to alarm his mother. Those large eyes of hers were always mournful as they followed him around. It's just habit, he would think. She can't help it. At least she kept quiet and didn't pester him with stupid questions as she did with the girls. He and his mother had an understanding. He gave her no cause for worry and she left him alone. He fooled her with great care, taking pride in his skill. If only her eyes would stop pulling at him! Now and then, not often, he would ask if there was any stuff she wanted fetching in. Though he tried not to admit it to himself, it pained him to see her on that hill with her shopping bags, loaded down like a mule.

She did ask once about the soft leather shoulder bag he brought in. That was different. He had his story ready. 'Trevor's brother gave it me.'

'Is it new? It looks new.'

'Yeh, great, in'it?'

'Doesn't he want it?'

'Nah.'

'Let me see.'

'You want it, Mam? Have it, go on. Look, it's got four zips, an' one with a lock.'

'I just want to look. What would I do with such a thing?'

'It's champion, Mam!'

The truth was, he had gone out one night with Trevor, stealing from cars for a lark. They went up behind the university where the streets were quiet, tripping past as if aimlessly, then sauntering, then doubling back and trying doors when the coast was clear. Trevor got a beautiful camera, a Cannon. The bag Johnnie snatched was half full of papers, documents, no money. He had visualized unzipping it, finding it stuffed with money, spilling out money. He ran with Trevor like a maniac through a maze of quiet roads, beneath well-established big trees and past large disapproving stone houses with richly curtained bays. Gasping for breath, he stopped to post fistfuls of documents through a drain grating.

Now he was about to meet Trevor and Darren at the sleazy bus station café. It was a favourite hang-out for kids. People sifting through restlessly, in transit, gave the place a raffish air. No one cared who you were, in the evenings especially.

He was the first to arrive. He picked a table in the middle, took his bag from his shoulder and dropped it proudly on another chair, to save it. He went up and bought a Coke and a currant bun. Sinking his teeth into the flavourless bun he realized he was famished.

He was still wolfing it down when a boy in a black studded jacket came over. The lad had a shaven head. He turned to wave over a runty boy at the counter, and Johnnie read the word 'skin' tattooed in biro on the back of his skull. The small boy arrived. His companion pointed to Johnnie's bag.

'Kick that out of the road.'

'Hey, no!' Johnnie cried. 'It's my brother's, he's comin'!'

As he spoke, Trevor and Darren pushed through the swing door. Their heads were dripping wet. Johnnie called, 'Hiya!' and waved.

Trevor marched up at once. He had a nose for trouble. He stuck out his neck, spoiling for a fight, his eyes working as he sized up the situation. 'Is this where we're sittin', mate? Room for us, is there?' His words were bantering and public, the tone uglily loaded. Johnnie loved him like a real brother. He grinned up at his friend and protector, his face bright. Trevor winked.

Glowering, the young punk and his pal moved to another table. 'See ya around,' the big one said, rasping it to save face.

'Is he talkin' to us or chewin' a brick?' Trevor said, loud and contemptuous.

Darren perched on his chair in a monkey crouch, his feet on the struts of the chair, left and right. They sat sniggering, heads close, planning moves for the evening. Darren munched through a bag of crisps. 'Yuh,' he kept saying foolishly every so often, like a goon, 'yuh!'

'Let's go round Broomhall,' Johnnie suggested. 'Yeh, eh?'

This was a game they played occasionally, lurking on a corner to see how many prostitutes they could spot. A splashy report in the *Star* recently, a follow-up the next day, told how the police were mounting a campaign to clean up the area, imposing fines of two hundred pounds and more. One of the women, interviewed by the reporter, said: 'They keep making it harder for us to make a living, that's all. We just have to get more clients, and we go underground for a while. They can't drive us away, the demand's there.'

'It's pissin' down,' Darren said, unexpectedly vociferous for once.

117

Johnnie, taken by surprise, laughed out loud.

'Go and have a look-see,' Trevor said, murmuring it with quiet authority.

Darren ambled out obediently. He came back looking blank.

'Well?'

'I thought it was pissin' down.'

'You know what thought did.'

'Eh?'

'Have you been on the loopy dust?'

'No.'

Trevor sneered. 'What did your 'ed in then?'

'Nuthin'.'

'Are we going or not?' Johnnie said. 'I'm fed up wi' sitting here.'

'Why, what's the 'urry?' Trevor sat where he was, an obstinate grin on his face, rubbing at his shocked damp hair.

'Aw, come on, Trev.'

'Yeh, come on,' Darren echoed. He had a pimply, trusting face.

'See the prossies, Trev.'

'See the prossies, see the prossies,' Trevor mimicked. 'Silly pair of twats.' Suddenly he erupted, flung himself off his chair and across the floor and was crashing through the swing doors ahead of them. 'What you waiting for, wankers!'

It was too early, so they rode the escalator rail for a while, until some woman up on the bridge crossing the street, a skinny shrew in her fifties, came running up, threatening to fetch the police. 'I'll have the law on you I will!' she yelled, gobbling it out, her arms waving.

They ran off and scattered, laughing, pleased to have created this flurry of drama. As it happened they were bored anyway and about to leave. The furious woman even chased after them on her lumpy varicose legs, startling passers-by. 'Hee hee, she's a nutter!' Trevor bawled. He spun on his heels and waved a mocking goodbye.

They re-formed and dived off in the direction of the

Wicker, a wide ramshackle thoroughfare of fly-blown shops, small workshops, a defunct cinema which had shown only soft porn, in the distance the looming brick arches carrying the railway across two barren roads and an intersection, always noisy with freight. Darren had some money. They bought a bag of chips to share, and marched in to play the space invaders next door.

'I'm skint now,' Darren said after a while. 'I am, yuh.'

'Any road, I'm fed up wi' this,' Johnnie said. 'Come on, let's have a race. To that corner, where the pillar box is.' He streaked off.

'I'm after yer!' Trevor howled, pounding in pursuit. Bits of dirt flew up.

By the time they had doubled back and got to the empty shopping precinct and the wilderness of new roads and traffic signs bordering the red light district, a soft sky was clearing. It was a mild night. The winter had petered out at last. They tore down a flight of steps into a tiled echoing subway, whooping like Red Indians, emerging from one tunnel only to plunge branching through another. Johnnie lifted his head to gulp down air as they surfaced. He felt the northern elation, close to frenzy, of a fresh spring night, sharp with a million stars, white seeds. It charged his skin with a buzzing astonishment.

They galloped up a ramp to the other side, to more concrete parapets, a muddy embankment, a line of fencing just creosoted, pungent and woody.

'I'm goin' up there!' Trevor shouted, pointing.

'And me!' Johnnie yelled, exultant.

'Yuh, yuh,' Darren was saying, and his tongue lolled out like a tired dog.

On an open paved space before the Co-op they paused to watch two long-legged West Indian boys cavorting gracefully on skate boards. They weaved around each other in tight circles. The tallest youth was incredibly lanky, grave and nonchalant, flexing his knees as if in his sleep, entranced with himself. Johnnie lingered, and on his own would have stayed for as long as the exhibition lasted. Those loops and curves and fine body swerves seemed to be expressing his sensations about the night

119

and his own inner balancing act with delicate precision. He soaked them up like someone drugged.

Broomhall was a devastated area of Victorian terraces, short roads full of potholes leading nowhere, the rubble of vacant lots, frowsty weeds. In the shadow of two ugly old high-rises were the signs of redevelopment, yellow bulldozers and a building site pegged out by surveyors. Many of the half-derelict houses were still occupied, some boarded up, others shattered and open to the sky, with whole end walls torn away. It was possible to look up into pitiful exposed rooms hanging in space and see the fussy wallpaper still intact.

At first there was no activity of any kind – not even a mongrel sniffing forlornly around. Then a car swung in from the streaming traffic and began nosing through. It cruised past them, went on for another twenty yards and stopped. A woman slipped from a doorway and got in. The boys watched the stalled car; cream, needing a wash, a low beetle shape. The woman got out again. There were raised, angry-sounding voices. The car went on. Suddenly the woman had vanished.

'That was one, hey!' Darren yelped excitedly.

'I ain't so sure,' Trevor said. 'Just hang on a minute. Keep your voice down, can't yah?'

Half an hour passed. They waited in a pool of darkness, where a street light was smashed, scuffing their feet, getting restless, aiming light punches at each other to break the monotony. 'Got any cigs?' Trevor said, sticking his face close to Johnnie's. He was always imitating Starsky and Hutch: the dark one with close-together eyes was his idol.

'No,' Johnnie said, 'I told you.'

'Want me to frisk yah?'

'Yeh, go on.'

They shushed each other as another car slid by, this time a bigger one, a shiny black job. It stopped outside the same house, by an overturned bin and a pile of squashed boxes. Johnnie wondered how it was that a car could move as steathily as that one seemed to do. It was evilly black, sliding under the few street lights and being swallowed up by shadow. For the first time he sensed the lawlessness of what they were watching, its taboo. What was happening now in that car? Did they drive out to a lonely spot, a secret lane, or were they on their way to somewhere swanky? And then what? He supposed the woman was stripped and given special underwear and then told to lie around showing everything like the pictures in *Penthouse*. Was that it? Then what? He couldn't visualize anything else. He had read the words but that was all it was, words. In order to make sense of it he needed to see a picture. He knew the crude details of what they did, in and out, but what then? How did you know when to stop?

A blonde ran out. As she did so, the car's nearest door opened noiselessly in invitation. The car drove off.

'See tha'?'

'It's only the same as last one.'

'She got in, though!'

'Shut thi' gob a minute.'

'Why should I?'

For a moment Johnnie felt the authenticity of their spying, the illicit business of the street thrilling him, including him – and then he lost it. The pile of garbage by the gate, which the woman had perhaps touched with her cherry-coloured coat, hurrying by so eagerly – that was him, waiting uselessly on the corner. It was a stupid thing to be doing. Then he was bored rigid; nothing to do, nothing to see. 'Stuff this,' he said aloud, rupturing the spell. 'I'm pissed off wi' this.'

They moved off in total accord as one, scrambling after each other, racing away as if they had received a message at precisely the right moment, one they were all straining to hear. Released, they broke into life, launching themselves into space. They took huge hops and jumps, leapt high and twisted, fell against each other and ran on.

Out of the corner of his eye Johnnie saw a girl entering a dilapidated porch who looked remarkably like his sister Sue. She raised her arm to knock and the skin of his face flamed. None of the others had noticed. He wasn't certain

121

himself. He told himself he must be mistaken, but refused to look again. All he wanted was to get clear of there, draw the others away.

Afterwards he blotted it out, or thought he had. For the next couple of days he didn't set eyes on her. Suddenly there she was, drifting around in the flat, ignoring everybody as usual. He watched her surreptitiously, a street spy, trying to decipher in her chilly features the clues to her other life, things he would rather not know. He couldn't stop, it was a compulsion. Finally she caught him at it.

'Are you satisfied?' she said coldly in her new supercilious manner, treating him like a man who was eyeing her up.

He flushed. 'What?'

'Stop staring at me, okay?'

'Who is? When?'

'Just then. Lots of times. Didn't anyone ever tell you it's rude to stare?'

'No.'

'Just you cut it out.'

He muttered something under his breath.

'What?' No answer. 'I'm asking you what.'

'Can't do with this shit.' He made a bolt for the door and was gone.

'Shut your dirty mouth!' she yelled after him.

17

Sue had seen Johnnie the other night. It didn't matter to her, though it annoyed her to see him, her kid brother, playing games in the street. She was beyond him, far beyond anything he may have experienced.

She saw herself as out in the world, scheming to make her escape permanent. She had been calling on a girl she knew who was also unemployed, but who always seemed confident of getting money. Money was the key to it, the quick way out. She sometimes daydreamed about money, thinking about the feel of it. When she had got hold of enough she would say goodbye, pack a few necessities in a brand-new nylon bag she had seen, a purple and green one, and folding her dresses into it with care she would walk down to the station and buy a single ticket to London. She had lived that scene a hundred times. In her magazine she had read an article about provincial girls and what could happen to them, homeless in London. She wasn't a fool. She intended to have savings in an account.

What was the alternative? Just under the surface of her calm skin ran the hysteria. At the thought of her mother falling sick again an hysterical panic would threaten to paralyse her. Her legs went numb and she started to freeze up. Yet she was always the one who was expected to cope. If what she feared did happen, the escape plan would founder and she would be trapped. There had never been anyone else but her, not really, not for years. As these fears swept over her she felt she *was* her mother, doomed to be trapped forever like her, simply because she had neglected to think of herself. She must never do what her mother had done – deny her own dreams.

Sue had a steady boy friend, Jason. She had brought him round a time or two, simply to prove to her mother that he existed. He drove a delivery van. He was sharply

123

dressed, with a sculptured haircut, and wore chunky white metal rings. Jason had style, together with a certain dark devilishness which had attracted her in the first place. He was fun to be out with, a good laugh.

An instinct warned her that it would be unwise to tell him too much. He put his hands on her jauntily, without commitment, to make a pal of her. They always swung along easily together, exchanging the language of surfaces by unspoken agreement. As a bright winking surface he was acceptable, not to be confided in or trusted. Only when they were in motion were they real to each other, and only then was he acceptable to her, joining her in a dance which never amounted to anything, returning her always to the same spot, the same spot exactly. His fixed bright smile, awful to her at first, was now familiar and nothing to do with being Jason.

She rapidly took on his jauntiness, seeing it for what it was, after the first few weeks when she imagined climbing into his van and heading up past Providence Park for the motorway, the South, the grey city falling away and blurring. Clearly that was never going to happen with Jason.

He was older than her, already a little staid. He was pleased with his routine and his good looks, he moved his head in a preening gesture of complacency, like the plump-necked pigeons in Fargate. He lacked daring.

Thinking once that it might be an Iraqi student who would guide her out, she had gone with him to his room, a squalid bedsitter off the London Road. Meeting him with a friend in a Wimpy bar, she allowed everything to proceed swiftly, touched by his shyness and the spell of his foreign blood, which gave him a dreamy, svelte glamour. He said touching, ludicrous things, made quaint mistakes, his English imperfect. She helped him along with her eyes, with trilling laughs of fear and amusement, her voice insinuating of its own accord. Hearing it she was surprised, sometimes failing to recognize herself. She wanted everything to be fast and inevitable. It was her first time, and must be unthinking. There was nothing shameful if you were taken out of your depth on the flood of a foreign boy's longing. How could it be wrong to take pity on someone?

Lying on the bed, she saw him by a chest of drawers that had several of its knobs missing. Seeing him sideways on, she was too horrified to move. A terrible mistake that would have been impossible to predict was about to take place. She submitted in a terrified silence, her eyes glaring, wide open. He was fumbling, hasty, embarrassed by his ineptitude. The transaction left him breathless and her horribly ashamed. Afterwards, as if happy to have regained his clothes, he took a childish delight in demonstrating his latest purchase, a massive transistor with twin speakers.

18

She sat on the glossy moulded plastic in the Wimpy bar
with her friend Angie, in a blare of orange and green.
She liked it there. It was brighter than anywhere else,
cancelling the outer drabness, and it was always spotless.
Everything conspired to cheer her up, decisive and young
like her, and at the same time it left her alone. They
sat against the window, in touch with the street, the
movement. Sue stroked the dark brown plastic of her seat
as she talked. It was like touching glass. If she examined
it closely, idly, she could see a mass of fine scratches.
'Listen,' she said to Angie. 'Hey, are you listening to me?'
  'I heard you the first time.'
  'How am I supposed to know that if you don't say
anything?'
  'Stop yelling, okay?'
  'Who's yelling?'
  'Keep your voice down.'
  'Well, answer me, I'm serious. This is urgent.'
  'I know that, Sue. You don't have to tell me that.'
  'I need to get some money quick.'
  'I'm thinking. Sue, it's no problem – only I got this
other problem, see, about my fella. He's on my mind a
lot lately.'
  'Sorry, yeh. Can I have a cig?'
  'Here, help yourself.'
  'Thanks.'
  'And stop worrying about it, okay? Look, you know
where my pad is. All you have to do is get yourself dolled
up and then come down there when you're ready. Any
Friday or Saturday.'
  'What's wrong with how I look now?'
  'Nothing, stupid.'
  'Oh good.'
Sue couldn't decide about Angie, whether she was on

126

drugs or just naturally twitchy. Her fingers twisted interminably at things, grinding her cigarette butt into the ash tray, tearing the paper napkin into tiny pieces and then pushing the scraps together into a cone, then demolishing that. 'Here, listen, if you want to make a *lot* of money, I mean really a lot, I've got a better idea. I've got a friend who's done it. Two in fact.'

'Done what?'

Angie laughed distractedly, but she had fixed Sue with her level, almost desperately serious stare. Her white peaky face looked under strain; it always did. She always seemed about to fall to bits, she had a sloppy quality about her, but no matter what happened to her, she bounced back. Sue would hear each time of some new disaster, yet Angie was able to boost her spirits, instil hope in her. She had hilarious tales to tell of her experiences round the corner, at the hotel next to the nightclub where she had once worked as a chambermaid. Sue was deeply impressed with her. Angie was intelligent, not just a silly tart. She could make you double up with her stories, always to do with absurdities, often with men. She was knowledgeable, experienced: what men were after, what they were prepared to pay for.

'You can earn two hundred and fifty a session as a stripper, did you know that?'

Sue hooted with laughter, rocking back and forth. 'Where?'

'Not round here. Sheffield's no good. You'd have to move up north, north-east. All you do is go to an agency, Newcastle's got one, and leave the rest to them.'

'Oh great. Oh smashing. Angie, you're crazy. I couldn't do that, I'd die.'

'My friend went up there and tried it, and she says it's so easy when you've done it once, just a job like any other. It's not you, it's an act, a performance. I can believe that.'

'Any other bright ideas?'

'Well, you did say you wanted plenty.'

'This is where I live. It has to be here.'

'Then you come round to my pad on Saturday. If you change your mind, it's no skin off my nose.'

'Okay, don't get huffy.'

'Who's huffy?'

Angie pulled out a pocket book of thin red leather, handmade, stamped with an elephant design in gold. It was bulging with bank notes. Sue goggled at it. 'Wanna burger or something?' Angie said. 'A milkshake?'

Angie's generosity gave Sue a nice feeling, and she knew her friend wasn't showing off. She spent as she talked, in loose emotional splurges, responding to the absurdity of the world around her. Sue had never known anyone so disorganized who was such a survivor, so hopeful, when all the evidence she trotted out was to the contrary. The emotional mess she churned around inside herself endlessly sounded terrible. Was it an element she manufactured out of herself, or did it descend on her?

Saturday was showery, a little chilly breeze blowing. At seven, Sue stood tapping on Angie's door, glancing round. This street in the twilight was like the aftermath of a bombing, with that kind of stunned silence. Broomhall was a mess, it always had been. She shrugged, turning her back on it. A strange woman let her in, a redhead whose hair was a drab brown at the roots. Sue asked for Angie and the woman merely jerked her thumb down the passage, sticking a cigarette in her mouth so that both hands were free. Then she stooped down to lift up the howling baby at her feet.

Sue found Angie sitting at a cheap shiny-topped table in the kitchen. 'Hi, you're early,' her friend said cheerfully. She sat gripping a mug. Sue went to sit down, first brushing off bits of toasted bread from a stool. She wore a new blue skirt, blue shoes, a pale blue fluffy sweater under her colourless see-through mac.

'When did you have your hair done?' She gazed appreciatively at Angie's two styles in one, brown natural hair short at the sides from the clipper, then a burst of wild blonde spikes on the top of her head. Really she liked it better as it was before. She thought this a mistake.

It wasn't Angie as she understood her. She asked about the woman who had let her in.

'Vera. She only came yesterday, I think from Nottingham, somewhere like that. That's where the bloke who owns this place lives. Or is it Leicester? – I forget. Last week there were six of us here altogether, but two went yesterday in a bit of a hurry you might say.'

Angie went out for food, coming back with hot dogs in a greasy paper bag. 'I got two with onions and ketchup, two plain. Which do you fancy?'

Sue said she felt slightly sick and didn't want anything. It was getting dark. Why didn't they switch on a light? She wished she was alone, perhaps outside somewhere, drifting along in the dark instead of here, her stomach clenching and her mouth drying. What was it, how did it go again, the sentence she said first? If the words failed to come, stuck in her throat, what then? She had kept on her mac; the kitchen was none too clean, even half-lit like this she could see how grubby it all was, and her skirt was immaculate. Sitting stiffly, listening to Angie's monologues and trying to will herself to relax, she missed her mother, the chattering television, and felt a pang of envious love for Eileen, so carefree, so childish and out of it.

She couldn't get the layout of this dingily lit house, telling herself to snap out of the daze she was in. They were in the kitchen but the window looked out on the street – how could that be? She remembered walking down a passage and turning a corner. Ever since getting up this morning she had sleepwalked, as if she needed a cocoon to wind around herself. The dazzling ultramarine skirt chosen in her sleep, enabled her to walk down to the Moor and over to Broomhall unsoiled, inaccessible, no matter what it looked like from the outside. She felt secure in her absolute blue, like someone else, a perfected vision of herself.

Angie stood at the window. Sue thought she looked older, grubbier. She jerked the curtains back over. 'Here you are then, kiddo, you can have this one.'

'Where?'

'Where d'you think? Hey, what are you nervous about?'

'Who said I was?'

'Jesus, I get it. This is your first go, right? You didn't tell me that but I ought to have guessed.'

'Well, it is, so what?'

'Why weren't you straight with me?'

'I told you. Money.'

'Are you bloody chicken? If you are, say so.'

Sue faced her friend coldly. 'No.'

Angie came over and touched Sue's arm, slipping her hand up and down the crinkly mac. 'Sweetie, after tonight you won't give a toss. Men do what you want, most of 'em do – remember that. You have to tell 'em. They expect that, see?'

'I know that.' How did she know? But it was true, she did. It was as though she had always known. Men at the centre of their beings were empty, and this surprising emptiness came into their eyes at unguarded moments, into their voices. They did senseless things, all the time asking, as a child asks its mother, for their inner space to be filled up. They were lonely, always bluffing, making out it wasn't so. They appealed by means of their helplessness to the mothers in women and then acted resentfully, brutal and stupid, writhing under obligations they had invited on themselves and then had to fulfil. No wonder the sorrows of women were never-ending. Men were just children with guilty secrets. She knew all this without thinking about it.

Right up to the door Angie was gassing away with advice for her, nonstop, as if something had broken loose. 'Now look, this is all new to you but there's nothing to it. If anybody asks you anything, like the police, if they try it on, try to suss you out, all you've got to do is act stupid and they haven't got a leg to stand on. You're out with a friend, get it? Nobody's else's business. Don't mention this address whatever you do –'

Sue interrupted her to say hotly, 'You never said anything about the police.'

'I don't know why I'm mentioning it even. It's you, acting so bloody nervous all of a sudden. Forget it – and for Christ's sake get a move on. He won't wait for ever, kiddo.'

19

The car door swung open as she approached. The man inside, hunched up in a suede top coat, looked straight ahead. They set off.

It was a new car, smelling of metal and leather. She sat as still as a doll, staring ahead like the driver. The man cleared his throat several times, his Adam's apple working. Was this it? Sue marvelled at Angie's words, telling her how simple it was. She was right. Even the sentence she had meant to speak was unnecessary. She had got into the car, and now another machine, just as impersonal, would draw her into love or sex with this clearly embarrassed stranger if she sat perfectly still and offered no resistance. The fear in the pit of her stomach dissolved and the next second she was ready to deny that it had ever existed. In its place was a rising tide of curiosity, a chattering relief that she struggled to keep in check. She flicked a sideways glance at the man, the customer, snapping a picture of him while her head remained rigidly facing the front. A bony man in his thirties. Scraggy neck. Deep-set eyes, glinting and dangerous in the dark under shaggy eyebrows; the eyes of a man involved in a drama, Sue thought.

'How much?' he said. 'The usual?'

'Yes.'

Then he croaked comically, 'How old are yuh, like?'

'Eighteen,' she lied.

'Come off it.'

'What?'

He drove on with nothing more to say. Finally he said, 'How long you been out?'

'Out?'

'On the street, doing this.'

'Yonks,' she said. The schoolgirl word flew out before she could stop it.

131

When he said no more, she asked. 'Where are we going?'

'I live in Hillsborough.'

'This isn't the way, is it?'

'There's a clever girl. I'm circling round a bit, like. Just in case.'

'I don't get it,' she said indifferently, her heart tight in her chest. Each time she spoke it was a studied, deliberate act, in which she took care to maintain the neutral tone she had decided on. She had sensed that anonymity was wanted of her, and it was what she ought to want.

'Well, you never know,' he said, gulping, losing his nerve. She felt sorry for him; her instinct was to help him.

'Never know what?'

He turned his head to look directly at her, and she lowered her eyes.

He drove on without answering. At a deserted crossing, waiting for the lights to change, the machine to mesh and carry them forward to the next mysterious stage, he suddenly laughed. 'You like to talk,' he said.

'Do I?'

'You like to ask things.'

His voice was homely. She imagined him in a pub, cheerful, nothing like this. It disappointed her to think that he had to be gloomy with her. His sudden laugh had astonished, pleased her. She liked the cheerful natures of men, their illusion that life could be mastered, even seen as a joke.

He was still unable to look at her, into her face. An awkward gravity seemed to be settling him down into his coat, the seat, and she was close enough to actually feel his discomfort. A little trance-like smile appeared on her face as her fears diminished. Once she caught him slipping a glance down over her thighs, her knees. That was better, easier to understand. The taut blue skirt composed and strengthened her, reminding her of her unaltered spirit, of the free bus ride down into town on the Clipper, when she had sat admiring it, smoothing her hand over it. This is only business, she thought. I may be changed after this, soiled by this man's business, but

132

how does it matter? My skirt will be the same afterwards and so will I.

'Nothing wrong with that,' she said.

'No.'

It occurred to her, with a flash of alarm, that she might meet him one day in the street by accident, walking along in broad daylight with his night knowledge of her. It struck her suddenly that this was why names were never exchanged. It was obvious. How stupid she was! Shorn of a name she was immune, she could cut him dead.

'Now I can see where we are. I know this road.'

He said doggedly, slowing the car and then parking, backing a little, 'You aren't like the others.' He parked with finicky manoeuvres, taking his time, like someone coming home from work.

'Why should I be?'

Again he laughed, giving her a thrill of triumph. 'Keep your wool on,' he said.

This was such an odd expression, one she hadn't heard before, that she nearly giggled. It was nervousness more than anything, coming and going in gusts like attacks of wind. He had said it considerately, not in a jibing sneer like some boys she knew. Men of his age had a weight to them, a slow sombreness. He fell silent again, leading up through the silent clean-smelling house and into a bedroom.

Shirts and a pair of trousers had been left where they had dropped on the cream carpet. There was a table of reddish wood that looked elegant, a modern tallboy, a wicker chair sprayed gold, with a soft cushion, and the unmade bed. Everything spoke to Sue of a woman's touch, a woman who was absent. On the table was skin moisturising cream. Without saying a word the man snapped off the light. A sick yellow glow from the sodium lamp out in the street entered the room through the swathed net. 'What about the curtains?' Sue muttered.

The man made no answer and she expected none. It was a need she had to hear the sound of her own voice. Suddenly she was acutely lonely, hearing the man's gasping breath, filling the room with his urgency, the unhappy desire men had to get rid of something, get something into you, to ease their bitter discomfort.

He was pressing against her with the front of his body, as if seeking a way out of his flesh through her. His sweat smell enveloped her, strongly acrid in her nostrils. She thought of what she would say to Angie, how much or how little, the futility of trying to convey the essence of this to anyone when it contained no element of surprise, as if known from birth, or even earlier in the womb. He was finished, lying on her like a casualty, like a street accident, struck down and waiting helplessly to recover, with strewn felled limbs. Sue thought of her absolved skirt, which she could see as a mere patch glimmering on a chair where she had left it, and of putting it on earlier with deep satisfaction and feeling clasped by it, reclaiming the source of her clean self. The man was stirring. As if abashed by her small bones he took the weight on his elbows. He rolled away and they each smoked a cigarette. This was the part she would remember, the film-like moment, when the face of the man grimacing above her as if in pain had been long forgotten.

'What about the money?' she asked naively – she should have found out what you said – and he replied at once, sluggishly, his voice surly, 'Look in your bag.' He must have put it there when she slipped into the bathroom. She didn't check. He let her out and at the door gave her such a strange look, his first. What was he saying to her? Did men have extraordinary words stuck in their throats or their hearts that they would like to utter?

The next time Johnnie saw her, he noticed that she had gone thoughtful. He was accustomed to a frozen, stuck-up Sue who put herself beyond his reach, with an insufferable disdain which made him feel like a crumb, and he would feel an urge to land her one on her sharp little hooter, bang. Now she was thoughtful. Even more remarkable, she took note of him, to the extent of giving him a funny direct look, as if working something out, or perhaps considering him. He was reminded of another Sue, lost to him for a long time. He had been fond of her. It took him back to the worst days of missing them both

134

terribly, Sue and Eileen. Trevor had said once, 'If you want to know what girls think about, I'll tell you. Absolutely fuck all.' Johnnie had laughed delightedly because it was so unexpected, and he saw Sue in a new light. Now though he wasn't so sure. He could see with his own eyes that she lived in boundaries different from his own, and that her very prettiness created space, distance. He could tell, though she inhabited a dream he dare not enter, that something was going on.

20

Tina mentioned to Marilyn Hunslett one day that she needed a baby-sitter; her regular had let her down. 'I wonder if your Johnnie fancied earning a bit?' She knew that Marilyn's daughter Eileen had an arrangement with someone or other.

'Oh, I don't know. I expect he would, yes.'

'Does he like money?'

'Johnnie? He's always after it.'

'Would he feel daft, d'you think?'

'I can ask him. If he wants the money he can feel daft for a few hours, it won't hurt him.'

'Never mind if he doesn't want to. Only I've been invited out for a little celebration.

Marilyn looked confused. She said timidly, 'Are you on your own now, Tina?'

'Yes and no.'

Tina Belcher spoke with a candour that Marilyn always appreciated, though she had reservations, wondering if it was wise for women to be so open. Tina went on to say that Nick had taken a bedsitter for himself, and now he had moved out they saw each other every other weekend. 'It eases the strain,' she said tersely. And then snorted, laughing gently at the other's expression. 'What's the matter?'

'It wouldn't do for me, Tina.'

'Why's that?'

'Well, it's neither one thing or the other.'

Tina laughed. 'It wasn't before.'

'Oh, I see.'

Tina laughed outright. 'You don't at all,' she said. 'Damned if I do either half the time.'

Marilyn glanced up and down. On the walkway where they were standing she was always strained. She hesitated and then said, 'Will you mention about, you know – what d'you think?'

It took a few seconds for Tina to comprehend. 'Oh, that.' They were quite alone out here, but she was used to Marilyn. Windows were open. 'It seems as good a time as any,' she said. 'If it's all right with you, Marilyn.'

'Oh yes, thanks.'

'Fine.'

'Shall you bother?'

'It's no bother, honestly.'

'I can't go on with it on my mind like this, day and night. Nobody could.'

'I'll see you later, love,' Tina said.

Entering her flat, Tina paused at the door to listen to a waddling top-heavy woman who was saying to all and sundry that the lift was broken again. 'It's disgustin', what about old folk up at the top who can't climb all them stairs? That's the third time this week they've had the men in, now it's broke again. Old folk go down in the lift and then are frit to death in case the lift's broke when they come back again, they'd rather stay in. It's disgustin'. I know a woman, seventy-six she is, haven't been outside her door for two months.'

'Jesus, no,' Tina muttered to herself, going in and shutting her door. She leaned back. Jan was asleep in the cot where she had left her five minutes before. She moved to and fro, picking up a trail of toys and books. If she didn't get out of here soon she would be like the others, moaning and bitching at lifts, at men, lost in the confusion of her fears like Marilyn. Poor bloody Marilyn. It wasn't how she saw herself, not for an instant, but the thought sent a jolt along her nerves.

That Nick. He was so unfair, depositing his guilt in her and then moving out as if under protest, making out it was her doing. She had a shrewd suspicion that the bedsitter idea had been in his head for some considerable time. He swore not, that she had driven him to it. She had done nothing of the kind. He sat at the table, hung his head in defeat, gently appealing for her sympathy.

137

Why should she give it? Why did he think he was entitled to it?

'It's not me, it's you,' she said.

'What is?'

'Nick, if we're going to have separate set-ups, that's fine. Only don't lay it on me. Be honest for once.'

'You're incredible.'

'Yes, honest. Tell me just for once what you want out of this. The truth.'

He got up then in agitation and his legs carried him around blindly, while she observed him. It was this cool detachment of hers that defeated him, this unassailable position she occupied, overlooking his antics. The more foolish he felt, the more he felt driven to acting like an imbecile in front of her. She would stare at him, with that look of a woman endlessly let down. What idiocy it was. If he screamed like a baboon and pounded on his chest, would she then wash her hands of him in total contempt? He sat down abruptly, to consider his next move. He had a wild craving to grovel and act the idiot in front of her, yet what she saw, insisted on seeing, was a man calculating his next move. That ironic smirk which so maddened her had come back, and in his eyes the sly expression which she particularly disliked.

He was stunned when she began to shake, at first imperceptibly, a tremor of the hands and shoulders. Then her mouth was trembling and collapsing, the whole edifice he had cowered under, that had seemed so impregnable. Women were incredible. 'Come on, eh?' he mumbled. He trailed over with his shame and then was afraid to put his hand on her, sad for her and himself.

'I'm so bloody tired these days,' she said.

'You need a break,' he said feebly. He fetched a box of tissues. 'Like your neck,' he joked, without conviction, lapsing into an old intimacy.

'Nick, I'm sorry.'

'Let's get in the bed,' he said, stronger. 'Take the weight off our minds. Talking runs out more easily when you're horizontal. Finds its own level.'

'Really.'

'Haven't you noticed?'

Following him there, she said with a touch of her sarcasm, 'I'm not too impressed with your solutions.'

'This isn't a solution. It's a place where you wait for one.'

'Oh, is that it?' She cried briefly again, undressing, peeling off her tights and pants last of all, before turning to him.

'There,' he said, between the sheets with her, equal again.

'Hold me,' she whimpered, in a broken little voice that overturned his heart and made him quail.

He strained against her manfully, a gruff father rocking his child into his chest. He felt grand and melted, aware of the anguish of his body. She was drawing the best from him. He held her responsibly, securely, this big amazing woman six years his senior who happened to be a mother, with a husband called Arnie somewhere in the world who had knowledge of her, with whom he felt a bond. He loved it that she trusted him at these moments, or was it that she had spiritual immunity, and no thought of being contaminated by his uncertainties? He was not weak, not mean after all. She returned him to his self-esteem.

God, she was warm and soft. Lying down, she seemed to shed years and he to gain them. She turned on her side away from him and he lay pushed up against her back, his arms encircling her belly. The stickiness of their skin produced a sweet suction, experienced whenever he was forced to ease the cramp in his arm; an old problem of his.

Where was her tough resolve, or his jerky reflexes, defending himself against – what? She had a tight grip on his hand, pressing it into the squash of her belly as if afraid. His fatherly concern dissipated, became nonsense, a sentimental feeling that her round hindquarters settling into his groin nudged away. He got half hard against her, letting it pulse unheeded on her thigh, on the back of her leg somewhere. She made no response. Neither did she let go of his hand.

'God, my arm,' he said, mumbling into that mass of hair. Then she released him, his hand fell down and straight into her, where she was drenching wet. 'Darling.' He knew when he entered she would exclaim 'Ah', as if he was the most unique and marvellous person, astounding her with his rigour. It was an unforgettable sound. And then other joyous cries, fluting up, out of such a big capable body. She lifted her right leg a fraction, a friendly, delicate movement. There was humour for him and also apprehension in it; she could be hurt that way. He gained access from behind and then was butting away too fast, anxious not to fail. A tiny thorn-sharp cry suddenly stuck into him. Chastened, he lost all his frenzy, afraid of what he was. He began slipping out. Perhaps to retrieve him, she stirred her inner petals around. In that swampy heat he came alive for her, rippling to her ripple. He moved against her back stealthily like a snake.

He sat in his clothes, looking at her with new eyes. There was a rosy lethargy on his skin. He was still intent on his plan to live in a bedsitter apart from her. He had to find out what he was, away from her disturbance, out of reach of her need for him. But he was no longer blaming her for anything.

21

It was another week. Ready for her night out, Tina opened the door to find Johnnie balanced impatiently on one leg, in his faded jeans and the *Heavy Metal* T-shirt he always wore. She was all set to leave, but not too sure that he would turn up. She said so.

He grinned, lowering his head to avoid her. 'I said I would, didn' I?'

This was hardly promising, she thought. His manner was shifty.

She told him there was Coke in the fridge. He was welcome to help himself to any food he fancied. 'You'll find a pork pie in there.' Jan was already asleep. He could switch on the television if he wanted and not be worried about the volume, she always slept through it.

'I doubt if I'll be late, Johnnie.'

'That's okay. No sweat.'

Discouraged by the contemptuous edge to his voice, she gave up on him for the moment. 'If she did wake up and get upset or anything, you could always nip up and fetch your mother.' She wondered if she was saying it to nettle him.

He gave her a look of disgust. She left.

After no more than a couple of hours she was back. Coming in, the first glimpse she had of him was his dirty trainers up on the coffee table. He was in the armchair, sprawled out of sight.

She wondered if he had dozed off, then saw a movement. He stayed put, while she closed the door, locked and bolted it from habit, even fastening the chain, and asked how it had gone. Had Jan cried out at all?

'Nah.'

She noticed the emptied Coke cans, one rolling on the floor at his feet, and on the table two tins of lager. 'Did you bring the beer in yourself?' she asked.

He snuffled out a laugh. Misgiving entered her in a rush. 'Did you?'

'I had a visitor,' he said.

She couldn't believe her ears, but said quietly, 'Who was that?'

'My friend Trev.'

'Why?'

'Don't ask me.'

'Did you ask him or what?'

'No, he come round.'

'But you must have told him you were going to be here?'

'Suppose so.'

'I'm not keen on strangers coming in here when I'm out, Johnnie.'

'Who says he's a stranger?'

'To me he is.'

'Well, ah. Sorry an' all that, like.' He studied the carpet.

'Not that I've got anything against him personally, it's not that.'

'Right, yeh.'

He was sitting up, looking at her with his head cocked, his legs drawn in respectfully.

'It's just that I live alone here, Johnnie. Now I do. I have to be careful. Do you understand?'

'He didn't stay more'n five minutes.'

'That's not the point.'

What was the point? She ordered herself to shut up, cantankerous bitch. She sat down on the sofa a moment while he grinned at her, his expression quizzical.

She calmed down. She liked him better now. His eyes were nice, fringed with dark lashes. He seemed reluctant to leave, looking at her with a strange hopefulness, clearly wanting to establish contact with her. She felt unequal to it, simply unwilling to cross over the great distance between them. Was it worth the effort? The futility of talking to him at all made her suddenly weary. She said frankly, as if to an adult, 'I'm tired, Johnnie. Let me give you the money. Is three pounds all right?'

'Great, yeh!'

'I'll get it.'

'Wanna coffee?' he asked hopefully.

Longing only for her bed, she was on the point of saying so. Her smile ached. But she couldn't bring herself to say more than, 'That would be nice. Do you know where it is?'

'On the top shelf.'

'Clever boy.'

'You said I was to help myself.'

'I did.'

She sat down again, listening to the sounds of this self-conscious lounging boy in her kitchen. His stubborn insistence would have irritated her in someone else. She hadn't forgotten her promise to Marilyn, but coming in she'd decided it was a waste of time. This Johnnie seemed stony ground. Now here he was making her feel she should be flattered. She *was* flattered, and she was curious. Why? She had no idea. It was too late, it was too much.

Carrying in the mugs, he made another journey to fetch the sugar. He asked her about her party, and was it a good one.

'Oh no, nothing like that. Just a lot of gab with an old girl friend, who I can't seem to make sense of any more.'

'How's that, then?'

'I suppose she's changed. Anyway, we drank to her birthday.'

He was looking at her intently; then a flush came on his face. Still, he got it out. 'Have you ever been a teacher or owt?' he said.

'No! Why?' she laughed.

He snorted. 'Nuthin'.'

'Come on, tell me why,' she coaxed. 'I want to know why you should think that.'

'One of my teachers sounds a bit like you,' he confessed, staring and obstinate.

'In what way? Explain it to me.'

He shrugged. He said in a peevish mutter, 'Can't.'

She sat back in her chair smiling and considered him.

A thought struck her. Comically dismayed, she said, 'God, you don't mean officious?'

'Dunno.'

'Is that how I seem to you, Johnnie, officious?'

'I don't understand that word,' he said angrily, clamping down on his teeth and shaking his head. He gave her a vicious little flash of a look.

She was at once sorry for her blunder. To make amends she explained about her school. 'Well, most of the teachers I remember got up my nose becausethey were so superior, they knew it all and they rubbed it in that you knew nothing, you were stupid, going nowhere. If you were a girl you were going to get married and have kids and be stuck in a bloody kitchen, and if you were a boy you would have some dead-end job, sorting newspapers or delivering meat or something brainless like that. That's the impression they liked to give you. Especially the headmaster. He used to stand up on the platform at Assembly and read us the riot act, tell us how useless we all were. Amazing! That's the kind of teacher I mean. I went to a lousy school, Johnnie, a secondary modern. I left at fifteen, I couldn't get out fast enough. Now look at me. I don't have an O'Level to my name. The only job I can get is at slave labour rates.'

Johnnie was round-eyed, absorbing this and what it meant. He shook his head solemnly. 'Ar, we got them like that where I am.' He stared at her with new respect. 'Our headmaster's a right fuckin' headcase, you should see him.' Then it dawned on him, what he had said. He gaped at her aghast. 'Sorry an' that. It came out, like.'

Tina laughed at his dismay. 'Oh, I'll survive.'

'Sorry.'

'Well, what is it then?'

'Eh?'

'How do I speak?' she cried. 'Tell me!'

He shook his head, either refusing or unable to say. It wasn't even how she spoke, it was an air she had of having decided something. And now and then an acid touch. He liked that. It was what he liked in Trevor. Girls in his experience never had it. They could be vindictive, bitchy – that was different. They went round squawking and fluttery and in front of adults they were disgusting, putting on a simpering act, and sometimes they put the needle in for no reason, for spite.

She told him humorously, 'I shall solve the mystery one day.'

'Oh ar.'

She could be airy, which came as a surprise from such a fleshy woman. There was something raw and overpowering about her build. The strong bones. It was funny that she was called Tina. She had a similar build to a singer he had seen in action on the box, Tina Turner. Only not blatant like her. Not her mouth. And he sniggered to himself at the idea of this Tina he knew jigging up and down in a slinky yellow frock covered in rows of fringes, staggering about as if half-cut with a lewd snarl on her face, legs apart, knees bent. What a headcase. Americans were like that. Crude. They could howl like dogs.

Tina Blecher sipped her coffee, and he did likewise, taking care not to gulp, watching her on the sly.

'What's up?' she said.

'Nowt.'

She laughed. 'Nowt?'

'Nuthin'.'

'No, I didn't want you to say that, I wasn't criticising. What you said is fine by me.'

'As good as owt else.'

'That's right, that's it!' They both laughed.

It was great sitting here and in her confidence, as he undoubtedly was at present. It wouldn't last; she was bound to snap out of it any minute now. Adults did that. They bundled you out of the door when it suited them. He bore her no resentment for being of that type, if she was. She looked a good sort to him. It wasn't her fault if she was getting on a bit. Though in her case that was a puzzle. How did she have the knack of tuning in, coming down to his level in the way she did? She wasn't old like his mother, and very definitely not the same sort of woman. Those lines on her forehead were not worry, they

145

were thoughts. She thought things. She was able to do that; airy thoughts came out of her. He sat lazily, sticking out his legs cautiously an inch at a time and hoping to spin it out. Sip, sip. Make it last. Those tits banging straight out, and the lumpy nipples, no bra, it looked like. She had a rumpled sort of face. Somehow the cheekbones, honest-looking, encouraged you to trot out a load of rubbish.

'Are you bored, sitting here?'

'What's there to be bored about?'

'Good!' she said. 'That's all right then.'

It was a ripe juicy mouth she had. Her eyes were sharp-pointed, and those eyes had witty thoughts in them. Her skin had a freckled appearance, and the remnants of a tan. Her sandy hair was in a tangle, exasperated-looking. He was puzzled by the desire he had to please her in some way, some picture which would remain with her, instead of dregs to wash down the sink with the rest of her evening. All his senses combined in the effort to leave her with a strong impression. He wanted her to take account of him, use those thoughts of hers on *him*. That body was tolerant, it had room for him. He strove to enter her bodily memory as a person she would not forget, who was important to her.

No, he was definitely not being edged out now he had done his stuff. He had been prepared to cut up awkward. No need. He stopped bracing himself.

As if reading his thoughts, or maybe to give her hands something to do, she picked up the vintage tobacco tin from the coffee table. He watched each move she made with a little grin of pleasure.

'I knowed you were one o' them,' he said.

'What?'

'As rolled her own.'

'How did you?'

'I just did.'

She looked at him, and said seriously, curiously. 'I wonder why?'

The tin she held was burnished on the corners down to the bare metal from years of intimate handling. When she had prised off the lid, taken out the Rizla packet of rice papers and rolled a cigarette, running her tongue along the glue line with a strange gleam in her eye, he asked if he could see the tin. She passed it over.

'Do you like it?'

'All right. If it worn't so old.'

'That's why I like it!'

He simply wanted to rub his hand over it. As he anticipated, it had a nice used feel. But as he rubbed it he looked at Tina. He had her tin. By her eyes she was thinking things. Now what would she say?

The way she came out with it shook him. 'You like a smoke I expect, Johnnie, do you?'

'Me?' He stared at her out a blank face, mouth stupidly open. This was what you did. With Tina it wasn't meant to put her down. A little joke was passing between them.

'On special occasions,' she said, murmuring it coyly. Now this is a funny business, he thought; Tina acting the coy bird when she is anything but. He continued to appear stupid while considering her game. It was no trap, he decided. Anyone else of her age saying that and he would have clammed up instantly.

'I expect so,' she said easily.

'Yeh.' He relaxed with a grin.

'With Trevor, eh? Not with me, though.'

'Who says?'

'I don't mind. Not if you don't feel right.'

'I'm a'right!'

She lit her draggly cigarette. She blew smoke at the ceiling. 'I'm only teasing,' she said. She smiled. 'Have a roll-up if you want.'

'Ta.' He set to work with a will.

Vastly amused by his gusto, she said laughing, 'Do you need any help with that?'

'No thanks.' He glanced up quite serious in the midst of his tongueing.

'I was joking. You're better at it than I am.'

'Nothin' wrong with yourn.' He moved a hand to her lighter, but hung there for permission. She waved him on.

When they were halfway through she took a deep breath and plunged in. 'Johnnie can I ask you a personal question?'

He narrowed his eyes speculatively, lounging back in imitation of a pub smoker. He was unsure, he needed a style; he had no vocabulary for what was happening to him. This was the life. She was about to ask him things, perhaps intrigued by the close secrecy of his life, its difference, hoping to be let in. It was leading to that. 'Yeh,' he said. He thought her curiosity about him perfectly understandable. In her place he would have been the same. It was boring, he imagined dimly, being a woman. If only Trevor was a fly on the wall and could see this!

She dropped her bomb. 'Have you been sniffing glue?' She had studied his eyes carefully – they seemed normal to her.

As if surfacing from a great depth with violence he plunged up rigidly and faced her. 'What if I 'ave?' he said furiously, his fingers working. He ground his cigarette into the ashtray and she was sickened, immediately in conflict with herself. It was a stupid gamble gone wrong. Up to this moment she had felt him liking her.

'Your mother's worried sick, that's what.'

'Gimme a break will ya?'

'A what?'

'Is that what this is, all this? Have a cig, Johnnie!' He sprang to his feet.

His bitter derision flooded down over her, so that she was forced to stand up. 'Don't be foolish. It's no game. Am I a friend of yours or not?'

'A what?' he jeered. 'Not 'alf you ain't.'

She stood her ground, her hurt rueful face and large pale eyes levelled on him. 'Yes I am. If you'll let me be, I am. I want to be.'

'Ah, shit,' he said.

She thought his disgust exaggerated. The little she knew of his history influenced her in his favour; she understood, he was going through the motions. Otherwise she would have dismissed him as just another

148

little brat acting big. God knows, you saw them around here every day, hard men in the making.

'If you have been, how much,' she demanded coldly. 'I'm asking.'

He put his thumb and forefinger almost together and waved them under her nose. 'That much.'

She said, breathing hard, 'It's a mug's game.'

'What if it is?' he said sullenly, and turned for the door. He was finished with her.

'Johnnie, listen to me.' She felt close to despair at being cast in this role, about to be left alone with it, when the whole thing had been thrust on her. How unfair. So much for doing someone a favour! There and then, in the space of a second, she began to suspect her own motives in agreeing to intervene. Was this another male impossible to reach whom she felt bound to flail at? Why the hell should she care what happened to him? It was Marilyn she was concerned about.

'I'm off,' he muttered, to his feet. 'Stuff this crap an' all.'

'I wish I'd kept my big mouth shut,' she moaned, beseeching him with her doleful sound.

'Yeh, well.' He blundered through the door and was out of there.

Instead of rushing off, he listened for a moment to her bolting herself in, barricading herself against him. Trudging away on the walkway, his legs seemed to be clogged with black sludgy thoughts. He became conscious of an indefinite emptiness, of a sore disappointment hurting his chest. To hear what it sounded like he said aloud, 'Who does she think she is?'

Passing the gaping lift, he stopped and got in. It was like a cell for punishment, litter and grime underfoot. One dim light. He rode up to the seventh floor and then down again, eerily, wishing it was a twenty-floor high-rise and he could ride up through the cooking smells in a desolate echoing solitariness. 'Who does she think she is?' he yelled at the walls.

On the ground floor, some tiles had been wrenched off a wall and there was one hanging loose, held by the corner. As he rushed out of the lift it was the first thing he noticed. His momentum carried him past, then he ran back and aimed violent kicks at it. As each kick landed he spat out 'Tina-Blecher, Tina-Blecher' in a rhythm, until the tile parted from the plaster and flopped to the ground.

22

In the middle of a hot summer, when Johnnie dropped a remark to his mother, though without exactly asking, she told him that Tina had moved out.

'Where's she gone to?'

'Highfield,' Marilyn said. 'I got her address here somewhere.'

A pang of loss, which made him angry with himself, confusing him, must have entered his voice. 'Don't talk to me like that,' his mother said.

He wanted to ask why no one had seen fit to tell him. Tina had noticed him, seen something. And she wasn't that old – she wore tight trousers didn't she? Even her interference was a sign that she expected things. He had been singled out by her. How could she disappear without a trace? A crazy voice urged him to run out and start searching for her now, this minute, so that he could tell her things he had told nobody.

His mother nagged him to eat a piece of cake. It was home-made, stuffed with fruit, the kind he liked.

'I don't want any.'

'You like it, Johnnie. Don't you? I thought you liked it.'

'Not now. Not hungry.'

'A drink then. Shall I make us a coffee?'

'Mam, I keep saying, nothing, I don't want nothing.'

He positioned himself in front of the television, switched on; a news programme he didn't see or listen to.

'What are you angry with me for?' his mother complained. 'Have I done something?'

'No.'

With melancholy, fearful intuition, she came into the living room and said, 'Why should I care where Tina Blecher is? Haven't I got my own troubles without bothering about her? You want me to care, is that it?'

151

'I never said that.'

'You're thinking it.'

'Rubbish. That's rubbish.'

He refused to turn his head and look at her. His mother's distress was in her face, permanently these days. Either he pretended not to see it or it was so familiar a thing that he was unmoved. Sooner or later though he always did look. He kept his face rigidly averted.

A bright, strained voice from the television was jabbering, a good-looking woman with hypnotic eyes, her voice running on insanely like a needle, stitching items together in a way that revealed the truth – and the truth was that nobody believed anything. Otherwise, why this – what did it mean? A train lay spectacularly on its side, several coaches strewn through the outskirts of a housing estate after hitting something and being flung everywhere as if by the blast of a bomb. The rapidly stitching voice of the woman was saying what a miracle no one was killed, there had been bad smashes before on this very bend, the train was travelling at eighty on a section with a forty m.p.h. limit . . . Johnnie found the extraordinary bird's-eye view of the diesel in somebody's back garden satisfying, and would have liked to have stared at it for a long time. It flashed off. He was left with his chagrin at the thought of his mother's news. A cold loneliness filled him up. He was excluded, of no account really. But Tina wasn't like that. No one was going to tell him that she was like that.

Tina Blecher had struck lucky a month ago. Through a friend of a friend she had heard of a poky unfurnished flat in Highfield, two rooms and a damp kitchen, the base of the wall near the sink stained with a black mould. The bathroom was shared, in a house of rented bedsitters. The street sloped down to a cluster of small shops and a motor-spares store, and then to the grimy brick railway bridge from another age, its inner walls shored up with iron sheets. Trucks and buses went bumping and crashing past all day. It was a barren district, no trees, drab tired buildings coated in dust, some of the street still with patches of cobbles from that Victorian time. All the same, moving in there gave her a surge of hope, a renewal of confidence in the grip she maintained on her affairs.

Providence Park had really begun to get to her. 'What don't you like, what is it exactly?' Marilyn had asked.

Without hesitation, she had said, 'It's the thought of Jan.'

The realisation that Jan would be going to school from there gave her the horrors. In order to stay on an even keel she had to keep reminding herself that she was not slipping or freaky or going over the edge, not yet. It was one long battle. Pushing out defiance day after day wore her to a frazzle. Discovering one day that she was almost insensible to her surroundings finally frightened and decided her. It was time to go. Looking round now at her tatty flat in Highfield, with its faulty wiring and old plaster and the dirt of a succession of tenants, she was still relieved that she had got Jan and herself out of that grim block. She would recall that half-destroyed hallway, the slogan sprayed on a fanlight – 'Beat inflation – shoplift' – and have no doubt that she had made the right decision.

Elated by her show of initiative, she went along one night to the local community centre with a woman from upstairs, Julie, whose voice had no expression and who never smiled.

'I'm Julie,' was all she said, the first time they met. It was like hearing a statement of the only thing that could be said for certain about herself as a person, the one proof of her existence. Julie wore old jeans and a coarse navy smock smeared with paint. Tina failed to place her accent. She had gone up to her bedsitter once for coffee; this was after Julie had silently helped her in with a few boxes and a trunk. Propped around Julie's walls on lumps of cardboard and rectangles of masonite were weird lurid paintings in dark colours, every one the distorted image of an infant. They struck Tina as shocking, too cruel and skinned. She recoiled. Yet they were only small, crude daubs. Some were mere foetus-like shapes, raw dark reds swimming in thick purplish-brown tunnels. Where had this woman been, what had happened to her? Everywhere in this art work Tina saw reflected the sullen morbidity of Julie's few words.

'I never had lessons,' the woman said.

That much was obvious. A dark, thin woman, she gave no information about her past, staring round at her own pictures as if bewildered, like someone denied a history. Tina thought it all creepy and felt stifled, wrong, longing to escape, but the obsessional, almost dumb woman, gazing lifelessly at her like an amnesia victim, put a spell on her. Tina thought she must be fortyish. She gave the impression of someone who had long ago stopped expecting anything, as if a vital organ in her had either ceased to function or was missing.

Tina was no joiner, but the woman had extended her an invitation and then relapsed into a sour silence. Tina wondered if the woman had some problem and needed a companion in order to get herself out of the house. She was rather appalled by Julie, who had normal, if monkeyish features, and yet was anything but normal. It was like Marilyn all over again, she thought. Except that this woman who was without apparent connection with anyone, who was clearly a casualty, made no plea, expressed no fears. She sat blankly stranded in a silence she seemed to generate endlessly as you watched.

'What goes on at this centre?' Tina asked doubtfully.

Julie cleared her throat. 'Friday night every other week is a workshop for writers,' she intoned. 'People come and read their own stuff. An old woman last time was talking about her autobiography. She had no education, and there she was writing down a record of her life. I couldn't get over it.'

Tina was astounded by this speech. Then she said, 'Yes, but wait – I can't write.'

'Neither can I. I tell them about these – she waved her hand around – 'if anybody's interested.' She paused so long that Tina thought she had finished. 'You just sit there and listen,' she went on. 'I do. If you don't open your mouth it's okay, they go on discussing things. It's a very casual set-up.'

Normally Tina would have needed a babysitter to go

anywhere, but as it happened she was due to take Jan to her mother's at Bakewell. This would be a yearly occurrence. Tina would come away every summer feeling giddy, set free for a week, gazing about zestfully with her new freedom like a girl. Time was a great luxury and she was unable to adjust to it. It would all get wasted. She trailed back sooner than necessary to collect her daughter, resentful and bad-tempered, asking herself what it was she wanted, what was the matter with her.

Partly it was the result of renewed contact with her too-bright, too-effusive mother. A jarring in the atmosphere tended to unnerve her. She had no idea what it was that her mother did, but assumed it was a consequence of her remorse and guilt at leaving Tina motherless as a child of seven. Nothing was ever said directly. As soon as Tina appeared the air seemed to vibrate dangerously. She wondered more than once if her mother was now afraid of her. No, if anything it was the other way round, Tina thought. Her mother would present herself as a helpless and unprotected person and this terrified her. For instance, she was about to allow a scrap metal dealer to marry her, an uncouth complaining brute with a thick pitted neck who kept insisting he was devoted to her.

'You're not going to, are you?' Tina said.

Her mother wouldn't say yes or no. Struggling on alone for years had worn her out, she explained. She had said no to Sam enough times but he came back, wearing a clean collar submissively to sit at her table, hoping one day she would weaken and allow him to stay the night. She might despise him but she was used to him, that was the point. And after all, he was a man. Marrying again would solve all the practical problems which never went away when you were a woman on your own. In the whole of her life she hadn't known what it was to be comfortable, to have what other women had.

Tina was against it, but because her objections were entirely subjective she said little. In any case, she felt sure her mother knew what was going on in her mind. She said once, 'Why don't you like Sammy?' She had this

155

babyish name for him which made Tina want to throw up.

'Don't I?' she asked sarcastically. Often she spoke in a bantering tone to her mother, who replied as if she hadn't heard.

'He has good qualities, though you might not think so.'

'I'm sure he has.' More sarcasm.

'I've always found him a very generous man. I like generosity in a man.'

'Any more virtues?'

'He's a considerate lover.'

'Oh for God's sake, Mum!'

'Well, if I can't make you like him I can't.'

Tina burst out at last, 'Tell him to stop coming the father with me!'

'What? Tina, you're very much mistaken.'

'Am I? I can do without that stuff from him. Tell him, will you? Oh he's doing it all right.'

'If he is, I'm sure he doesn't intend to. He's not aware of things like that. Men often aren't, Tina. He's probably just trying to please me.'

'Can we stop talking about it?'

She had had a stepmother, now she was about to have a stepfather. Sam's heavy, dull flesh took no account of her. She had nothing against him but his dull assumption that they were now important to each other because of her mother. Why should she have to fake an interest in a man she cared nothing for? She suffered under his crass, heavy gaze, furiously suspecting him of seeking to add her to his ménage. He had two sons by a previous marriage, and an aged mother living with him. Tina had other, unanswerably physical objections to the man, to his hands for instance. They lay in his lap and looked blind, like scarred unearthed tools, dug up from some awful cindery hole. She would try to blot out his hands. What sort of creature was he, to come reaching for her mother with hands like that? And she – what about her? Her mother would actually grin – that half dirty monkeyish grin that women often flashed at such moments, when they were found out and didn't give a damn! As if their scruples had never been more than a pretence.

Was everything about her mother a lie?

She wouldn't see her for months, thankful to be a good distance away, nothing to do with her mother's endless compromises. A letter would come. At the sight of the handwriting, all loops and giddy swirls, the reluctant tenderness she sometimes felt for her girlish mother revived. In the funny absurd way she had of putting things was her mother's brave spirit as she dealt doggedly with life, coping with problems single-handed and always keeping up appearances. Behind the trite words lay a ridiculous hope, a peculiarly stubborn belief that things would get better, that some shining, enticing event would one day dazzle and transport her. It was a dream she had had for as long as Tina could remember. Tina sighed. There was a bond between them after all. If she stayed away, it was fine, she could appreciate and even care for her mother. Unlike her, though, she refused to use the word love, or even think it.

23

With Jan away, she was free to accompany Julie to the Centre. They went under the ponderous bridge that was always trickling with damp and turned sharp left, up a steep exposed road flanked on both sides by demolition sites, heaps of rubble and old blackened timber stacked in jagged piles. High on the ridge ahead stood a row of ugly buildings, among them a modern church, faced with a knobbly yellow composite stone; it hung over the deep crater they were toiling to leave. Beside the church to the left was a cheap new building, a low structure with tinny black gutters.

'There,' Julie said, pointing it out. 'That's the Centre.'

Near the top Tina paused on the broken pavement to catch her breath. What a surprise! The years she had been here, yet this city was still full of surprises. Every winter the gloom and grit seemed to descend from the sky, then she climbed another steep pavement and glanced over her shoulder and saw this! Streets clambered over the hills exuberantly, laid out at risky angles, slanting away and criss-crossing, clumps of green showing, and so pretty and spangled with its ribbons of lights twinkling. The squalor and gloomy thunder of traffic, all the restless jabber of a big city would be wiped out, hushed to a mere murmur, lit magically with fairy lights. Tina, her gaze rolling around as she looked, swung this way and that, saw again that it was an exciting place in which to live, a bubbling cauldron of possibilities. Something exhorted her to give it another chance – things *could* happen to her here.

The two women marched together in silence towards the raw new bricks of the Centre. This is crazy, Tina thought; I might as well be alone here. It was like walking along beside the husk of someone. She began to suspect that. Julie was consumed with something, perhaps a dreadful secret or a crime, and this inner burning ate up all her energy, even her voice, so that on the outside she was horribly lifeless and indestructible, like a beetle.

She followed Julie down a line of new flagstones to the rear, through the blank shiny doors painted a sharp lime. They went along a short corridor that echoed and into a bare barren room, the floor covered in new vinyl and containing only a semi-circle of black moulded chairs on metal legs. Her crepe soles squeaked on the floor. She joined the half-dozen people on the chairs. A young man with prominent eyes was speaking in a low hesitant voice to an elderly woman. The woman leafed through a big dog-eared jotter stuffed with loose sheets that seemed out of control and was only half-listening to the young man, who sat back finally and crossed his legs, smiling as if to comfort himself.

Tina was waiting for Julie to introduce her to someone in charge. There seemed no one present like that. Maybe they were waiting for him – or her – to arrive?

The young man coughed loudly and then stood up. He said a few foolish things and the others watched him, showing him no respect but not appearing to mind, perhaps glad it was him and not them. Tina sank down lower in her chair. The way these people seemed isolated from each other, coldly and hopelessly self-engrossed, struck her as repellant. She felt caught in a circle of futility and wanted to break out of it and escape. She was a fool to have come. She would go away and feel hopeless and mediocre, and she was not. The young man said, 'I think we should start now, if you agree. Are we all agreed?'

He had the earnest, didactic tone of a teacher. An older man with a scalded, angry face said, 'What about Elsie?'

'Who?'

'Elsie Watson. She's coming. I saw her yesterday.'

'Is she coming?'

'That's what she said yesterday.'

'Then in that case perhaps we should wait for a few minutes.'

'I've got to go at nine,' a blunt-voiced woman said.

'Well, we'd better start, then. What do you all think?'

159

No one said anything. Tina sat embedded in their stony silence, disliking them indiscriminately for making her feel so utterly dismal. She was commonplace, as they were, an ordinary person, a no-hoper. Now these people, hanging on grimly to their private papers, were forcing her to feel guilty about her ordinariness. How many times had she sat on buses among packs of ordinary people, jammed in, staring straight ahead like them, conscious only of her sameness? Her worries were like theirs, her aches and pains the same. Here was a group of people intent on emphasizing how special they were, drawing attention to their self-consciousness about themselves. Before they opened their mouths she knew this was what it meant. Resenting them was unfair but she did resent them. They had got sick of moping around in their rooms and so here they were. She feared them, and what they represented, these quietly desperate ones. She would rather not know about them, they were unthinkable, like their underclothes, she had a horror of them. Her skin crept as she sat among them and saw how pallid and tight-lipped they were. They were going to reveal themselves if it killed them. She dreaded having to listen to their lonely thoughts, their illusions, their disappointments and truths. She was a fool not to have realised beforehand what she was letting herself in for. And where were her papers, to prove who and what she was? She had no identification. She felt they were indifferent to her. They were even indifferent to each other. It was deplorable and she hated them.

The young man, Michael, read a series of verses in a peculiar, special voice that was droning and melancholy like a priest's. When he came to the end of a poem, people nodded foolishly. He went on again. The use of words was clever, Tina thought. Nothing touched her. She hoped desperately that she might be stirred, wrenched out of her unfairness. It was just words to her, strung together for effect. She believed that Michael was similarly unmoved, even bored. The energy was low, guttering down in him. She stopped feeling embarrassed and felt sorry for him, for the loss of his illusion. At least he didn't plead; he expected nothing. He sat down quietly, without any fuss, and Tina, watching, believed he was perfectly aware that it was a pastime which he didn't greatly value. He looked across brightly, enquiringly – it was the elderly woman's turn.

She was a rough diamond. She read clumsily, with some emotion, from a memoir of her childhood in the slums of Liverpool. It was a direct, simple narrative, describing one thing faithfully and then another. There was no interior life, no irony, just this charged flood of reminiscence running on without end. Murmurs of appreciation greeted the odd bits of spunky humour. Tina felt a little better, although she was uneasy at being included in this bald confession. The woman bulldozed on and Tina was forced to listen, weighed down and deflated by this tenaciously remembered luggage from a distant time, that was too personal, and uncreated; she could do nothing with it.

A little later, the same woman requested loudly, with the brutal candour of an old person renowned for speaking her mind, 'I want to hear Julie reading out about her paintings.'

Julie smiled bleakly. 'I read it last time, Molly, remember?'

'Yes, well, I wasn't listening properly. My back hurt.'

'I haven't got it with me.'

Michael spoke up. 'Perhaps you could tell us in your own words, for the benefit of those of us who missed it?'

There was a painful pause. 'I can try.'

'Please.'

The man with the inflamed face nodded amicably at Julie. So did the old hard-eyed woman, who smiled the smile of someone used to getting her own way.

'I haven't been to art classes, nobody taught me what to do,' Julie began slowly in her dragging monotone. 'I make it up as I go along. Until my baby died – it was a cot death – I never wanted to try anything like that, it seemed nothing to do with me, with my life. I had somebody living with me then and when they moved out they left a box of paints behind. I thought I would try it.

Who cares what I do anyway? Who is there to say it's right or wrong? I started because it was so quiet, and I had enough of quiet. I got a piece of board and picked up a brush and started. If I had known what it was like I'd have done it ages ago. I loved the dark colours especially, the darker the better. If anybody comes in and sees my pictures for the first time they are always frightened, even though they don't say. They look shocked, then frightened. I paint what they have hidden, buried in the garden and won't remember. I dig it up and it shines for me in the dark, in the quiet. That sounds terribly morbid, you will say. I can't help that. If I knew how, I would make wax dolls the size of babies, with real hair and teeth. Is that shocking? As it is I paint babies, it's all I want to do. I can express everything that way, so why not? We start as babies, we end up as babies – have you ever thought of it? I sometimes wonder if this earth we live on is a baby. If the stars are babies. I can see how this frightens people, of course I can. Anybody is welcome to come and see my pictures, and make friends with them if possible. It means a lot to me if they like them. What they are liking is my true self. There is an exhibition of paintings and drawings at the University in October and they are going to hang up three of my pictures. I don't want to sell them but I should like them looked at.'

Tina had been sitting quite still and astonished, listening to this revelation of Julie talking, listening almost against her will. At first she had thought, what a horrible exposure to be making, Julie naked, the room sterile, the listeners indifferent. As it went on and she sneaked a glance sideways now and then at Julie beside her and at the faint smile on her lips, hearing her friend's strange satisfaction, suddenly she felt tears shaking in her. Curiously upset, she sat as still as she could, even smiling constrainedly herself.

Later, getting back in and shutting the door on the event, she denied her own feelings, deciding angrily that the evening had been hateful from start to finish and a gruesome mistake. But going back down the steep street with Julie in the dark she had found herself able to accept

162

the woman's stony silence without resentment. It had been like listening to a medium, an instrument. She wondered now if she was mistaken about her, if Julie's dull face, frozen hard, tired-looking, made her appear much older than in fact she was. She shivered to think it. What had this woman survived, what had befallen her?

'They're a friendly crowd, aren't they?' Julie said inexplicably, as they parted in the hallway.

'Oh yes.' Tina gave her a meaningless smile and went through her door. Her feelings bewildered her, violent gusts of reaction bending her out of shape. Her instinct to condemn, to have no sympathy for those people because of their stigma, their taint of unhappy isolation, made her feel a fraud. How was she any less alienated? They attempted things, even completed things, and what had she ever completed?

She went to bed depressed, and in the morning woke up with a fierce determination to act. It took her a while to know what it was. Sitting over her breakfast, the trance of sleep ebbing from her slowly, in the sensuous trickling way she liked, with the sensation of rich deposits left behind in her consciousness that she would later use, she made up her mind. She had considered it before and it had awakened no response in her – she had thought it too long-term a plan. She was going to join a class and obtain an O'Level in English. When Jan began school this autumn she would be free to do it. This would qualify her to join a course later studying literature, novels, the Romantic poets. She wanted to learn how to read the big, difficult nineteenth-century novels.

The jumble of her mind distressed her. She only had to think of poor Marilyn, milling around in her jumbled-up mind. In libraries and books was a world of order, which she would enter and stroll about in one day. As a girl she had read avidly, voraciously, during a period when she was casting around for avenues of escape. Now she wanted to learn how things were ordered. She loved to think of the adventures waiting for her in libraries, in the polite aisles of books.

The first step was simple. All she had to do was enrol

163

at Mylor Grove on the appropriate date. She went out and rang the office. A homely, unsurprised Yorkshire voice, a woman, told her to expect the information in the post the following day. Stepping out of the booth, Tina glanced around sharply. Suddenly she was immensely pleased with her decision, her action. This pleasure affected the way in which she saw her surroundings, as if by one simple act she had sharpened the outlines of buildings, altered the slant of light.

24

Her mother had taken Jan for a fortnight. Tina, immersed as usual in the frustration of a freedom she could only watch dribbling away, heard a knock at the door one day and found Nick there.

Since her move here he had been just once. She missed him badly, nursing a sad ache, but was too proud to write. Who knows, maybe he was staying away out of pride too? How stupid. Now here he was, looking as if he was at a loose end.

She looked out wryly at him there in the street. He had his old grin ready. Nothing had changed that she could see. Yet a magical quality he had for her still lingered about him. Her heart speeded up. He hovered there on the pavement outside the gardenless house, light on his feet, looking comically as if he had just landed from outer space and was dusting himself off. He was young, vain about his appearance, in need of appreciation. Why it was she had no idea, but he touched her with this transparent need. Right now he was laughing at himself, at the day, the noisy treeless street. 'Come in!' she said.

In the room she said, 'Now I can see why my mother gets in a dither over unexpected visitors.'

'Called round the other morning, whenever it was,' he said vaguely. 'A week ago.'

'That's funny, because I'm always here. Unless I was out shopping.'

'I called, anyway. No Tina,' he said mournfully, putting it on.

'Poor Nick. When would that be?'

He shrugged. 'Haven't a clue.'

'Ha, what am I thinking of?' she exclaimed. 'I must have been in Derbyshire, taking Jan to my mother's.'

'Of course,' he said.

'That's where she is now.'

'I see, yeah.'

She began to feel a little cramped with him, in this dingy room where she spent so much of her time. She said eagerly, 'I feel like going out – it's claustrophobic in here. Shall we go for a drink?'

He looked solemnly at his watch. 'Too early.'

He had carried in something that was flat, in a brown paper bag, propping it against his chair. She asked what it was, if it was anything exciting. With an air of reluctance, he said, 'A record. Only a second-hand one. From 'Rare and Racy'.

Tina pointed to her music centre. 'Put it on if you like, if you want to hear it. Have you heard it yet?'

'Only from way back. It's Miles Davis.'

'Don't you want to play it?'

'Not really,' he said. 'Not in the mood.'

She stopped trying so hard. He was a pleasant sight. All the same, to see him sitting there inspired in her a craving for movement, to have a destination in common with him. She studied him a moment. 'You're looking at me strangely,' she said.

'Am I?' he said. 'Sorry.'

'Hey, let's go to Mr Kite's for coffee, how about that?'

'I've just come from there.'

She came to a halt with him. 'Oh, all right,' she said. 'So what shall we do? Talk about the weather? How's the weather been where you are?' She was smiling hard, cursing herself; as the words flew out of her mouth he sat studying a high corner of the room, staring absorbed up at the ceiling.

'The same as where you are,' he said.

'I don't even know where you live. By the way, do I sound jumpy to you? Am I talking too loud? I know I do that sometimes. I'm alone a lot, you see. Don't let me make a meal of you,' she pleaded.

'You aren't doing that,' he said. Before he ducked his head she saw his cruel little smile. He was amused by her.

'Where do you live? I might feel like dropping in to have a look at your bedsitter. Is it any good?'

'Awful,' he said.

'How about if I helped you with it? We could fix it up, perhaps.'

'Nobody could.'

She thought his joky neutrality a futile thing. Her teasing was going badly wrong. Let it, she thought savagely. They sat a long time in a strained silence, while she contemplated him. Prolonging this encounter was a danger, yet she had been glad to see him. She still was. Then she made up her mind and said slowly, 'I don't think you want me to know where you live. Is that true or not? If it is, say so. Tell me that at least.'

He looked at her for a moment. 'I don't want you to,' he said.

'I see. I get the idea. It stinks but I get it.'

'No you don't.'

'All right, I don't. Explain it to me.'

He shook his head. 'There's nothing to explain. We've said it all. Didn't we spend hours chewing it over? Did I dream it? We agreed, didn't we?'

She laughed. 'I thought I was the jumpy one. I always think it's me. It's you, you are.'

'Tina, no arguments.'

'I suppose it's my fault.'

'When I came in I felt fine.'

'That's why I wanted us to go out. We aren't going anywhere, are we?'

'If you like,' he said evasively.

She paused. She went to the bathroom and came back. He was in the same position exactly, stuck there. 'How are you getting on, really?'

Nick didn't stir. 'Why?' he asked, startled.

'That time you came round looking for me, when I wasn't in.'

'What about it?'

'Oh nothing. I just wondered what that was about.'

He seemed unwilling to answer. 'I was miserable,' he admitted finally. He even managed to sound forlorn.

'Why?'

'I can't remember.'

167

She sniffed. 'Anyway, you're all right now.'

He stared at her, his eyes working. 'Oh, I get it. You mean on my own, away from you. Yes, Tina. I'm a big boy now.'

She stood up then in a rush, took a deep breath and shouted at his head. 'This is terrible, I don't want this, I can't bear to hear any of this, go away please, it's pathetic.'

At the door he turned and said carefully, 'If you want the truth, I came round to see if you were okay. All right, I'm moving from where I am. Is that clear? Just don't get the wrong idea.'

In spite of his defiance he seemed half-ashamed. He went out. In a strange suspended anger she saw him slipping past her window and it occurred to her suddenly that he was a drifter, a hanger-on, a time-waster. She had not seen this clearly before. He was so impossibly childish. In a passion of disgust and disappointment with herself, hardly knowing if her anger was meant for him or her, she cried out through the glass, 'You creep. You shit. You rotten fucker.' It sounded unhinged but she was beyond caring. She wished she had thrown something, hit him with something. She clutched a handful of curtain and waited for the shaking bits inside her to settle, dizzy with their tumult, saved from wailing by a picture she had of herself clinging by the claws like an animal, a dry-eyed, interesting creature. She was intact, she still had herself.

One Saturday afternoon Tina was in town. It wasn't a good place to be with a small mardy child. All the way up from the Moor Jan grizzled, tugging in spasms to get her hand free, till they reached the fountain at Fargate.

They stood by the railings and stared at the play of water which fascinated them both. A crowd restlessly on the move milled around them. Then they stopped again to see a martial arts class in action – twenty youngsters drawn up in an arc in front of an instructor. Mats were laid over the flagstones. There was a demonstration on combat; the children were arranged in two lines, big and small, both sexes, pumping their arms and counting aloud, at a certain point yelling out the same weird cry in unison and bending forward on one knee. Tina watched one figure, a stocky little girl of about ten, yellow hair and buttery face. Eyes glued to the instructor she put everything she had into it; she was a ferocious frowner. Tina laughed, but she was impressed. Such a determined little demon!

They went on through the thick scrum, aiming for Boots. A boy burst out from the mouth of Chapel Walk, almost landing at their feet, staggering.

'It's Johnnie!'

He was alone, so he stopped. 'Hiya.'

'Where are you off to in such a hurry?' Tina asked, smiling.

'Nowhere much.'

'At that speed?'

He shrugged, grinned. 'Ah wusn't,' he said, scratching his head. When he was caught off balance he always talked broad.

She laughed with pleasure to see him. 'I'd know that T-shirt anywhere.'

'Yeh, right,' he said naively. 'I got two.'

'Really? I thought it might be twenty-two.'

'Why, what's up wi' it?'

'Nothing!' She laughed in his face. 'Listen, how's your mother?'

His face clouded; he was staring at his feet. 'I s'ppose all right.'

'I must come round and see her one day, I really must.'

'Yeh,' he said, and sounded indifferent.

They were being jostled and forced apart – it was a ridiculous spot to hold a conversation. Johnnie seemed on the point of drifting off. Tina saw again his funny habit of crimping his mouth, as if swallowing his lips, when he was at a loss. His stationary body had a resistant, welded look. She said, with an attempt at playful seduction, 'Are you still in the market for a bit of baby-sitting?'

'Yeh, I might,' he said. 'Why not?'

'Next Friday I could do with one. Well, every Friday.'

'You're on,' he said toughly. He was about to turn on his heel.

Tina cried, 'Hang on – you don't know where I live now, do you?'

'Expect me mam does.'

She shouted it after him anyway, between the startled faces of impatient shoppers. 'Know where that is, Johnnie? Can you find your way there?'

He flashed her a grin of male scorn, which she also remembered. 'That was Johnnie Hunslett, that was,' she told Jan as they mounted the stone steps of the crowded store, pushing in on the next wave.

'What's baby-sitting?' her daughter asked.

Tina went up for her prescription. It was for sleeping pills, and she was afraid of getting hooked. A bout of insomnia had driven her to the surgery. Lying awake for hours she would be at the mercy of doubts and fears. Nevertheless, she hoped the doctor would dissuade her. Instead, he scribbled on his pad before she had finished trying to explain, tearing off the sheet and asking her in a bored voice if there was anything else. Pills, that was all they knew.

PART THREE

25

It was August, a bad time to be trapped in a city. The traffic, banging and senseless, hardly ever let up. In shops nearby, Tina heard them gossiping about the holidays they were about to have or ones they had returned from. 'The sea was cold, too cold to swim in,' she heard a tanned woman say. The sea! With her inland upbringing, Tina had never got over a first glimpse of the sea when she was a child. She was with her mother and father before they were divorced, so she must have been very young. The coach shook itself free of the trench-like lane, rose and dipped over the brow of a hill and there was the sea, an immense wall of deep blue that slowly flattened as they approached. A ship lay on it, a mere toy, far out. This was Cornwall. The name itself was a sound full of sea.

Standing there disaffected in the sunless fruiterer's to buy salad stuff, Tina made a vow to get to Cornwall next year. Somehow or other she would do it. She would ask her mother to take care of Jan and then take off. It was fierce as a lust in her, the craving. As for money, she had ideas about that. For instance, they wanted a woman right now at the San Remo in Division Street, lunches only. Then there was bar help, more difficult for her to manage as it was evening work.

She would take Jan another time. Strange, whenever she indulged in such dreams she was always alone. She wondered if Johnnie liked the sea. She took it for granted that, unlike her at his age, he had seen it many times. These days the kids did it all, poor or not.

Remembering how they had bumped into him, she felt glad, and also oddly disturbed. She had wanted to detain him, definitely. Why, when they had nothing for each other, no words, no experiences? Maybe it was something he did. Once or twice she had caught him tugging at her

173

with his eyes, as Jan tugged with her hand. Only in his case it wasn't to get free. He was in need of attention, she thought. Was that it? He didn't hate her, then! If she had had time she would have felt uncomfortable at the memory of the glue-sniffing interrogation, but it had happened too fast. She thought now that he was absolutely right to be mad at her.

He came round on the Friday as arranged, and he was on time. He paid no attention to her new surroundings, merely remarking that it was early to be going to a pub.

'That's true,' she said. 'My friend arranged it. Anyway, how would you know?' A risky remark, so she smiled.

He sniffed. 'Why shouldn't I?'

'I'll be back no later than ten. Help yourself to anything.'

He nodded. And now he was glancing curiously here and there, in a bored fashion. Tina had dolled herself up in brown fishnet stockings and high heels, and when he looked briefly at her legs she was pleased. Any notice was better than none, she thought wryly. Lately she had begun to feel drably invisible.

Along the London Road she sat in the Globe with her friend, a glum red-head of her own age, estranged from her husband but still living with him. Tina was acquainted with the man, Norman, and had to admit she liked him. She pitied them both, and would avoid calling on Jenny if it was a family situation. The deadness in the atmosphere made her feel dejected, and then angry at her own dejection. Walking out as soon as possible she would direct her anger at them both in her thoughts, in retrospect, for wasting her time with such pointless misery. As if she wasn't perfectly capable of doing that for herself. Afterwards she experienced remorse. Nothing was ever simple. Jenny's solution was to immerse herself in local politics. She had a branch meeting tonight at eight-thirty. 'Okay, I'll stay till nine,' she said.

They had a small table to themselves at this hour. 'That's a big responsibility you're putting on me,' Tina told her.

'What is?'

'Keeping you from the Party for half an hour.'

'Drink up and less of your lip. Cheers, Tina.'

'I could do with getting drunk tonight.'

'Something wrong?'

'I'm not sleeping very well. Even with those bloody pills.'

'It's your mind. It won't stop churning away at the problems. I've been through all that.' She raised her glass. 'This is the best analgesic, for my money.'

They sat over their gins, not yet prepared to laugh at themselves. They knew each other pretty well. Tina had bellicose moods when she would become exasperated and urge her friend to make a move, overturn the whole show and be done with it. Jenny always listened ruefully and said it was not that simple. 'You'll be saying that when they screw down the lid,' Tina said.

'Charming,' Jenny replied.

She seemed trapped by her own nature into waiting humbly for developments which didn't happen. Tina urged her now and then, not out of malice, to concentrate on the shortcomings of her own politics instead of the Party's.

'Have you ever thought that he's doing the same as you, waiting?'

Of course Jenny knew that. She and Norman had an unspoken agreement to sourly wait and see. Meanwhile Norman was seeing someone or other, she believed, only half-heartedly concealing it.

'You can't be sure,' Tina suggested.

'I'm sure.'

'I suppose you're both waiting for the children to grow up.'

'That's one consideration.'

'Is it, though?'

Once Jenny said, her eyes uneasy, 'I think we stay together to avoid the risk of involvement with anyone else. One failure like ours is more than enough to cope with. We've lost our nerve.' Tina was chilled and disturbed, hearing this.

Now Jenny asked Tina about her mind, and what was in it that refused to let her sleep. 'A bad conscience?'

'Definitely.'

Tina was half-serious. Jenny said this puzzled her. 'You've got nobody other than Jan to feel responsible for. I don't get it.'

'Guilt comes in with your mother's milk.'

'Oh Christ, I know,' Jenny said. This was such a mournful utterance that they laughed briefly in each other's faces.

Tina then confessed to nightmares, and a feeling of apprehension in the streets sometimes. 'As if I'm walking about stripped naked, about to be attacked for it.'

'You mean late at night?'

'How would I be out late at night?'

Jenny considered her friend. When her mind seized on a problem she worried at it like a terrier. 'Tina, hang-ups aren't what I associate with you.'

'I'm going nuts, is that it?'

'Don't be a prat.'

'Shall we have some music?'

Jenny stood up. 'Tell me what.'

'No, you choose. Surprise me.'

While Jenny studied the juke box list, Tina fetched more drinks. The music started, Dexy's Midnight Runners, the raucous beat of their hit 'Come on Eileen'.

This changed the mood like throwing a switch. Jenny smiled – a rare sight these days. All her youth swooped back. She said, 'Come on, Tina!' and raised her glass as the song belted along, changed tempo, gathering speed irresistibly.

'Come on, Jenny,' Tina laughed, responding gladly. They touched glasses. 'Doesn't it make you want to dance?'

Jenny looked at her watch. 'I ought to dance you off to this meeting with me. It's an important one. Somebody's got to get this government out, they're lethal.'

'Is that what you're doing tonight?'

'Complacent bastard.'

'Jenny, it's not my thing. You like committees and that stuff, admit it.'

'If you want to know, sometimes I'm bored out of my mind.'

'Anyway, my boyfriend's waiting for me.'

Jenny opened her eyes wide. 'Why, is Nick back with you again?'

'Who mentioned him? This is a new young fella.'

'Stop teasing. Give me his age and any other credentials.'

'I think his mother said he'll be fourteen in October. She doesn't like him out too late. Didn't I tell you about my nice baby-sitter?'

Jenny changed her tone. 'At least at that age he won't get across you with any nonsense.'

'I sincerely hope not,' Tina said. They exchanged bawdy grins.

Jenny said quietly, after a pause during which they munched away at crisps, 'Tina, I have an awful feeling that if Norman said he'd found a woman he could be happy with, I'd welcome the news. His depression at times is such a load of guilt to bear. Who knows, it might all be me.'

'No, it's not, Jen. What you're saying means you still love him.'

Tina sat watching her friend, who shook her head. 'I can be the cruellest bitch,' Jenny said. 'You've no idea. I've made him squirm more than once just for the hell of it, and the joke is I don't give a damn.'

'Let me get you one more.'

'This is my last. I can't sit gabbing here for ever. You bugger, you want me slurring my words, I know you.'

They came out, and on the pavement embraced before separating. Tina was aware of plunging forward at an angle as she walked, and once she said aloud to herself, 'Jesus Christ Almighty.' Ordinarily at this time of night the streets would seem bleak and cold-smelling, favouring couples and so hostile to her. She would feel mocked and lonely, no one ahead but Jan and a baby-sitter eager to leave. Now she felt the exhilaration of strange company installed in her rooms to greet her. There was payment involved, which she chose not to take into account. She leaned forward and hurried.

26

It was good to see a light shining from her living room. Because of Jan she let herself into the house quietly, though all was still. She expected at least to hear the television.

Opening the room door, she gazed in on a repetition of the previous occasion. She saw the top of Johnnie's thistly head and his dirty trainers parked on her coffee table. Advancing closer, she noticed that the magazine he was leafing through was her *Cosmopolitan*. He raised his arm to acknowledge her, a gesture stolen from some film. Face to face he couldn't have carried it off, she guessed, and smiled.

'I'm glad you feel at home,' she said amicably. 'You certainly look it.'

He put his feet down on the carpet. 'Oh yeh.' Then he half-looked at her, closing the glossy mag.

'It's early yet,' she told him. 'No need to disturb yourself. Unless you're bored and want to be off.'

'That's what you said before.'

'What did I say?'

'About being bored an' that.'

She sat down heavily, sighing with relief. 'I may not have been long but I'm slightly squiffy,' she announced. She smiled to herself, thinking she must look foolish. It was very pleasant not to have to bother about how she looked. With a man she hardly knew it would have been tense, a matter of being guarded, not giving anything away too soon, preserving your image. Finding out if you were liked for yourself, if you liked the man and were willing to make moves with some common end in view – it was such a strain and no one was ever sure anyway what was going on until it was too late. None of that here.

'Slightly what?' he said. He shifted his legs, as if her remark had caused him to be uncomfortable in his body.

'Pissed,' she said brightly.

'Yeh, right.'

'I'd like to be more so. That's the truth.'

The boy stared at her animated face with interest. 'Who's stoppin' ya then?'

'Who's stopping me?' she echoed.

'Yeh.'

She snorted. 'What a good question.'

'Have you got anythin', like?'

'Let's see. Cider, there's some cider in the fridge. Are you going to join me, Johnnie?'

'Wha'?'

'Do you like cider?'

He grinned insolently. 'Course I do, yeh.' Then he remembered himself. 'Thanks very much.'

'Look, you don't have to be polite with me. I'm not sounding like a damn schoolteacher again am I?'

'Aw, no.'

'That's what you said last time,' she accused, softening the remark by smiling at him.

Confused, he dropped his gaze. 'Huh . . . not a teacher I didn't mean . . . '

'I'll forgive you, thousands wouldn't.'

He frowned. 'You think I'm stupid,' he muttered, and began twisting around.

'Oh for God's sake, no I don't.'

She jumped up and went to the kitchen. She knew she had two flagons of unopened cider in the fridge. Lifting them out, she found one had a quarter missing, but said nothing. His glass was there on the draining board. She ignored it, opened a cupboard and brought in two glasses.

'You think I'm thick in the head,' he said stubbornly.

Tina shook her head at him. 'I do not.'

'That's okay,' he said, with hate in his voice, 'I'm used to it.' He slung his right leg over the arm of the easy chair, while his body sought vainly to avoid her.

This made her even angrier than what he had said.

'Johnnie, I am not going to be told what I think, not by you, not by anybody.'

'Towd? Towd what?'

'If you want to believe what you say, that you're an idiot, then believe it. If it makes you feel good, fine. I'm not in the habit of asking stupid idiots to stay for drinks. I wouldn't be very interested. I won't beat about the bush.'

'Interested?' he said. He was looking queerly at her. She felt despised for her word, and disliked him very much when he scowled at her. She would give him one drink and then say she was off to bed.

'Yes, interested.' Damn you, she thought, picking me up on my words. She was not drunk, but relaxed enough not to care what she said. 'You interest me. Yes. But not when you try to tell me what I think.'

'Ar, right,' he sneered. It was clear though that she had placated him. 'Are you goin' to have a drink wi' me, like?'

She laughed at his nerve, feeling a little wild and reckless. She splashed out two large tumblers of cider and picked up hers, enlivened by sunny gold. He was crazy if he hoped she was going to get annoyed with him. Was that what he wanted?

'I suppose it's been quiet here, or you'd have said,' she remarked.

'A funny woman called.'

She stared. 'Who would that be? Funny? Did she say who she was?'

He shook his head, bored. He seemed to have trances, when she lost touch with him altogether for perhaps half a minute. She just drank and waited, having nothing better to do, feeling pleasantly amused by him and by herself, having this conversation about nothing with an undernourished kid who couldn't decide whether to stay buttoned up or not, whether to trust her or not. Or maybe he couldn't care less.

'Describe her, this woman.'

'Just a woman.'

'Women are different, they aren't all the same, or haven't you noticed?' She shook her head in mock despair over him.

Suddenly it was all hilarious. So was this room, she thought. All at once she was struck by the ridiculous air of self-importance the drawn curtains assumed. She felt laughter bubbling up and going ping in her breath. She parted her lips, showing wet teeth. Problems, what were problems? Look at this kid. One of the first things she'd do, if this boy was anything to do with her, would be to get some decent meals inside him. She imagined the junk food he consumed. When he came to peel off that bomber jacket and the T-shirt, how much was left of him? Did his shoulder blades stick out? He was too white, the skin of his face too stretched. His tight frayed jeans and skimpy cheap jacket only worsened the impression of deprivation. Bony ankles. One of his sneakers split across the top.

He guzzled at his cider as if it was a drink of pop. Tina filled up his glass, then her own. Taking another greedy swig, he said, spluttering, 'She wanted me to look at some pictures.'

'Ah, that'll be Julie. Did you go?'

He looked affronted. 'I come here to look after your nipper.'

'Yes, I know,' she said solemnly. 'I only meant for a quick visit.'

'She a headcase?'

'No, and don't say that.'

'She looks it.'

'That's cruel.'

'She a friend of yours?'

'Not exactly. I hardly know her. And neither do you.'

He gazed at her with shrewd eyes. 'You think she is an' all, I reckon.'

'No I don't.'

'I bet.'

'Are you telling me what I think again?'

This time he didn't take his eyes from her face, and didn't blink. He told her slowly, 'So's my mother sometimes. Think I don't know that? What people say is shit. What you are saying is shit.'

'Is that so?' She sat and considered this statement, as if he had offered her a compliment. She drank now without

182

noticing that she did, but remembered from time to time to fill up Johnnie's glass. They were travelling somewhere together, moving pleasurably and successfully through time. She lifted up the heavy flagon. Finding it empty, she blurted out laughter. 'Here y'are,' he said, passing over the full bottle.

'No, you're wrong, Johnnie.'

'Eh no, I aren't,' he said comically, labouring drunkenly at the words. They were arguing now like old friends who understood each other, happy to make endless allowances.

'All right, if you say so. Only don't jump to conclusions. Wait till you know Julie a bit better.'

'I'm not talkin' about her.'

'Who then?'

'People . . . '

'Well.'

Lunging sideways, he scooped up her *Cosmopolitan* and flapped it in the air, then let it drop. 'Whoops, sorry.'

'That's not very nice,' she said mildly.

'It slipped.'

'Have you been studying it?'

'What's that?'

'My magazine.'

'You like that stuff?'

'Oh well, bits here and there. I suppose I must. To tell you the truth, Johnnie, I like the glossy feel of it. Is that what women like? Luxury, that's what I feel. Richery. That's as near as I ever come to it. I buy it one month and then think, what rubbish, never again. Then one day the feeling comes over me again, I want to see the colours, touch the glossy paper, read the smart silly features that don't come within a million miles of the world I inhabit. You have to be frivolous now and then, Johnnie, in this life.'

'What's friv'lous?' he said, pronouncing it with difficulty, frowning.

She threw back her head and laughed. 'Oh Christ, how can I explain, I'm too drunk. What questions you ask.'

She gazed softly at him, and after a moment he had to look away, abashed. 'Ask me another day,' she murmured.

She was touched by him, pleased with him for remaining in her company from choice, free will. She had asked nothing of him. In the midst of her hilarity there was a resolve, to make no move of any kind that would prevent him from leaving whenever he wished. Then a thought struck her. 'What time does your mother expect you home?' she asked, too fuddled to put it more diplomatically.

'I do what I like.' He was glaring at her. 'See?'

'You mean you've got a key?'

'I ain't going home. That surprised you.'

'Yes,' she admitted. She waited, determined to ease up on him.

'I'm staying at Trevor's tonight.'

'Oh I see.'

'Satisfied now?' he said, leaning at her.

She glared, then laughed. His truculence was hard to take, when she kept taking pains not to offend him or his little ego. Really though she was past caring about his tender feelings. He rubbed round his face, a harsh scrubbing gesture, exactly the one his father used in moments of stress. Tina took in for the first time his bitten fingernails and the exposed balls of soft flesh, which gave her the shudders. She wondered when it was that he gnawed away hungrily at himself – never in front of her. She said, scoffing, 'It's none of my business, love.'

At this he began to roll round in his chair. 'What are you on about now?' he mouthed.

'Watch it, Johnnie. Don't push your luck.'

'I never had any.'

'Well, that's tough. That's very sad. But not a good reason for bad manners, in my opinion.'

He said again, 'What are you on about? I thought you were worried about me?'

'You've got it wrong. I'm worried about your mother.'

'Why's that? Why are you?'

'Because I like her.'

He began rolling around some more, then rocked to and

184

fro, his face screwed up, flushed. 'So do I,' he mumbled at last.

'Good.'

'Can I have a roll-up?'

She told him yes. He couldn't seem to see the tin, and this made her giggle. 'You're staring at it. On the table.'

He made a clumsy grab at it; perhaps he was shamming. It flew out of his hands and landed on the carpet. 'You spill my tobacco and you can watch out, my lad.' He was struggling with the lid and asking for papers. 'Inside the tin,' she told him. 'If you ever get it open, that is.'

'What the fuck,' he spluttered, actually laughing at himself. 'No nails . . . '

'Give it here.' She prised off the lid. 'Okay now?'

When he set to work he did a reasonable job. He made a cigarette for himself and one for her. 'How about that then?'

'Not bad for a young 'un,' she said.

This wasn't to his liking, not with the cider in him. She saw now how far gone he was. Perhaps she didn't want him to like it. A funny mood possessed her, to put on a record and dance before him. She sat where she was, dragging deeply on her cigarette.

'You think you're hot shit,' he managed to say, stumbling; then failed to look her in the eye.

'I'm what I am, good or bad, take it or leave it.'

'Would you like to kick my arse?'

'What for?'

'You would, wouldn't yer?'

'Not just now.'

'Why not? Why wouldn't yer?' he demanded.

She sniggered. 'I'd probably fall over.'

He sat gaping at her, on his face a look of blank cunning. Finally he said, 'Right-o.'

'Let's be friends, eh Johnnie?'

'We are, we fuckin' well are,' he cried out in alarm, in a strange passion.

They sat then in what to her was a pleasant stupor for a while. She saw a grin break on his face, then shatter into something troubled, a cloud. At last she stood up.

She said, 'I'm so tired, my knees are giving way, it's no good. Listen, are you telling me the truth about Trevor?'

'I can allus stay with him.'

'Goodnight Johnnie.' She spoke with an effort, wobbling where she stood. 'I must go to bed now, this minute, pronto. I really am knackered.' She stood in the bedroom door.

He seemed to acquiesce. But he lumbered up and faced her. 'I'll come an' all.'

'Ha.' She regarded him sadly, beyond caring, weary.

'See if I ain't goin' to.'

'You aren't man enough.' She left him and walked carefully into her bedroom.

Through gritted teeth he swore painfully, 'I'm comin' in! Hey, Tina, I'm comin' in there!'

Tina was standing by her double bed, already half-undressed, nearly falling to sleep as she stood. 'Oh, do what you bloody well like,' she sighed in a fuddled voice. Then she pointed warningly at Jan, asleep in an open-sided cot by the window, and touched her lips with an upright finger. 'Wake her up and I'll brain you,' she whispered fiercely.

Johnnie seemed to have got stuck in the doorway. He was gazing as if famished at her big succulent breasts and gulping hard.

'Have you seen a ghost?' she mocked. Instantly contrite, she added gently, 'Come in, then. But for Christ's sake be quiet.'

He couldn't keep his eyes off her biscuit-coloured suspenders and the lacy belt. Both his sisters wore tights. He had even laughed once at Eileen as she stood ironing her skirt in the kitchen – he said she looked like a frog. Tina noticed: she made one of her suspenders slap against her leg, and said, 'I wear these when I want to be glamorous, okay? So what do you think?' She rotated her hips slinkily, very fluid and curved, and struck a show-girl pose. 'To make me feel sexy. They're for me, my pleasure. Though walking in these you feel a bit like a trussed chicken.'

The boy went on staring and staring with his lost,

reddened face. 'Come over here, come on,' Tina urged softly. 'Don't bump into anything.' She extended an arm in invitation and he moved to her in a limping movement, pulling off his clothes. He had trouble with his Y-fronts, which were orange, trimmed with white edging. He finally freed his ankles and reached her, still in socks and shoes.

'Tell me what you like. Touch these. Go on, it's allowed.' She hissed jokily, 'Are you afraid they'll bite?' As the naked boy stood before her, swaying, Tina crowed in drunken elation, 'Down in the forest something stirred' – something she had said many times before. In his case he was nearly hairless, merely a soft fuzz in his groin. He was stumpily pointed at her. She touched him with humour and kindness, like a greeting.

'You know what you did? You called me Tina.' Afterwards she would wonder if she had dreamed hearing her name called.

She faced him boldly, taking off the belt and panties. He watched every move she made in rapt silence.

Lying in her bed he trembled all over like a dog, as if unable to control anything now that his hard image was shattered. Seeing his white face seized with shame, Tina was troubled. She felt hurt by a sense of her own foolishness. Johnnie's predicament upset and sobered her. What could she do except be nice to him? In between the sheets he looked like a baby. When he had stood helplessly before her, thin and small, very white, the skin pulled over his rib cage, she had felt an impulse to touch every outlined bone. Now he stared up from the pillow in a panic and his long dark lashes fluttered. Unable to bear the confusion of his body she clasped his round head and roughly stroked it, in a wash of boozy sorrow for them both. Her instinct was to draw him out of his cold, to bury him in warmth. She felt his neck in the dark and was shocked by how thin it was, like her own ankle. 'Come on to me, love.'

'I know what you do, you do this –' He wriggled and jerked against her, like a terrier he had seen once in the park frantically rubbing its stubby red prick in the grass.

187

'That's what you do, it is . . . ' Tina's belly heaved under him. She was laughing and spluttering. 'Oh you daft kid,' she said, 'steady.' The boy spurted on to her somewhere, far off the mark. He lay still, a landed fish.

In the morning she was woken by Jan running in and out busily as she usually did. Johnnie lay in the bed beside her, snoring lightly, only the crown of his head visible. She uncovered him to the shoulders, then lay back and groaned.

'Look, look,' Jan said.

'What is it?'

'Who's that in there?'

'Johnnie Hunslett.'

'Is he your friend?'

'Please, love, I've got a headache. You'll wake him up. Talk quietly to me.'

'Does your head hurt, Tina?'

'It does, darling.'

'How does it?'

'You mean why.'

'Is Johnnie Hunsla your friend?'

Tina sighed. 'It looks like it.'

The child said gravely, nodding, 'Looks like it, it does.'

Her mother gave herself five minutes and then hauled herself out. She groaned, clutching her head.

'Oh God.'

'Why does your head hurt?'

'I don't know. It feels like it's coming off.'

'No it isn't, it can't come off, don't be silly. Your head can't come off.'

'Well it feels like it.'

When Johnnie found her in the kitchen she was recovering, able to smile ruefully at him. Standing in the doorway he sniffed up the aromatic coffee smell. She took hers black, he saw. Jan, perched on her high chair, said, 'You're Johnnie Hunsla.'

'S'right.'

Tina invited him to sit, and asked what his preference was. He said coffee. He watched her arrange the cone of

188

filter paper in the yellow plastic funnel. She spooned in the ground coffee and brought over the kettle of freshly boiled water. The ritual was all new to him. When she was finished he grunted thanks and shovelled in his three spoons of sugar, adding plenty of milk. She guessed this was his first taste of real coffee. Amused, she said, 'Like it?'

'Not bad,' he said doubtfully.

'How's your head?'

'Great.'

'I've got a hangover.'

'Oh ar.'

'Trevor's going to be mystified.'

'Why's that?'

'Well, you didn't turn up, did you?'

'That's nothin', that. I changed my mind, it's a'right.'

'If you say so.'

Through the window she could see a sunny morning. The idea of filling up this boy who was such a scrannel with a cooked breakfast appealed to her. When she suggested it, he made no objection. 'Bacon and egg and some fried bread all right for you?'

'Smashin'!'

'Can you eat two eggs?'

'Easy.'

She heated up the frying pan and prepared his meal in silence, only asking if he would like another coffee. He said yes to everything, which suited her. She put the willow pattern plate of breakfast before him and enjoyed watching him tuck in with relish, getting up to bring a bottle of sauce and again to retrieve her half-burnt toast from the grill.

'Is that all right?'

'Yeh.'

'Nice?'

'It is an' all.' He looked up. 'Aren't you havin' some o' this?'

'This is all I want.' She scraped butter on her toast, then allowed herself a gobbet of marmalade. 'You can have some too if you want. I'm making a bit more.'

189

'When you're ready, like,' he said, his mouth full.

Jan suddenly asked, 'Why are you having breakfast in this house?'

'Cause I've been axt by your mam,' he said between mouthfuls.

'Tina you mean.'

'That's it, ar.'

At the door, leaving, he made a business of peering up and down the street, shifting his weight from one foot to the other, his eyes downcast. 'I'll see ya then,' he got out, nodding.

Suddenly she remembered. 'Wait, your money!'

'Gi' it me next time,' he said grandly, making off.

'Mind how you go,' she called after him humorously, with a touch of affection.

He went down the street hunching his thin shoulders in embarrassment, then stuck up his arm in a salute as he turned the corner. Tina closed the door.

Back in the kitchen, Jan asked her mother what she was smiling at, and got the reply, 'Nothing.'

27

Soon it was autumn. Tina loved this season. She would wake feeling heavy with it, gravid, and when she walked into town, to the hectic greengrocer's in Chapel Walk, the line of beefy girls shouting 'Nex! Nex pluyse!' and the heaps of fruits facing her, she had to force herself to concentrate and remember what it was she needed.

The new school term began and she took Jan along to the big sandy building on the London Road for her first day. It was an immigrant area. Lots of Asian children flocked together on the playground, excited heaps of them, the girls very dainty and bright in vivid silky trousers and embroidered tunics, their hair caught in glistening black braids, plaited pigtails. How large their eyes were!

She went next to her own English class out at Mylor Grove. The group was composed entirely of women and girls, a whole range of ages. Two young girls sat meekly, smiling shyly and saying nothing. An energetic elderly woman wouldn't stop talking, glaring aggressively at the lecturer, another woman. Others chattered in happy rough accents at every opportunity, laughing nervously and loudly.

Tina was astonished by their vehement determination to succeed, and upset by their sudden attacks of nerves, when their shaky confidence deserted them. They were so much like her, flapping wildly, unsure of their powers, scared of making fools of themselves, but there anyway and going through with it. Tina was caught staring at them as if transfixed before a mirror. Their violent releases of energy, when they laughed and chattered all at once, threatened to overwhelm the lecturer. Tina herself felt slightly hysterical, on the verge of giddiness. Such a din they all made together with their fears!

At the end of the session it was announced that they

could look forward to a visit by a writer who lived locally, a real live poet, Harrison Coombes, three weeks from now. For some reason this encouraged them to be ribald. 'Is he coming to look us over?' one bulky housewife shouted. 'What do his friends call him?' another hot-faced woman called breezily, cheered on by several half-shocked classmates who were delighted by this show of cheek.

'Harry, I believe.'

'Oh I say! He's going to read poems to us, is he?'

'That's the general idea,' the lecturer said dryly. She seemed torn between reasserting her authority and joining in the fun. It was understood that these sessions of mainly mature women were bound to be informal if they were to work at all. The problem was one of attendance; how to keep things afloat and moving along academically, on a rising tide of gossipy reminiscence, without frightening off the more timorous. The older women especially loved swopping anecdotes with each other. It was as if they had to remind themselves repeatedly of who they were; that although their homes were real, this too, wonder of wonders, possessed a reality and an importance for them. Tina left feeling strangely stirred, by them and by herself, her fate.

She sat dreamily on a bus trundling back into town. At a bus stop she became aware of a young boy scrambling on in a muddy anorak, and she thought of Johnnie, worrying about him vaguely, but not seriously. What had happened on that second evening was pleasantly unclear, even funny, and no more than an accident of his presence, her despondency, the nirvana reached through the drink; all that. All she had now were blurry memories. If it had led to other times, why should she worry? It was only that a certain attitude he had towards her remained in her mind to bother her. Was she an influence on him? Next time she saw him she would find out if he was going to school regularly. Marilyn had said he had done plenty of mitching, though not lately. But she was easy to fool.

The slow lumbering progress of the bus, stopping and

192

starting, and the stuffy interior, put a trance on her which she could have snapped out of, but did not. It occurred to her that what Johnnie was seeking was no more than the warm awareness of his early days, when his mother and father and two sisters were all one, before it went wrong. She knew next to nothing about him, just a few facts about this boy reckless of himself, blind to his acts.

Since that drunken evening he had called round every Friday, coming to her door as if they had made a permanent arrangement and he was expected. The effrontery of him made her smile, though she had fixed nothing with him – she had even told him to expect nothing. Guessing he would come, she would have cider for him, and treat herself to a bottle of vodka, her elixir, which she mixed with orange or pineapple juice. Once he took a sip of her drink and declared it to be too sweet for him.

Each time they would get drunk slowly, each time they lay on the bed together. Although she no longer went out beforehand, she made him leave around ten. A curious unacknowledged relationship had begun; that was how she explained it to herself. A ritual. She realized that she was getting used to it, looking forward to her Friday.

His knock was distinctive, a sharp double rap. She would open the door to his small obstinate figure. He looked at her oddly, deadpan and cold, out there in the street where his other life was lived. Even in private sometimes his face thinned, or seemed to, as she gazed at him. That must be his antagonism sharpening against me, she sensed; it was hardly a thought. Whether she reacted or not depended on her mood. After a few drinks it seemed absurd and a waste of time, getting worked up.

Strange, if she thought about it seriously, deliberately: they didn't complement each other in any way that she could see. In bed they were a ridiculous combination, his bony rib cage and hard little head pressed against her blossomy thighs and breasts. Nothing matched. Why didn't it matter – was it the drink? It was beyond her. Just like a grown man, he seemed to lose his bearings when he took off his clothes. She felt she was guiding someone who was sightless, someone blinded by her. He took his cue from her, even in the odd moments when he tried to assert himself. It all stemmed from there; she accepted that. She had to be responsible for his vulnerability, and the burden this put upon her meant that she had to drink.

The bus halted at a busy intersection. Inspired by her class, Tina wished she could break through and confide to Johnnie the lovely moment of clarity she felt, her life unfulfilled and yet responsive to change, able to germinate, stir with seed. Talking with him would always be difficult. At least now he was less suspicious of her, though without trusting her completely. But he kept coming back.

She smiled to herself, as if recognising it for the first time as a simple matter. He sought her out. Maybe he was feeding off her. Evidently he liked the privilege of coming to her as an equal, no questions asked. However, once she broke this unspoken rule. 'Tell me what you're thinking,' she said. It was a mistake. He sat lower, hung over his football magazine, set resentfully against her.

She got off outside the City Hall and began to walk quickly, still energised by her class, waiting for the lights and then passing the fountain on the clean paving of the precinct. She glanced at women shoppers with interest and sympathy, curious about their lives, at the same time wondering if her secret feelings and expectations lay visibly on her face for everyone to see. She could read nothing on theirs except weariness and strain. Was she kidding herself – had her experience deluded her?

She had heard it said that you were bound to bump into someone you knew in Fargate, and here suddenly she saw Nick moving in her direction, at almost the very spot where she had run into Johnnie that time. She was a few yards away, unnoticed. He had a girl with him. In the loose throng it would have been easy to avoid him by dodging away sideways. Perhaps still under the spell of those wilful, elated women at Mylor Grove, she kept going. Anyway, she was curious. It had been a long time. Though her stare was frankly inquisitive, and she saw him now for what he was, with clarity, she no longer felt critical of his behaviour. He was what he was. She saw everything in an instant, so free now and strong. He loped along with his young hard purpose, still affecting her. She understood at last that his life had never included her.

On his way past he came to a halt, nonplussed. 'Where did you spring from?' he said, alarmed, on the defensive at once. Tina stood waiting, all smiles, enjoying his consternation.

'You were miles away.'

'I don't think so, no,' he said huffily. As an afterthought he introduced the girl, who was smiling around prettily at nothing. 'This is Dawn.'

'Hi,' the girl said. She opened her mouth as if to laugh, but didn't. A tiny gasp came out. She was black-haired, not quite a beauty, nervously conscious of herself, with flat surprised eyes.

'I've been to my first class,' Tina told Nick, and explained what that was.

'I always knew you were an achiever.'

She laughed. 'What have I ever achieved?'

'It bugs you that you haven't.'

She shook her head. 'The same old Nick. I don't think I want to go where this is leading.'

'Where's that?'

To the girl, Tina apologized, 'Just ignore us. We have this knack of tying each other up in knots at the drop of a hat.'

Dawn tittered. 'I wouldn't know I'm sure.' She put her arm through Nick's and he appeared not to notice or mind. Tina suppressed her irritation.

'How are you making out?' Nick said, forcing a smile. Clearly he would have liked to be on the move.

'I'm fine,' Tina said, politely, angrily. What was the point of this? Why did he have to do this? She was impatient with herself for stopping in the first place. To be sentimental about him was foolish. They had nothing for each other, no trust. She thought she had always been wary of him, even when most attracted. She feared there would be nothing left when he was done with her. A dream had misled her, of opening a door and finding a certain man, at a certain time. She realized suddenly, with a cold shock, that whatever they had had begun to end as soon as it started, and her heart tightened as if she was still in danger, standing close to him with his bored girl – wanting now to get away with her discovery about him and examine it.

'Is the new place better for you?' he enquired. 'You were worried about Jan in the Park.'

'It's not scary. I'm a free woman now, with Jan at school.'

He whistled. 'She's started? Jesus, time flies.'

'Did you move after all?'

He was immediately depressed, in need of sympathy. 'No, not yet. I'm still looking.'

Without approving in any way of what she said, Tina suggested that he call round some time with Dawn to see her flat.

'I've been, remember?'

'I mean both of you.'

Afterwards she asked herself whether it was to prove that she was now immune. She doubted very much that he would take her up on it. But he looked at her familiarly, with even a touch of affection, saying he probably would. 'When are you in, or out?'

'Friday's the one night to avoid,' she said, and went off feeling better, more in charge of herself, even though the precious clarity she had been carrying inside her like a secret was gone, blown to bits by the excitement entering her in a rush at the sight of him. She shook her head, exasperated, jumping on another bus that was just leaving, lucky to get it because she was late now to meet Jan out of school.

28

She could now meet Jenny in the week for lunch, on those days when her friend was clear of politics. They sat in a pub or at her house in Nether Edge. Tina would go up to the bathroom and glance idly into rooms where the doors were left flung open. Every room in the place seemed to be in chaos. Tina saw this as a contagion, spreading from the unrest of the parents until the whole house was in a state of pandemonium, the children taking it for normal, leaving everything strewn round in the weird blast which no one had actually witnessed. The kitchen was the least disorderly room, so the two women sat there. A Beryl Cook poster up near the cupboards, the colours bright as a parrot's, of two women dropping coins in the hat of a busker, seemed to be telling them that life could surprise, be joyful, funny, simple pleasures lying around for the taking. It had been there for some time and now they forgot to look at it.

Tina had spoken more than once of her need to get some money saved, and Jenny mentioned a friend of hers who modelled occasionally for a life class in the Hays Building, a few yards from the Crucible. They were a large group of amateurs who met on Thursday mornings and were always hard up for models. Tina said she was free, but doubted whether she could cope.

'You mean you're bashful? An ex-nurse?'

'No, I mean I lack the ability to keep still. Imagine the agony. I'd get cramp.'

'This friend of mine knows the instructor, Ralph Newsome. You could have a word with him over a drink.'

'What have I got to lose?' Tina laughed, shaking her head. She saw nothing outrageous in the idea – it was only that the world of art had no reality for her, except for pictures in the Graves Gallery over the library, or paintings reproduced in books. The notion of art as an activity, taking place in this city where she lived, startled her. How could it be relevant? What were people who lived here seeking in odd corners that they did not already have? She was only intrigued to the extent that it had been suggested to her, and maybe she ought to see where it was leading. Mylor Grove was one direction; maybe this was another. 'Now what am I getting into, do you know?' she asked her friend, laughing. Jenny was a fixer.

When Johnnie stopped coming she was not exactly surprised. A boy of that age forgot, became easily bored. She went around with mixed emotions, feeling, as women often did, that the fault had been hers and now she had nothing to blame herself for.

The little ache of loss remained, and pricks of conscience. She decided she was glad, yet felt sorry, trying to remember something offensive or tactless she might have said. He could be a touchy little devil at times. There was also the worry that he could be in some sort of trouble. Marilyn had told her bits of his past, not much. Tina put this fear out of her mind with the thought that he had survived plenty so far, and in any case, good God, she had no parental obligation, no role of any kind. A doubt lingered as to whether this was strictly true.

On the day of her fourth class she was preoccupied with a messy jumble of memories, a combination of Johnnie and Nick – and Nick's attractive body. She found herself staring rudely at a stocky little man who had come in with the lecturer. This was Harrison Coombes, poet. Asked if he would prefer to be left alone to run the session as he wished, he said yes, his grin ironic, his chubby face clever and likeable. Women were almost leaning at him, some of the more avid with gobbling eyes. Tina felt shame for them, wanting to disown her own vulgar curiosity.

Coombes opened his mouth and at once began walking about, working his shoulders and gesturing energetically, hacking at air with the edge of his hand. Tina promptly lost her embarrassment. This man was at home, in his element; he could take care of himself. In fact he lapped up the captive audience. 'I come from Bradford,' he said, evidently making a comic statement that was at the same time a boast. 'You need to be a brave man or a lunatic – which you can say are one and the same – to be a poet in Bradford. But I have a clever mother, and she used to say, "Harry, you can get away with blue murder if it's funny." She's right. Otherwise it's best to leave. Like Delius. Know him? He wasn't very funny, by the sound of him. One of these days I'm going to write a poem about how unfunny Delius was.'

He wore a dark blue knitted pullover and his white shirt was open at the neck, ironed back in wide wings like a clown, an angel. Tina thought that this heavy-armed cherub was around her own age, possibly younger. His patter was fast, young, ebullient. The preambles to his poems were entertainments in themselves, and very appealing; the poetry when it came something of a let-down, with sad notes and subtle indigenous effects. It was necessary to sit down and tussle with it.

The group of women rocked and hooted, unable to believe their good fortune, intrigued by this young man who stood his ground and had the impudent vitality of a billy goat. Tina was reminded of Nick for some reason. Harry Coombes had the appearance of a certain type of student, who worked hard at a gregarious manner but who lived in secret, from a hard lonely core which was anything but friendly. Harry seemed able to call up warmth at will, and this charmed them all. Once or twice, Tina felt she was being mocked at; but he was mocking himself, she saw – a stylish character who was in the business of selling, not buying.

Part of his brief was to get them to write something of their own there and then: a shock tactic. 'This won't hurt much. You'll feel better for it after.' He laughed and coaxed, his face damp. 'I'm going to ask you a simple question and I want you to answer it in your own words and without hesitating too long. Ten minutes I'm giving you. So what do you know? – that's it, that's the question. Think about it for just a minute. What do you know after all these years? Get a piece of paper and scribble down your answers fairly fast. Don't fuss. Start each sentence with the words "I know . . . " and then just tell me. Is that clear?' He gave one example: '"I know when I wake up in the morning I feel terrible and then it gets better."'

Seriousness and anxiety descended. A woman asked, 'How many sentences did you say?'

'Ten minutes worth. Starting now.'

'Oh God,' another woman bleated, at a loss already. Others laughed, and bent to the task, nudging each other and giggling.

When the time came to read out their efforts, Tina was touched by the plain truth of some lines, the groping, sad admissions of others. One woman in her fifties with a leathery kind face brought her close to tears when she read out slowly and deliberately in a strong accent, 'I know I shall never feel young again or have children of my own. I know I am not hopeful about life as I once was. I know I did not expect to be sitting here doing this. I know that the thought of my approaching death frightens me . . . '

They worked round in a ring, expectant, appreciative. Few were confident enough to risk jokes. A tough, jolly woman whose eyes slanted like a cat's had written, 'I know it would be a waste of time entering a beauty contest . . . '

Tina's heart beat wildly as they came to her. She wanted to object, but had no grounds. She swallowed hard and then declaimed, in a voice which cracked with fear and quavered horribly and then somehow steadied itself, 'I know I am not satisfied and that is why I am here. I know I am too selfish to be a good mother. I know very little, and even less about myself. I know that anything is possible after a few drinks. I know . . . ' She tailed off. 'I can't read any more. I didn't realize we were going to have to read them out.'

She had written, but not read, that she now knew she had difficulty in maintaining a relationship with a man. An intense glowing woman to her right, radiant with her own momentary liberation, urged her to finish. 'We're all friends here, don't be shy.'

Tina shook her head. 'I'm not shy.'

She left feeling she had been manoeuvred into revealing too much of herself to these strangers, many of whom she liked as individuals. In a group they tended to fuse into a nosy alarming animal with one greedy eye. She walked off feeling less intact then when she had arrived. She was the first out in the street. A bus was coming, she jumped on.

29

One day, a Thursday, there was Johnnie at her doorstep as if he had never stopped coming. He came in.

She had just put Jan to bed. At her back she could hear her daughter babbling quietly to herself, casting spells on her dolls.

'Where have you been?' Tina said.

'Nowhere.'

She tried fixing him with a hard reproachful stare, then gave up. He was looking and not looking; his usual pretended indifference. The wall. What a funny little devil he was. She had missed him. Everything was as before, to be gone through in unhurried stages. She asked, 'Now what do you want?'

'Nuthin'.'

'In that case,' she said, 'it won't take you long to get it.'

He stood inside the room where she spent so much time, looking around questioningly. She was put in mind of a curious, shamelessly sniffing dog, poking around for any changes, anything new. As far as she knew it was all unchanged. His intense scrutiny made her begin to wonder.

'Why are you slaggin' me off?'

'I hate that expression.'

'Why are you? Don't howd it back, tell us.'

'Just ask yourself.'

'Ah doan' know,' he moaned, putting on his most miserable thick accent for her benefit, either to sound pathetic or to mock her, she thought.

'Because I was worried, stupid. Anybody would be.'

He sniffed. 'Who worries about me?'

'I've told you. Your mother for one.'

'That's diff'rent.'

'Why is it?'

'Ar, she can't help it, like.'

He watched Tina sit, and followed suit, thumping down.

'Make yourself at home,' she said sarcastically. She looked him over, thinking yet again that he was impossible, his tightened thin shoulders anticipating rejection. She was glad to see him, and groaned; it came out as a sigh and a soft smile. The lapse of time meant that they were back at square one. She would have to start again with him. Not feeling up to it, she reached out for her tin of tobacco.

'Have one of these,' Johnnie said, pulling out a dented packet of Rothman's.

She would have preferred her own makings, but said as if gratefully, 'Thanks.'

Gradually the constraint lessened. She wondered again why he had come. They were left sitting silently in mock contemplation of each other, which he seemed to enjoy, playing the adult; until he got bored and rose to stretch his legs. On his feet he would overcome his puny stature by moving with a city prowl. It amused her to see it indoors. Out in the street it would give her a pang of dismay as he made off, slipping along close to the wall in a cold slither.

His words were even fewer than usual. Leaving, poking his head warily into the street, he said as a matter of fact, without emotion, 'Bastard 'ole, Sheffield. I'd like to get out.'

'You mean like your sister – like Sue?'

Not answering, he shot her a look so remote that her heart froze.

She mentioned that she could do with some baby-sitting in a week's time and he nodded, as ever non-committal. She went in, telling herself again that it was a long slog with him and why bother, glad to turn from the scummy gruel of his disgust.

Yet when she sat down it was with a sense of loss. He was on her mind. Something about him, his loneliness or his bitterness, had flowed into her. The television when she switched it on mocked her with drama, steamy scenes between actors whose faces looked sacrificial, gruesomely suffering for her in close-up. She took one look and then killed them wholesale with a single snap. She found she was gritting her teeth. Let them flay each other without me, she thought.

At the weekend, another surprise was Nick, turning up with a blocky, beaming girl for her to meet. Josie was wrapped in a fringed shawl. Under one arm she nursed a bulbous crash helmet that looked enormous, gleaming and purple. A glittering new motorbike was propped up at the kerb.

'Come in!' Tina invited, trooping behind them in wonder and shutting her door. A little later, with Josie in the bathroom, she asked Nick what had become of Dawn. 'I still see her,' he said, airily evasive. 'Don't go making a big production out of it.'

'Who's making anything?'

'I know you.'

'Oh, I doubt it,' she said dryly.

He sneaked wry glances at her. 'A little of Dawn goes a long way,' he said, wistful for something else.

'Poor little bitch.'

'What's that supposed to mean? She's dim.'

'I feel sorry for her.'

'You don't know the first thing about her.'

'I know you.'

Josie emerged. Soon she was pressing Tina to come down to the Peace Centre, a large blackened building, once a masonic hall, opposite the main library in Sussex Street. Three months ago a mixed group of anarchists and nuclear disarmers had established a squat there. Once in the early spring Tina had come down the library steps and noticed the handmade posters and black draped banners, and seen lit candles wavering bravely at windows behind the caked grime. 'We're about to be evicted,' Josie said. 'Next Friday night there's an open meeting to rally support and discuss ways of fighting back. Come round. I'll show you over the place. It's really huge in there. They're lovely people, too. Please come, Tina,' she ended warmly, with a direct appeal. Tina, won over by the girl's shining idealism, said all right. 'If my baby-sitter turns up,' she promised.

Johnnie did come, in a good humour for once. He actually ventured a smile. Tina was amazed, more than ever reluctant to leave. She explained where she was going and why. 'I met this girl, Josie. She's a unilateralist.'

'We had one o' them but the wheel come off.'

'Very funny. Now where are you going?'

'To have a crap.'

'Charming. Go on then, I'll see you later.'

She went out impatiently. Well before eight she arrived outside the Centre. Ahead of her was the town hall, a great elaborate cliff, prettily illuminated by spotlights. She glanced up at its clock tower and then went inside.

The Centre was wide open, candles burning on shelves and trestle tables, nobody about. She thought she could hear low muttering. As she listened, it ceased. It was so quiet and deserted that she could listen to her own breathing. The exterior of the building looked impressive: inside it was smelly, down-at-heel, crudely partitioned. Temporary doors were everywhere, daubed in childish colours. A wind blew in from the street, flapping a wall surface stuck with notices and exhortations. Tina shivered. She heard the slap of sandals and then Josie came round a corner. 'Hi – I was up there!' She pointed towards the roof. 'I just happened to stroll over to the window and looked down in the street and there you were – fantastic!'

'I just got here,' Tina said needlessly, wanting very much to like this breathless girl and yet failing somehow. 'I didn't realize how big this place was.'

'You should see upstairs, Tina. There's a magnificent ballroom, it goes the whole length of the building. I'll show you later if you like. Come and meet these friends of mine, they're great, they want to make your acquaintance.' As they went off to the left down a short corridor, between more plywood walls, Josie said that she didn't live here herself, her situation wasn't desperate enough. 'Most of them here are in families, and they're homeless.'

'Is that so?'

'Oh yes. This is it, through here. By the way, Tina, what's your last name?'

'Blecher.'

'Meet Tina Blecher, a friend,' Josie said in a loud announcement to the stark windowless room.

It was a rudimentary kitchen, a bare, littered table in the middle and a dirty sink over at the far side. A pressure lamp with an incandescent mantle shed a hissing yellow light. The high discoloured walls were in deep shadow.

A girl at the table who sat holding a baby smiled at Tina vacantly. Two men, one balding, sat cross-legged on the boards passing a joint back and forth. They didn't raise their heads. A man childishly dressed in dungarees and a bright green T-shirt, whose face was lined and ferrety, scratched between his legs and gave her a wave. He sat in isolation and seemed much older than the others.

'Want to sit down?' the girl with the baby said. She was sweet and dopey, spooning mush into her child with a white plastic spoon. Giant plastic hoops, multicoloured, dangled from her ears.

Tina sat on the rickety hard chair. 'When is the meeting?' she asked Josie.

'There ain't one,' the lone man beside her said at once. 'It's cancelled.'

'Oh no,' Josie cried. 'I didn't know that.' She laughed. 'Nobody tells me anything.'

'Yeah, well, they've gone to Manchester,' the same man said laconically.

'Why, what for?'

'A demo, perhaps. Haven't a clue.' The bitter-sounding man hung out of his chair to ask Tina, 'This your first visit?'

'Yes.'

'I've only just got here myself. From Durham.'

'Oh?'

'Guest of Her Majesty. Got busted, I did.'

Tina, disliking the man on sight, pretended interest.

His angry reddened eyes frightened her. Each time he spoke he seemed to be insinuating something vaguely obscene. Tina felt herself smeared over and yet there was nothing definite that he did. He was called Vince. An instinct warned her that he was spoiling for a fight with someone. 'I was in for three months,' he said. 'Ever been in prison?'

She thought he was joking, and said no.

'Not even a visit?'

'No.'

'Three months,' he said. 'Think of it. I wrote a lot of ballads in that time. Wanna see some?'

He pulled out several tattered school exercise books from a canvas satchel while she nodded miserably. The pencilled scrawls veered about wildly, slanted and changed size, nose-dived, petered out. 'They're all about the same thing,' he said. 'Songs of freedom and confinement. Got that? And peace, yeah. What d'you think, eh? Any good?'

Tina went through the motions of appreciating, unable to focus because the man was hanging his face nearer, dragging his chair closer. She feared him. 'There's a lot here,' she said hopelessly, leafing through one soiled page after another.

'Just what I said,' Vince muttered. All at once he was apathetic. 'That's three months' work, that is.'

'Very good.'

'You reckon?'

Josie asked her if she would like to see upstairs. Tina jumped up thankfully and went out with her, up a grand, filthy staircase and into an immense, echoing space which had an enormous chandelier suspended in it, dangling from an ornate plastered centrepiece. A sandy-haired man poked his head round the door. 'Keep your voices down please,' he said officiously. 'Children are asleep behind here.'

'Yes, sorry,' Josie said meekly, rolling her eyes at Tina. They tiptoed out again.

An exhibition of pictures had been hung around the wide landing. Josie said what a beautiful woman the artist

207

was, and weren't the paintings gorgeous. Many of them were portraits of children, huge-eyed, clasped by proud coloured women in native dress. 'They're for sale. If I had the money I'd buy them all.' Tina wasn't keen, but thought it might be her mood.

On the staircase she said, out of her melancholy resistance, that she would have to be going, she had someone waiting for her at home. Josie apologized again for her mistake.

'It wasn't your fault, surely.'

'No, but all the same . . . '

If Tina felt any resentment, it was with herself. A dark frigidity, mixed with impatience, was on her. Johnnie's coming had generated an excitement in her, which she had chosen to walk out on to come to this. At his surprising smile her own smile rose to answer, from deep within, putting to flight the curious strain he sometimes caused. She had felt like a woman.

Making for the bus stop, she realized how badly the atmosphere of squalor and lethargy in that building had depressed her. It was good to be out in the night air, active and moving again. Clouds packed over a dark sky. She thought of the seething man with his indecipherable ballads and hated him afresh, his smell of rot. As she walked she took deep angry breaths, feeling a perfect fool for having let herself in for the visit in the first place. And where was the passionate beliefs she had heard so much about? In Manchester maybe? She saw Josie as a well-meaning butterfly, dipping in and out. She passed one bus stop and headed straight for the next, rushing on without dignity, feeling pointless, wanting to put more distance between her and that futile scene. 'If that's peace,' she muttered aloud to herself, 'give me war.'

30

The next morning, Saturday, Tina woke up and at once felt an urge to do something real and concrete. She would call on Marilyn and find out how she was. Why not? It made sense, it was meaningful. Johnnie had mentioned going to watch football, and yes, today was Saturday. That settled it. She would go in the afternoon and hope to catch Marilyn by herself. Underneath this decision was an uneasiness to do with Johnnie, which she tried to keep submerged and hidden from her consciousness. But it lurked there, and maybe because of it she was drawn to Marilyn. Maybe things would clarify; or maybe they would say nothing but she would come away easier, happier with herself.

Tina came out of an underpass which had graffiti all over its dingy concrete. It was just after three. She skirted round suspicious-looking puddles. Litter blew around her feet.

She tramped on up the steep approach. The great bulk of Providence Park hung over her, a gigantic dead weight. This was her first time back. She had expected to feel nothing, but was gripped by a mixture of excitement and dread. She thought exultantly, I was here in this hideous place and I got out alive! Her heart pounded violently and she couldn't stare hard enough at everything. What did she hope to see? Were there shreds of herself still clinging to doors and window frames in here, was that it? Nothing had happened to her, yet it was like revisiting the scene of a crime, a rape. The disaster-struck block – that was how she saw it – looked as it always did to her when she approached, on the point of collapse, the high walls about to quake and cave in.

Of course it was her imagination, that and her sense of unreality, filming over her eyes. Once inside, she nearly laughed hysterically. That smell! She climbed the stairs and her senses were clamouring with recognition at every turn and she saw marks and cracks, a burnt-out heap of junk, broken glass. All her memories ran loose. She let out little gasps of amazement, her heart so flooded with vile and vivid impressions that she wanted to weep. As she reached Marilyn's door and stood rapping on it, Tina understood that nothing she had ever done in her life was lost, each morsel was inside her, being carried about. This sensation, which made her feel immeasurably rich and wonderful, was also, she felt suddenly, a strange joke. It was funny, terribly sad, and at the same time a great secret pleasure.

A strange moon-faced, big woman opened the door. Over this woman's shoulder Tina could see Marilyn.

'I was just leavin',' the woman said. 'Ta-ra, love,' she said to Marilyn.

'Marilyn, it's me,' Tina said. All at once she was unsure. She lost her bearings completely.

'Well I never,' Marilyn said.

Tina stepped into the room. 'Is it all right?' she asked.

Marilyn was staring fixedly at her, as if struggling to remember who she was. Tina thought how terrible she looked, with black marks under her eyes. Had she forgotten what Marilyn was like? Was it that long ago?

Without preamble the unsmiling woman said, 'That was Muriel from next door.'

'Yes.'

'Sit down.'

There was a three-seater settee covered in greasy moquette, an unpleasant dark red expanse, almost sinister. The side nearest the door had a long jagged rip in it. Tina went over and sat down. She still felt unrecognized, floating. If Marilyn would only use my name, she thought wildly. Perching there like a total stranger she even wondered if her friend was ill or perhaps suffering from amnesia.

'I thought I'd come and see how you are.'

Marilyn sat down and said flatly, 'I'm not very well.'

'Why, what's the matter?'

She ignored this, and said, 'Johnnie's a lot better now.'

'Better?'

'Behaving himself.'

'You mean at school?'

'Not only that. Easier to handle, like.'

'Well, that's good, isn't it?'

'When you came, when I saw you at the door, I couldn't remember who you were for a minute. One day I won't remember my own name. I've been feeling peculiar this week.'

'We all get those days, Marilyn.'

Marilyn got up abruptly and mumbled something about making a pot of tea, leaving the other woman stranded. 'Are you sure you don't mind?' Tina called out anxiously. 'Were you going out?'

Hearing no response, she waited. When Marilyn had put down a tray of tea and a plate of sweet biscuits, Tina asked her again.

'You know I never go out Saturday afternoons.'

'That's what I thought.'

Tina now felt identified, but no longer trusted as she once was. This could have been due to absence, if she hadn't also felt the loss of the friendship which had grown up between them. They were never intimate friends but they had come to like each other. Now Tina believed she was being resisted. It seemed far-fetched to conclude that Johnnie was a factor in this change of atmosphere, but a voice warned her not to dismiss it. All she could do was wait and see. She suppressed a longing to talk freely about Johnnie to his mother.

'You know Sue's gone?'

'Left home? No, I didn't know that, I had no idea!'

'I thought you would,' Marilyn said meaningfully.

'How?' Suddenly Tina had had enough. Perhaps if she waited long enough she might be accused, confronted, then there would be honesty instead of this sullen caginess. It didn't work. The other woman remained stubbornly silent. Irritated by this absurd silence, Tina forced herself to say placidly, 'Where is she, Marilyn?'

'London.'

'Good lord.'

'What she want to go there for? She couldn't go much further, why as far as that? Don't make sense. Stupid, I call it.'

'Is she on her own?'

'Sharing.'

'Does she have a job?'

'In a supermarket. In Shepherd's Bush.'

'Well that's all right. That's something, anyway. I wouldn't worry too much if I were you.'

'She don't write, hardly.'

'Oh, kids are like that.'

'Why all that way? Couldn't she do that round here?'

Tina laughed, but felt sorry, hearing the bewilderment in her friend's voice. 'It's not so far, you know. Two and a half hours on a fast train. She's young, Marilyn, you have to remember that. She wants to try her wings.'

'What did Johnnie say?'

Here it came. She answered levelly, 'To me? Not a word.'

'He likes you.'

'I hope so.' Startled, she exploded a laugh. 'Sometimes I wonder, but if he does, that's nice.'

'He repeats things you say. He looks up to you.'

'No, really? I'm surprised. What kind of things?'

'I can't remember.'

'I'm glad he's more amenable now, anyway. To you, I mean.'

There was a funny silence. Marilyn worked away in this silence, hidden, and then said heavily, her eyes fixed on Tina's face. 'I don't like him seeing so much of you.'

Tina took a moment to answer. 'Why?' she asked.

'I don't think it's right,' Marilyn said slowly.

'What isn't?'

'You know.'

Tina sat there shocked, struggling with herself. 'Do I?' she said in a choked voice. She felt baffled, so in the dark, not knowing if she should feel insulted or not, or simply take pity on this fear-ridden woman. She sat painfully knotted, in conflict, seeing Marilyn's frustration. She would have preferred outright hatred, an attack, screams even. If Marilyn launched herself across the room and hit her, at least everything would be over.

'Coming round like he does,' Marilyn was saying. 'Botherin' you.'

'But I don't mind, honestly.'

'Have another cup of tea,' Marilyn said.

'If you don't want Johnnie to come round, then tell him,' Tina said, using a level, penetrating voice. 'You must. It's up to you.'

'He does what he likes.' Marilyn sounded depressed. She was looking down at the carpet. And Tina remembered that this was exactly what Johnnie had told her, almost word for word.

'Shall I tell him what you said?'

'No!' Marilyn cried at once, frowning, shaking her head in fear.

Tina said gently, as the thought dawned in her, 'Marilyn, somebody's been getting at you.'

'What?'

'That's what I think. Somebody's been giving you advice. I'm right, aren't I?'

'Yes.'

'Who is it?'

'Muriel.'

Tina sat back, accusing herself of hypocrisy, wanting to set Marilyn's mind at rest, to console her, knowing this was impossible. She began to think of leaving, before something unforgivable leaked out. The two women sat together intimately and yet without any means of communicating with each other. It was a hopeless situation.

'Never mind,' Tina said ruefully, and even smiled.

'I wish I could have a holiday.'

'How do you feel in yourself?'

'Awful.'

'I'll come and see you again, shall I?'

'If you want.'

Tina was unhappy with this reply. 'Would you like me to?'

After a long difficult pause, Marilyn said, 'Yes.'

213

Tina saw to her distress that her friend was crying. Her first impulse was to go to her, touch her. She couldn't move. It was then that she understood how their relationship had deteriorated, how compromised she was, and felt terrible.

Marilyn asked her where Jan was – an innocent-seeming question. But now Tina thought the suggestion was being made that Johnnie was sitting secretly in her flat. She flushed. 'She's with a friend of mine called Jenny,' she stammered.

'Bring her with you when you come again. I like to see little ones.'

'Right, I will.' She got up to go.

At the door, Marilyn spoke her name. 'Bye, Tina.'

Tina laughed in embarrassment and affection, moved to give the older woman a kiss but failed to make the attempt definite enough. The two women wavered, and Marilyn began closing the door.

Tina was downstairs and out of the building before she knew where she was. The situation was miserable, rotten. Most of the way home she castigated herself. She even resolved to turn Johnnie away next time he came. Muriel's big reproachful face loomed up in her mind like a sour moon, and she forgot her wretchedness and let herself into the house angrily. What business was it of that interfering bitch? Now Tina had to turn round and go out again for Jan – she should have gone there in the first place. She was acting like someone in a state of delayed shock. Yet at Marilyn's she had felt in perfect control of herself. What was she doing? Maybe a clear-out decision was called for? One thing was certain – no one else would do anything. She kept seeing Marilyn stranded in her predicament, and the contamination of her fate, fearing that she, Tina, would become aged and tired, and become in the end indistinguishable from her. It was a fear that shamed her.

In a flood of anger she hurried out again, angry now with Johnnie for letting her in for this, using her in his ignorant way. Walking along rapidly she reminded herself yet again that she had initiated nothing. But when she tried to trace things back to the beginning, the sheer nebulousness of everything caused what reality there was to slip through her mind. If Johnnie were to bring up the subject of his mother, that would be different. Until then, all this soul-searching was ridiculous. What had she done, anyway? It was nature, blind forces, factors beyond her control. Life flowed through her like everyone else, like the people in this street, hurrying like her, or drifting, like a girl crossing the road ahead of her in her pencil skirt, looking as if she had all the time in the world, sunk away inside her own skin. Why ask her, or anyone, what was going on? Nobody had the answers.

31

As she expected, Johnnie was silent on the subject of his mother. Unless asked casually about her health, he didn't mention her. Tina saw no reason to cross-examine him; he had had plenty of that already in his short life, apparently. She just said, lightly, 'I went to see her, you know. Last Saturday. Did she tell you?'

'Ar, she said summat.'

'Were you surprised?'

'Why should I be?'

The dark nights closed in and she found herself thinking more and more about him, yet without getting anywhere, only admitting to herself that she and Marilyn were now related in a way she could not have foreseen. Like it or not, they were involved.

Each time he came she experienced a mild shock of surprise. He was now liable to arrive at any hour, even a Saturday, in fact whenever it suited him. (Once he turned up with Trevor – so that his friend could see how at home he was in her set-up, she suspected; how he had the run of it. She didn't care for the sly malice in the older kid's eyes, or his mean mouth.)

When Johnnie left, she soon found she was missing him. She saw him without illusion as a cunning, sometimes sweet boy. She made no special effort to please him, and he seemed to like Jan, turning over the pages of her picture books for her if she insisted, grunting out words to identify objects as if he was at the same stage himself. Out on the pavement he pushed her up and down on her tricycle while she stuck out her legs in a wide vee. If she threw a tantrum he just stared at her, interested. Once or twice Tina wondered if they were in a secret alliance against her, the adult.

Yet he still came back.

'Back again?' she said once, opening the door in surprise.

'Shall I clear off, then?'

'Don't be daft. Come in if you're coming.'

Surely he did like her? Anticipating his visits enlivened her days. Sitting alone, she cast about in her past experience, asking herself why he seemed to get more from being with her than the others had done. And yet neither of them, she reasoned, were in a love relationship. She could not understand what he must be getting, unless it was a certain intimacy, something his ordinary life had not known, for which he had no vocabulary.

The others had seemed to want intimacy too; then they would feel threatened and begin erecting fences. It was a pattern she had come to expect – so far and no farther. Afterwards she tended to blame herself for a failing, for something she wasn't aware of that she did. It could be that Johnnie didn't feel his freedom endangered because a blissful ignorance saved him. Or was he way beyond her in his imagination, breathing a different air entirely? What was a boy of his age likely to think of her? That she was a tart? Harmless but mad? The idea of womankind as another breed, to be stalked like an unknowable animal with a strange smell, this was a notion she kept in fascinated suspense whenever she tried the game of swopping places with him in her mind. Did he ever laugh at her? With Trevor? These speculations took her in a circle and she would end as she began, in a sort of tender exasperation at the thought of him.

If she concluded anything, it was that he got whatever he wanted from her by being near her, absorbing her in waves – something she was quite powerless to prevent. She smiled, thinking of his bitten nails, his hard little buttocks. The sex was more cuddling in the dark than anything else, no closer to the real Johnnie than at any other time, and for it to be carefree she had to get drunk enough; otherwise her conscience hurt. This was mere common sense, like taking aspirin for a headache. She might be anyone, she thought sometimes, supplying him with his taste of intimacy. But when he used her name, though it was a rare enough occurrence, it affected her strangely, like a love sound. She recognized it as weakness; he revealed his weakness to her and that was love.

Once, fairly drunk, suddenly aroused, wanting him inside her like a man although she was too wide, she squeezed her thighs desperately together and actually kept him there. For a brief interval they were a couple. She whispered that she was sorry her nails had dug in. He lay limp, unanswering, hugged tight to her belly. Making the coffee afterwards as usual, she felt something oozing down her leg. It gave her joy. She had to resist giving him a kiss, for which of course she would have been hated.

He was puzzled by her classes. 'Eh, you've gone back to school,' he said, accusing her.

'Not really.'

'You have. After what you said an' all.'

'What did I say?'

'It was rubbish, your school. That's what you said.'

'So it was. That's why I'm going now, to make up for it.'

'Right-o.'

'Are you bothered?'

'Why should I be?'

'Well then,' she said, 'ask me what else I want to learn.'

He looked at her with cunning. 'You were making out you never liked it, learning an' that.'

His mock antagonism amused her. She raised her eyebrows. 'I never did, not then. Now, there are things I want to know.'

'What about?'

She thought a moment. 'Myself,' she admitted, surprised and moved to hear herself saying it. Then because he looked interested she felt a fraud.

'How d'you learn that?' he asked curiously.

'By studying how characters behave in stories.'

'Oh ar.' A vague look passed over his face. She was glad he remained sceptical. Her real motives were too obscure to explain, and complicated now by her feelings for the other women, many of whom she admired tremendously. Some of them had terrific obstacles to overcome, and she found their determination not to miss a class contagious.

'What about you?' she asked. 'How's school?'

'Same as last time you asked.'

'I don't remember asking,' she said, 'but tell me again.'

'Diabolical.' The big word was from Trevor. He rolled it round in his mouth in the act of saying it, pleased with its crude sound.

'Are you still going?'

'Yeh,' he said.

'No mitching?'

'Course not!'

There was no evidence to support this, nothing for her to go on, but she chose to believe him. He took pride in speaking his mind, she thought, influenced by her. At any rate his answer satisifed her. More often than not, she felt, she got the truth from him. What was evident now at last was his growing trust in her. She loved him for that, and recalled what Marilyn had said about him taking note of her. If he did trust her, saw her as a friend and not a danger, then this confirmed her hopeful picture of herself as a good person who blundered, made mistakes, but who should not be blamed, whose intentions were honourable. If Johnnie's dealings with others had steadied as a direct result of his contact with her patience and her affection, then how could that be bad? One day Marilyn would see her in that light. Jealousy was such a senseless thing.

In the New Year, her mother's new husband fell ill – she refused to acknowledge him as a stepfather – and was taken to hospital. Tina went over to see her mother but wouldn't go with her on hospital visits. 'You know how I feel,' she said stubbornly.

'That's unkind, Tina.'

'It's truthful.'

'He'd love to see you, dear. He'd be so pleased.'

Tina said savagely, 'Stop kidding yourself.'

'My God, how do I come to have such a cruel daughter? It can't be me you take after. You're like your father, it's the same cruel streak he has.'

'I'm not saying anything about Sam. I'd feel a hypocrite sitting there by his bed, that's the truth and I can't help it, so that's that. I'm sorry he's ill but it doesn't make any difference, how can it? I don't like the man. You know I don't, you know perfectly well. Mum, it's you I've come to see.'

'Oh all right,' her mother said. 'Anyway, it's nice to see you looking so well.'

Tina laughed sadly at the touch of spite.

A month later she heard that an aunt, a sister of her father, someone she had not seen since childhood, had died and left her five hundred pounds. Her mother wrote with the news. Tina replied that it was like something in a book – she found it hard to believe such things happened to people like her. When the formalities were completed and the money paid over, she came up with one reckless idea after another for getting rid of it. She intended to have a holiday abroad. Another day, she thought, why shouldn't I buy some dresses, a carpet? Finally she went with Jenny and bought herself an old worn-out Vauxhall, ignoring her friend's advice to wait until Norman could look it over. 'If I don't get it now, I shan't get it at all,' Tina retorted. 'I'll buy a set of bloody saucepans and a vacuum cleaner instead.'

32

On Saturday Johnnie found her in the street outside her
front door, cleaning an old grey car. She had a bright
yellow plastic bucket on the pavement and was sloshing
soapy water over the black roof with a cloth. The boy
came up and stood staring at the rusty chrome bumpers.
He poked his finger at a scab of blistery paint on the
nearest wing.

'Hey, careful,' Tina warned.

'What you doing with this old jalopy?'

'Cleaning it – what does it look like?'

'It looks clapped-out to me.'

'It's not!'

'It ain't yourn?'

'Mine.'

'Straight up?'

'Yes.' She was enjoying her moment to the full, and
felt young.

'When did you get it?'

'Last week.' She straightened up and faced him. 'If you
want to help, go and look under the sink for something.'

Johnnie went into the house. He came out with some
rags and set to work on the other side from Tina.

'You don't have to if you don't want to,' she said.

He sloshed away energetically in silence for some time.
At last he said, 'I didn't know you could drive.'

His eyes were serious. She smiled. 'There's plenty of
things you don't know about me, boy.'

She took the bucket and rags indoors and came back
outside. Johnnie was intent on examining the windscreen
wipers. The wet glass gleamed and winked.

'Now what are you up to?'

'Checkin',' he said.

He lifted up the bonnet and peered inside. He pulled
up the dipstick and slid it back in.

'Very impressive,' she said, watching. 'Do you know what you're doing?'

'Gimme a break!'

'I didn't know you knew about cars.'

'Plenty you don't know about me,' he mimicked, and she laughed.

He carried on checking, or pretending to. He let the handbrake out and brought it back up smartly on the ratchet, sitting inside the streaming car. He adjusted the rear mirror.

'How much they sting you for this heap?' he asked.

'Oh, two hundred.' It was nearer four. Even so, she expected criticism.

'They seen you comin'.'

'I don't care,' she said. 'I'm fond of it already.'

He curled his lip. 'Where you goin' to go in it?'

Tina said without a moment's hesitation, happily, 'Cornwall.'

Johnnie engaged the ignition, snapped on the car radio and a blast of pop music came out. He stuck out his lower lip and nodded. 'Something works.'

'Get out of my car, you,' she said, 'and we'll have something to eat.'

'I wanna ride. When can I have a ride?'

She said with relish, 'You can come with me to Jenny's and pick up Jan. Apart from her you'll be my first passenger. How does that grab you?'

'Great.'

He beat a tattoo on the wheel rim with his palms. She saw his pleasure with satisfaction. How good it would be, she thought, surprised by her excess of feeling, to take him on a trip one day and startle him with something new, the moors, a coastline, opening up his horizons and sharing this vision of freedom with him, like a new dimension.

She soon found that he was two jumps ahead and waiting for her, a mad gleam in his eye. On his next visit he asked straight out when she was going to Cornwall.

She avoided answering. In the night there had been a fall of soft snow, already melting and running down the gutters after a few hours of daylight. It was a raw Sunday, the house still locked. Letting him in, she said jokingly, 'I shall have to get a key cut for you.'

He shot a glance at her, expectant. He had taken her seriously. He wiped his feet thoughtfully on the mat, as if he was now a member of her household. Bundled in his Taiwan anorak he stood there a moment, his thin cheeks bright with cold. He pressed his hands together and rubbed, making a dry chafing sound.

'Right-o,' he said, following her in.

Jan ran up to him in the kitchen. 'Johnnie Hunsla, Johnnie Hunsla!'

'That's me.'

'You'd like that, wouldn't you?' Tina said.

'Come again?'

'A key to this place. You'd really like that.'

He stared at her. 'Ar, I wouldn't mind. Orright!'

Holding his steaming mug in both hands he asked again about her trip to Cornwall.

'I thought Easter.'

They were three weeks away. He dipped his nose thoughtfully, in and out of his mug. Jan went into the other room, playing a counting game of her own invention. 'Wi' me or her?' Johnnie said, grinning up broadly at her. She thought she detected a note of anxiety in his voice.

'On my own,' she said.

He questioned her with his eyes like a small child and gave a nod in Jan's direction, shrewd as an adult. Tina told him in a low voice she intended to leave Jan with her mother. 'Only for a few days,' she said defiantly. 'I could do with a break.'

He shivered inside his anorak. 'Cold in 'ere.'

'We've only just got up. The heater's on.'

'Why aren't I comin' with you?'

'Drop it, Johnnie,' she said, not sharply, letting out a little gasp. She had heard her voice pleading with him and was annoyed. Why should she always feel guilty, and why about him?

'I wish I wus.'

223

'God, don't you ever give up?'

Then he dropped the subject, she hoped for good.

The following Friday evening, he said casually, 'Why do you want to go on your own, anyhow?'

She sighed. 'No choice. Anyway, I don't mind my own company.'

'Not much fun in that.'

'Johnnie,' she said sharply, 'you're not coming.'

'Right-o.'

'You're being stupid. It stands to reason you can't.'

'Why can't I then?'

'Do I have to spell it out? Your mother.'

'I bin on holiday before.'

'Where?'

'Devon.'

'When was that?'

'I was in this Home, an' we went on a camp to Dartmouth.'

'Lovely. What was it like?'

'Orrible. They put these older kids over us, strappin' buggers, real slave-drivers they were. Worse than the ole geezer in charge. Like a chuffin' concentration camp it was.'

'Where was your mother?'

'Dunno. In hospital I s'ppose.'

'You poor little sod, you.'

Johnnie gazed at her with sly interest. 'I never thought I'd miss Sheffield but I did. I was real homesick. I wanted me mam. I only remembered what me mam looked like when Eileen brought me a photo.'

Tina glared at him. 'Stop that. Lay off me, you bastard.'

'You what?'

'I can't take you to Cornwall and that's final.'

'I don't see no harm.'

'No, you wouldn't.'

'I'll ask her, shall I?'

'Oh no you won't.'

He sat still, like a dejected cat, until she felt quite woebegone. 'I bet you can't change wheels if you get a puncture,' he said hopelessly. 'I changed a wheel once.'

'For Christ's sake!' she groaned. 'Ask her then if you like.'

He gave her one of his rare smiles. 'I already 'ave,' he said.

33

Good Friday morning came. Tina was all ready to set off. Had she forgotten anything? She locked her two doors, inner and outer, and sat fretting behind the wheel of her serviced car. The tank was full, the MOT test in the glove compartment. She had fixed the departure time, ten o'clock, and Johnnie was nowhere in sight. Had his mother kicked up a row at the last minute, or was she sick again?

Tina no longer regretted her crazy impulse to say yes. Ultimately she believed that whatever made a person happy carried its own sanction, provided no one suffered in the process. If Johnnie failed to turn up she would of course still go, her resolve was so strong, but her disappointment would be the keener because she was now so identified with his enthusiasm. Sharing with one another was the top thing with her. Soon now she would watch his eager eye, feel her heart quicken, laugh to see his city feet scampering over the sand of a beach. Why it should be so infinitely better than hugging the experience to yourself she never understood, when she was as selfish as the next person. As for Jan, she would enjoy being spoiled by her grandmother, but if Tina told the truth she wanted to feel single again, not a parent. She sat ready to snatch her handful of free days, pained to think that he might have found his friend Trevor more attractive company. Yet surely that was right. She was old, thirty-two – what was he doing with her?

He came sloping round the corner, swinging a white plastic bag marked 'International'. A rough wind hit the car in gusts and rocked it. Now and then a fitful sun shone palely, a sudden shower of rain flew against the windscreen and stopped within half a minute. The whole sky was restlessly on the move, in a tearing hurry to get somewhere fast. Tina approved of it, her mood fully in accord. She couldn't wait to get going.

Johnnie climbed in beside her.

Tina asked, 'What have you got in there, may I ask?'

He shrugged. 'Pyjamas. T-shirt.'

'What else?'

'A kagool.'

'Anything else?'

'A toothbrush.'

'Fasten your seat belt,' she ordered.

He was looking with approval at her long boots of soft yellow leather, thick-soled, with black laces all the way up. 'Are them new?' he said.

'No, I've had them ages.'

'Great, they are.'

He even took notice of her earrings and made a comment, saying he would have one of his ears pierced when he left school, and did it hurt. For once she was at a loss, feeling a childish thrill at having pleased him with her appearance. She wore an old blue duffle coat with the nap worn off – she felt happy in it. Underneath, though, she was dressed for spring, a light striped blouse and a pink skirt. In a bag on the rear seat she had stuffed a thick sweater, make-up in a pretty satchel, toilet things, and a plastic box containing pre-cooked chicken pieces and tomatoes for the journey. Johnnie dumped his carrier behind him. He stared straight ahead through the wet glass.

'Got plenty of petrol.'

'I've got everything,' she said. 'Here, take charge of the maps.'

They drove into town, down into the roaring hollow before the train station, entering the streams of traffic smoothly without having to halt once and climbing steadily past Providence Park, up on the heights above the city. They passed the abbatoir, then large dreary estates on either side of the road which could have been anywhere. 'Here we go, here we go!' Johnnie sang out in a football chant. Near the city boundary they sped past a huge grassed-over mound on their right – she had never

227

known what it was – and into flat blackish fields, swampy industrial stretches which always seemed under thick cloud. The dark northern green came back. They joined the motorway and were soon rushing along it, under an exultant sign in blue and white, 'TO THE SOUTH', holding to a steady fifty-five. On the inclines they overtook grim, grinding trucks and felt the vibrations as they went in and out of their shadows. The shuddering height and the weight and the enormous flailing wheels always made Tina nervous. She called, 'All right, are you?'

'Orright!'

She wanted to feel heroic but she knew herself too well. She felt cheerful, glad, and thought her expression must convey sharp expectancy. 'They can't stop us now,' she said, just to hear something crazy.

The boy beside her was silent, concentrated on the road and movement, in a bright tension of excitement. Tina caught it, smiling to herself. 'We've escaped, we're out,' she said, not fooling herself for an instant. Was it her own child who was somehow with her, or another child, herself, as they went racing free down the road? Yes, she felt childish, in a childish delight, while paradoxically wary, nervous. You were always being caught by life, caught out. As she drove she congratulated herself on her nerve, her decision, blowing the best part of her windfall on this old tank instead of sticking it in a building society like a prudent mother. Travelling like this, after being stuck in a street for so long, made her feel light-headed. Memories flashed by like fence posts, the trees, the exits. She marvelled to think that as a young girl she had been so demure, keeping her eyes downcast in company like an oriental, having nothing to say for herself, going about with no confidence, guts in a quake. Now here she was, in control, at the wheel of her life!

Driving, she was well aware, brought out a latent bossiness in her. She felt in the mood to indulge it impishly, carrying away this boy whose presence beside her she had sought to resist, secretly possessing him for a moment.

'What's that noise?' she said suddenly.

'I can't hear nothin'.'

'Listen,' she said again, more urgently. 'There it is again – hear that?'

'Nah.'

'Like a knocking noise. There, I heard it again! Hear that, Johnnie?'

'Think so. The engine just fell out.'

'I'm serious – listen, you slob. Concentrate, will you? I thought you understood about cars.'

'Shurrup, I'm listening.'

'I'm getting off this motorway soon, otherwise I'll go nuts. God, I hate these things. Do you like it?'

'It's fast.'

'It doesn't even feel fast. I don't feel I'm getting anywhere. I'm going to turn off soon.'

'Right-o.'

'There!' she exclaimed. 'Hear it now?'

'Oh ar.'

'What did I tell you? Could it be serious d'you reckon?'

'Could be.'

'Gee thanks! What a comforter you are.'

'I wouldn't bother though.'

'Thanks very much. Terminal, is it?'

'Why slag me off?' he said comically. 'It ain't my knock.'

'Look, you want to go to Cornwall, is that right?'

'I 'eered it then!'

'Never mind, I don't care. Quick, look on the map, find me an exit.'

'What?'

'Exit, exit. You don't know what an exit is?' she taunted.

'You think you're hot shit,' he muttered, his finger moving as he pored over the map.

He located their position and she praised him extravagantly. 'I'm hopeless with maps. You're a real asset, you know that?'

'Bullshit,' he muttered, embarrassed.

How could she explain that she had begun to lose a sense of herself on the motorway? They swung off to the left and the road narrowed, she was human again. Back there she had felt a horror creeping on her, of not knowing what she did, why she was part of this beating river of traffic, most of it commercial, aimed at cities and ports, the continent, none of it to do with her bid to reach Cornwall. Now she breathed easier; she could handle this. Beside her sat the kid who had been entrusted to her, naively alert now for the next sign. It was irrational, but she had imagined them being crushed and flung aside by a heedless steel flood, edged from the road and smashed against fenders for using these channels without permission, impeding the race of all this thundering blind industry.

'Motorways, they're built for lunatics, must be,' she said, half to herself. 'I was turning into one.'

She pulled off to the left again, and the dual carriageway dwindled to a road narrower still, a road like any other. A film of sweat hung on her brow; she wiped it off with the back of her hand, which she noticed had a slight tremor. It had been a long time since she had embarked on such an ambitious journey. I'll take it easy from now on, she vowed.

Driving lightheartedly she crossed a boundary and was in Staffordshire. She was looking keenly ahead and soon saw what she wanted, a track to the left which ran parallel to the road. They pulled in, bumped over the potholes and halted by a screen of young ash trees. Johnnie got out and climbed a gate. He came jogging back.

Tina said, 'What's it like out there?'

'Perishin'.'

Tina emerged briefly to stretch her legs and arch her back, groaning with extravagant satisfaction. She got back in. 'That wind's pretty fierce.'

He nodded amiably. She asked him if he was ready for a bite to eat and he said yes. Inside the plastic box, when she prised off the rubbery lid, were buttered rolls as well as the chicken pieces and tomatoes. She shared out the food. 'We'll stop again soon and have a drink somewhere, shall we?'

Just before she set off, Johnnie said, 'Hang on, I think I need a slash.'

Seeing him return with his head bent, bouncing over

230

the ruts as he fastened his zip, an urge to question him came over her. After all, he was her captive, she could ask him anything and there was nowhere for him to run. As he settled and belted himself in, she turned to him. 'Tell me,' she said quietly, 'what your expectations are.'

'Come again?'

'What are you looking forward to? Tell me, Johnnie. What do you want from this trip?'

'I don't get you.'

'You were keen to come, weren't you?'

'I might'a bin!'

'Well, when you didn't seem to be coming, I thought you'd decided against it. To tell the truth I imagined you having second thoughts about spending so much time alone with me.'

'I never did think that,' he said hotly.

'So you're glad, then?'

'I don't know what you're on about,' he confessed, puzzled.

'You aren't sorry you've come?'

Sometimes she moved her eyes over him critically, but this was different. Her look was curious, penetrating. Hanging his head, he mumbled, 'Why should I be?'

'No reason.' She stopped pressing. He was looking distinctly uncomfortable.

'How do I know I'm goin' to like it, till we get there?' he said laboriously.

'Oh, it's nice,' she promised. 'You'll see.'

' 'Spect so,' he said, sounding to her like someone obliging an auntie. It made her laugh.

'Right, here we go, Luigi.' They were moving off.

'Okay, boss.'

'Did we shake 'em off?' she joked.

'I can't see nobody.'

She was backing down the track and he kept an eye on the road, twisted round in his seat. As they went forward again and gathered speed he asked her if she fancied a rake-up.

'You'll find the tin in the glove compartment,' Tina said.

231

'That what it's called? I never knew that.' He shook his head, marvelling. 'Wheer you keep yer gloves!'

'Something else you've learned.'

'Ar, I 'ave.'

She did her best not to ply him with any more unanswerable questions. After a while she got bored and wondered aloud if Marilyn was happy with their jaunt. He answered in a rush that his mother had other things on her mind at the moment to think about. 'Such as what?' Tina asked curiously. Flicking glances at him as they sped along, she thought his eyes were jumpy, wandering everywhere.

'Such as our Sue wrote us a letter. Well, it were a postcard. She's havin' a baby.'

'No!'

'That's what she says.'

'Oh God. She's too young yet to tie herself down.' She was dismayed for the girl, and for Marilyn, though her body reacted differently, sending through her a distinct pang of envy. 'What does your mother say about it?'

'Same as you,' he said dreamily, as if the road unwinding was a gift he must attend to, both a continuous surprise and the only reality there was, and this talk of his mother and sister came from a dream, another planet.

34

Skirting Birmingham, Tina drew into the forecourt of a pub and stopped the car. Preoccupied with her thoughts and concentrating on the road she had fallen into a long, detached silence, stirring heavily from time to time as they ate up the miles, yet unable to break out without help, as if she was drugged, her eyes veiled from her passenger. The onward rushing movement had deadened her responses and the stale air made her drowsy. She was aching painfully at the bottom of her spine. The boy at her side sat blankly, staring ahead, in the capsule of his own remoteness. She made a huge effort and slowed, swung in and stopped the car.

She had a brandy, then a large coffee. Johnnie drank two Cokes in quick succession and sat devouring a bag of crisps. Tina looked at him and smiled wearily, still with the curious reluctance to speak.

'I wish you could drive,' she said to him. 'Why can't you drive?'

'You can teach me.'

'What's the use if you're under age?'

'We could have a drive round in a field. Can I?'

'I don't see why not,' she said indulgently. 'We'll see. Let's get there first.'

'I reckon I could drive anyway. Looks easy.'

'Well, it is. It's even easier with a new car I expect. Still, what d'you think of my old banger? Good little runner, eh?'

'It gets you theer.'

'It's like you, isn't it?'

'Me?'

'A good little runner.'

Bemused, he said, 'Ow d'you mean?'

'Pay no attention to me, I'm babbling. It's what I do when I'm tired.'

With her resistance lowered by fatigue, she was overcome suddenly by a senseless anxiety. She said tensely, 'Did you notice whether the tax disc was still in place? It fell off the other day and I thought it was lost, then I found it down by my feet. The glue doesn't seem to work, something's the matter with it. Was it up there?'

'I don't know.'

'You realize what I'm talking about, that round disc on the windscreen?'

'Think I don't know what a tax disc is?'

'The police watch out for that, I don't want to lose the damn thing.' Her irritation and tiredness, and the touch of fear, created a distance between them.

'It's there, yeh.'

'You said you didn't notice it!'

'I just remembered. It's up theer all right.'

'Thank God for that,' she said gratefully. Then she looked at him, disgusted with herself. 'What's the matter with me, what am I getting uptight about, d'you know?'

Again she spoke to him as an adult, forgetting to take account of the gap of years. To her great surprise he said, 'You're just tired. Our mam gets worked up when she's tired.'

She was so gratified, she risked putting her arm round him as they walked out. How thin his shoulders were! He walked along stiffly on the gravel, submitting.

'Soon be halfway there,' she said jovially, as much to comfort herself as anything. He nodded philosophically, climbing back in and fixing his seat belt. 'All right, kid?' she joked, made shy by the moment of physical contact with him.

'Yeh, boss.'

They rode along and another silence descended, this time an easier, lighter one, which she believed she was sharing with him. And she began to feel differently, now that he had acknowledged an awareness of her. Somehow he was no longer a burden. The journey they were on together in this cramped space was so intimate that she was able to consider him differently, as someone in touch with her sensations. All this distance they were covering

234

seemed part of a process, working away to give them things in common.

They entered the rolling Cotswolds. Tina parked her car and they had another break. 'Fancy stretching your legs?' she asked.

'Don't mind if I do.'

A sign pointed to a public footpath and gave the name of a hill, Dover's. The sky cleared, they climbed up to a stile and over to a broad uplifted field swept by a strong cold wind. It was too chilly to stand about admiring the view. Tina turned back, as the muddy ground sucked at her boots, but Johnnie grabbed her coat to prevent her, and she halted.

He ran on ahead and disappeared completely in a hollow, with Tina plodding reluctantly in pursuit. 'Not too far!' she shouted after him.

They were so high up, the biting wind was making her ears hurt. She pulled up the hood of her duffle coat. Johnnie stood waiting in the next dip with a grin on his face. 'That's far enough for me' she spluttered, staggering, clutching at him for support, and in fear. Not far ahead was a herd of young bullocks.

Clambering back up to the hilltop Tina's foot slipped on the cow track they were following and she let out a shriek. Johnnie got behind her with his head down, butting her upwards like a goat. She laughed and protested, her abundant body an encumbrance, while he scuttled around her, grinning and impish. Straddled above, he gave her sleeve a violent yank. On the level she was suddenly high-spirited in the whirling sharp air, snatching his hand and charging forward recklessly. They stumbled slithering down the other side hand in hand like lovers.

Nearly at the car, Johnnie stamped his right foot down in a puddle instead of stepping round it. Water shot up, splashing her clean boots. 'You mucky sod! Why do boys have to do that?'

Crestfallen at once, he said, 'I weren't wettin' you on purpose.'

'Who said you were? You're a dirty bugger all the same.'

He took offence. 'Shurrup, you,' he said, and sounded genuinely hurt.

In the car he repaid her with interest. Her breasts rose and fell after the exertion, and he asked why she was so out of breath.

'Because I am.'

'You oughta lose a bit o' weight.'

She aimed a slap at his head. He drew back like a snake, so that she missed. 'That's not the way to talk to ladies. Want to get out and walk?'

'No, lady.'

'Then watch it.'

'I am,' he said solemnly. And added, to her amazement, 'Your chest.'

'What's the matter with it?'

'It's still goin' up and down.'

'I think we'd better move. Find our route on the map, and behave yourself. Gloucester we're heading for now.'

'Right-o.'

They sat still a moment. After the buffeting of the wind and cold, it was an enchantment to be sitting there, protected and quiet. Just as they were about to pull away, Tina found herself saying, the words rising up of their own accord, 'Be kind to me, Johnnie.' Odd though it was, she had felt compelled to say it. Coming out of nowhere a forlorn misery gripped her.

'I am.' He didn't know where to look.

'Am I kind to you? I want to be.'

'Orright!'

'Are you happy, Johnnie?'

'Why shouldn't I be?'

They were plunged again into an interminable silence, for which she took full blame. It's unfair, she warned herself, to let out your spasms of loneliness on a young boy. What could he possibly do about it? She searched his face contritely now and then as they travelled on, ready to win him back with a smile if he met her eye. But he seemed hypnotized once more by the road winding itself under the wheels, sitting mute and glassy as if alone. A flicker of anguish told her how precarious their undertaking was and how solitary she was in it. Her mouth registered a grimace. As they entered streets again she shook off her morbidity, glad to be forced to concentrate on signs and lights.

He too woke out of his dream and took notice. 'Ever bin here before?' he asked, turning his head this way and that.

'No, never.'

He remarked that it didn't look much of a dump. She disagreed, liking the softness, the bits of run-down Georgian, musing half to herself that she could imagine living here.

'If you was old,' he said.

She let that pass.

It was mid-afternoon, the centre was busy. The car edged through the little bustling city and was soon cruising again. The boy fell silent and Tina was content. Once it would have meant quiet hostility from him, a stubborn refusal to speak – even his smallness seemed at times to convey that – and she would have been setting her wits against it in a struggle to win him over. Now at the very least he was quiet with the indifference of youth, ignoring her as he looked out with flicking, unsmiling eyes. When he did venture a smile in her direction she felt her skin coat over, filmed with gladness. Was it her achievement, or simply the result of a whole series of accidents? Better not to ask; he came from such an unsmiling world.

'What's it feel like to be having a holiday?'

'Suits me!'

'Suits you, does it,' she laughed. 'You *are* a funny tike.'

'I aren't funny.' He sounded so indignant that she laughed again.

'No funnier than me,' she told him.

They reached Devon at last. Passing the sign at the verge she let out a shout. 'Jesus, I thought we'd never get here. Glorious Devon!'

'How far now?' Johnnie asked, staring curiously as they ran past a row of crumbling thatched cottages.

'Less than an hour, if we strike lucky with the Torpoint ferry.'

At Devonport, a mass of traffic and men leaving the dockyards choked the streets. They were soon crawling, forced at times to a walking pace. They rolled down towards the river, just in time to see the ugly iron ferry clanking away on its grim chains, a huge, clumsy raft packed with vehicles. An identical craft set off from the other side of the water.

Johnnie scrambled about, eager now to get across. Tina sat where she was, then got out and followed reluctantly, rubbing at the bottom of her spine and limping. She waited by the wall, while he prowled restlessly up and down. She had booked a small holiday flat at Penlee which had been advertised on a card in her local post office, taking it for a week, the shortest period possible. If he gets bored, we'll move on, she thought. Johnnie had not even thought to ask where they were going to stay. She sighed, smiling. What a thing it was to be young! She tried and failed to imagine a time when she had been as feckless about what now seemed to be vital necessities.

They crossed over the dark, tugging expanse of water, and on the other side got going again. 'Were that a river?' Johnnie wanted to know, because it was the biggest he had seen.

'We're at the mouth of it, near the sea.'

'Why, wheer's the sea?'

'Round the corner, that way.'

At long last they drew up outside the address she had taken out and checked several times – a ludicrous thing to do, she realized. Nothing could have been easier to find. The place was only a few twisty streets, no more than cobbled alleys and stone staircases, all tangled in a knot. Thin white houses and fishermen's cottages, either tarted up in smart colours or mouldering, were squashed together in a heap on what ground there was against the hill, before a tiny cove with a pebble beach. The tide was out and a small area of sand was exposed. A headland dark with trees sought to enclose the little bay on the right. To the left was a great jumble of slimy rocks. From one street an unimpressive clock tower poked up, behind a stone wall bearing the sign 'Library and Institute'.

'Is this it?' Johnnie said. He got out as though he couldn't believe his eyes.

'You like it?'

'Yeh, great,' he murmured.

Near the Boat Café was the house she was looking for, perched on a slab of rock at the edge of the beach. At full tide the sea swirled around the base of it, judging by the water mark. When Tina located the owner and was let in to the so-called flat, she saw that they were in the cemented cellars of the house above. How strange, to be sunk underground at the sea end, hearing the wash and slap of it, and with a door and window opening on the street, more or less at ground level. Inside it was icy and dry, by the look of things only recently converted, with rush matting, white plastered walls and the minimum of furniture.

At first shocked by the frigid walls, Tina was soon pleased with the austerity, grateful for the merciful cleanliness of the minute apartment. She asked if they were the first tenants and was told no, the second. There was no bedroom, only an alcove containing a three-tiered bunk bed, brand-new, and another bed which seemed three-quarter size. Behind a room divider was the cooker, a varnished pine table, two chairs, a bookshelf with a few paperbacks, thrillers and romances.

The moment they were alone, Tina collapsed in the one armchair and groaned with the dubious pleasure of her aches and pains. 'Home sweet home,' she crowed. Johnnie seemed completely unmoved. Soon he was at the spyhole of the half-round window sunk in the stone, watching the street.

'Can you see anything? Any sign of life?'

'Nah.'

'What are you expecting, smugglers?'

'There 'in't any now.' But he kept fixedly staring out.

Tina glanced at her watch, saw it was two minutes before five-thirty and cried out that she was off to a shop she had spotted round the corner. Johnnie jumped up and ran on ahead. He gesticulated wildly at the grocer pulling down the blinds. The man swung over his indicator to read 'Closed'. 'Friendly here,' Johnnie muttered, and gave a prod at the air with two fingers.

'Stop that,' Tina warned. 'We can make do, come on.'

On the journey down she had purchased a few items, and now she beat three eggs for scrambling, adding grated cheese. They drank teabag tea without milk, using artificial sweeteners from her handbag.

'Will that do for now?' she asked him when they had eaten.

'It's summat, any road.'

As darkness fell it grew very cold. They found a one-bar fire, then ran out of slot electricity. Tina sat huddled in her duffle coat. Johnnie was acting tough, but looked blue. When they stepped outside to experience the strange empty night, by the pure water under the clear Cornish sky, hearing as they stood still the shuffle and beat of the sea on the shingle, Tina exclaimed that it was warmer out than in. Going inside again, the air struck her and she gasped, 'What is this, what have we come to?'

'A fuckin' igloo,' Johnnie said.

This was so lugubrious, so unexpected that Tina's eyes widened and she broke into laughter. 'Young man,' she gurgled, 'there's only one thing for it.'

In the bed they hugged each other fervently for warmth, yelping at the cold sheets. 'God, you're bony,' she muttered, not for the first time. 'Come here, I'll warm you up.'

In this alien, distant place, with only themselves to think about, Tina forgot about her need for strong drink at these moments. She caught him to her with bold arms, lifting him higher in fun and being shocked anew by the fragility of his skeleton. How little there was of him!

Johnnie responded more freely than he had ever done – she could only guess why. For the first time he opened his mouth against her flesh. His hands moved about, to know her. This was so surprising that she exclaimed, 'Oh.' Even in the dark she could tell he was fascinated by her skin, following it where it led him, shyly, then not so

240

shy. She felt sharp love, as if for a real lover, unable to see him curled on her like a baby. 'Oh, you!' she crooned, and rocked him to and fro. Animal heat spread from her to him, wrapping them both. She gave herself up to the night, her bone-tiredness, him. The grisly grey morning light when it came found him wide awake on the same pillow as her. She slept on. He got out, dragged on his chilly jeans and a sweater and let himself out stealthily to explore the little beach. Wavelets of translucent sea were ebbing away, with tiny shushings.

He came in to find the electricity flowing, the kettle on. She had been to the shop and now was sponging herself with a flannel over the washbasin, her big soaking wet breasts tipping and rolling. He hung in the doorway to the poky bathroom and she ordered him to clear off, this was private.

'What's the door doin' open then?'

'I forgot.'

'I like lookin'.'

'All right,' she said, touched, 'only I'm a bit shy.'

Ignoring this, he said, 'I wish I could do that.'

'Wash me?'

'Ar.'

'Another time, maybe. Don't you want any breakfast?'

They sat down to eggs and bacon, fried bread and a pile of toast. 'Oh, I'm hungry. Are you hungry, Johnnie?'

The question was unnecessary, but saying it made her feel homely. She thought of all the things she might be doing at this moment instead of what she was doing, sitting here in this cold white cell at a wobbly table with a boy who seemed to accept whatever was put in front of him, wherever he was.

Oh, but she liked to feed him and see him eat! Her heart warmed, it was a good feeling being here, a good thing they were doing. She felt peaceful in his company, she gained virtue by serving him, yet was curiously sufficient, satisfied in herself.

'Are you or aren't you?' she cried. 'Speak to me!'

Famished, his mouth full, he nodded at her with a

comical expression on his face, wolfing away at his breakfast.

35

At the weekend they went on a series of unplanned excursions by foot, only returning to their cell-like room for meals. Tina was prepared and willing to use the car, even to take a trip into Plymouth if Johnnie expressed a wish for something livelier. He made no mention of anywhere but the beach, which seemed to magnetise him. In the village they saw numbers of people who appeared to be holidaymakers, gazing around and pointing. The one and only beach café still had its shutters up. A stringy man showed himself in a doorway with a broom in his hand, and Johnnie asked him in a nice voice if they were opening for Easter, starting with, 'Excuse me.'

'No,' the man said. He shut the door promptly.

Johnnie began to mutter under his breath and made a show of picking up a rock to heave, weighing it in his hands. Tina wasn't fooled. She led him away firmly with his hurt pride.

The weather remained quiet, cloudy but dry. Now and then a pale sun made a showing, and sometimes the bright sunshine seemed to blow at them in gusts, coastal fashion. They walked out to the ruins of a fort which could be seen half a mile away on the shore line as they rounded the first bluff.

'When were it built, this fort?'

'I'm not sure if it was the Great War or the last one. Anyway, to repel an invasion.'

'Who by? The Germans?'

'That's who we were fighting, yes.'

'Could have been the Italians.'

'Never. They were the ones who advanced backwards.'

'Tha's clever!'

The fort when they reached it was nothing much, vandalised for its scrap iron and left mutilated; shattered heaps of concrete lay everywhere. Behind it, just visible in the trees and rhododendron, was a solitary house surrounded by wild gardens. The lane from inland ran down past this house and vanished in a patch of grass, in the middle of which stood a spick-and-span piece of apparatus, grey-painted wood and metal, for emitting fog signals. Tina and Johnnie came upon it from the ankle-twisting rocks of the foreshore, and Johnnie ran forward eagerly to examine it. Tina wanted to walk on and see the house at close range. 'Hey, look, imagine living there,' she breathed.

'Creepy,' was all he said.

On Sunday they set out in the other direction. If they kept going, they would come to the farthest point of the headland and confront the open sea. From the cobbled square where the local bus arrived and turned, they found a gap leading to a railed, earth path and went tramping up behind new bungalows, each one with a view of the bay.

'See these coastguard cottages we're coming to, Johnnie?'

'These 'ere?'

'Yes. They were built in the last century to keep an eye on the beach.'

'What for?'

'Because of all the smuggling that was going on.'

'Did they catch any?'

'Not at first. If you got caught you could either spend five years in the navy or three in Bodmin jail.'

'How you know all this?'

'There's a book about it in the flat.'

Soon they were high over the village, on a long, straight track tunnelling deeply through trees, with pines below their feet towards the sea, dizzy poles of trunks zooming up at them. Far below they could see rocky fissures churning with mad foam. Johnnie kicked exuberantly at the rotting leaves as they swung along. 'Look!' Tina cried, pointing. A grey squirrel shot along a branch in ripples like a snake.

At a spot where the track forked and narrowed, a

signpost told them to expect a coastguard station down the lower tunnel. They kept to their level route and went on. Bluebells flowered in a dim, ghostly mass, shining, steely blue sheets spread over the upper slopes. Elms and sycamores rose out of them in the lovely peace.

'Where's this come out in the end?' Johnnie wanted to know.

'On the Point.'

'You read that in your book an' all?'

'Yes!'

Out of the woods and on the nibbled turf of the Point, Tina was at once intoxicated by the light and air and the huge mysterious body of water ahead, a sea that was lead-coloured like the sky, which silenced them by its presence and seemed too immense ever to be able to move, and yet was clearly, stunningly alive and stirring, from far below right out to the horizon. Johnnie took a brief, startled look at it and then tore over to a concrete bunker sunk in grass and brambles. He disappeared. She heard him calling excitedly through the gun slits. Later, when Tina asked what he had liked best about the day, this was the high spot for him.

Easter Monday she remembered later as a terrible day. A cold wind blew off the sea, but Johnnie was set on a swim even if he froze in the attempt. 'All right,' Tina said, 'but not far out. I don't know about here, how safe it is. There might be dangerous undercurrents. It looks harmless enough, but who knows? If you sink, what am I going to tell your mother?' She laughed, uneasily.

His noncommittal reply, and something fugitive about his expression, caused her heart to contract. Why was he shutting her out? She lost him altogether and her heart chilled, so that she had to ask, 'Did your mother raise any objection to your coming with me?'

'Did she wha'?'

'I'm asking if she minded.'

'Don' expect so.'

'What sort of answer is that? Johnnie, stop playing around and give me a proper answer.'

245

'Can't.'

'Can't what? Why can't you?'

'Cause I don' know.'

'Don't know?'

'I left her a note, see.'

'You did what?'

He began to mumble. 'It worn any trouble. It'll be a'right. No use arguin' with her, like,' he whined. 'Stop lookin' at me like that.'

'You said you'd asked your mother. You said so!'

'When did I?'

'Are you saying you don't remember? Because if you are then you're a liar.'

'No I ain't!'

She was glaring at him now with hatred. At the top of her voice she yelled in his face, 'Oh, fuck you!'

'What's up wi' yer?' he muttered, and went white.

Immediately she began to rush about, packing. 'What you doin' that for?' he moaned.

She swung on him viciously. 'I'll make it short,' she said. 'We're going back, now, this minute. Hunslett, I wash my hands of you.'

'I ain't goin'.'

'What's that? What did you say?'

'I ain't goin' nowhere with you.'

'Here are the car keys. Go and get in. I've got to hand over the keys of this place and then we'll be off.'

'Not me,' he said.

Tina reddened. 'Why, where are you off to, little man?'

'I dunno.'

'Stop talking rubbish and do as you're told for once.'

'I'm takin' off.' He stared past her, as if down a road or out of a window, his mouth set obstinately against her.

'You're doing what?'

'Takin' off. Ain't you ever heard of runaways? I'm one o' them.'

'Oh are you?'

'I bin one before.'

'I don't care what you've done before. Do you hear me? You're with *me* now and you're coming back with me.

246

That's what you wanted and now you're stuck with it. You're my responsibility. What you do after that is your own business.'

'You can't mek me.'

'I shall go mad in a minute,' she said. 'I really will. I can't stand this.' She took a deep breath and then screamed at him, 'Don't you think of anybody else ever, for a single minute? Aren't I in enough trouble with your mother already? You're not supposed to be here, I shall get the blame for that, and now you think I'm going to go back up there and tell her you've disappeared, you've gone missing, I've mislaid you somewhere – is that it? Is it? Well you've got another think coming, boy. Now get in that car and shut up!'

He stood where he was. She left him and went to hand over the keys and explain that they were leaving early.

With the car started, she asked him whether he was getting in or not. She was beyond caring what he did. Johnnie refused to look at her. When he did, his eyes were without light, his mouth tight and curdled. He walked up to the car stiff-legged with disgust and opened the rear door. Inside, he sat directly behind her and as low as possible.

He stayed there, motionless and ugly like a gnome, sunk in speechless gloom, all the way to the Midlands. They pulled in to a garage forecourt for petrol and she twisted round to him.

'I'm a horrible bitch. I'm sorry.'

'You can't 'elp it.'

She began to cry, then pulled herself together. 'You gave me a terrible fright,' she confessed.

'Why?'

'I don't know. I hadn't expected it, that's all.'

'No.'

'Please come and sit with me,' she said humbly. 'Is there a box of tissues back there?'

On the move again, she asked him in a small voice why he had done it.

He said bitterly, 'What else could I do? Think me mam would have said yes? No chance.'

247

'But what about me? Couldn't you have thought about that?'

He said nothing for a while. She imagined all the interviews he must have had, sounding exactly like this. He said, 'I wanted to come, didn't I?'

'You certainly did. Oh boy.' She smiled wistfully at him.

Descending into the middle of Sheffield, oddly moved to see familiar sights, she dropped him off close to the estate. She said she would appreciate knowing how things were and he said yes, he would be round later.

She was far from sure. She was fairly certain she had seen the last of him, as she drove sadly in the direction of home.

38

He came on Thursday afternoon. Tina was having trouble
with the gas. Always nervous of it, she had smelled what
she thought might be a leak and informed the Gas Board.
They had promised to come at once; that was six hours
ago. She opened the door in a thick sweater. Johnnie
came in rubbing up and down his arms. 'Cold enough to
freeze a brass monkey's in here.'

Tina observed him warily, then forgot her misgivings
when she saw that his teeth were chattering, his colour
sickly. 'Aren't you well? Have you got a chill?'

'Might have,' he said plaintively.

'Then you ought to go home and get into bed.'

'We keep rowin'.'

'Who does?'

'Me and me mam.'

'I'm not surprised. Was she mad at you for going off
with me?'

'Not 'alf.'

'Oh Christ. I hope you told her the truth, that I thought
she knew. Did you say that?'

'Yes.'

'Go home and get to bed, Johnnie.'

'Can I get in yourn?'

'Why, what's the point? You'll only have to get out
again.'

'Can I?'

'Oh, go on.'

In a way she was glad. Seeing him now made her
a little sick with apprehension, and she was afraid her
resentment might compel her to say something hasty
which she would afterwards regret. She wanted to ask
him things but decided to wait for a calmer time. If she
had felt more composed she wouldn't have panicked
about the gas. For the first time since Nick had moved

out she wished that, instead of being alone, she was with someone who made sensible unemotional remarks and scoffed at her attacks of nerves. She wished she was dull and safe in a routine like everyone else, absolved from herself.

An hour passed. There was a loud knocking on the street door. Expecting the gas men, Tina went into the hall, opened the door and found Marilyn standing in the street, her face curiously altered, making weird gobbling sounds.

'Is Johnnie here?' she kept saying.

'Yes he is, he's here . . . '

'Where is he then?' She pushed angrily past Tina.

'In the bedroom,' Tina said, very angry herself now, and shocked. 'He doesn't feel well.'

Dazed, as if trying to wake up, she followed Marilyn inside. Johnnie was sitting up in bed in his T-shirt. His jeans were thrown on the carpet. 'What are you doing in there?' Marilyn said. It came out in a strange gobble. Her body blocked the doorway.

'Keepin' warm.'

'I'll see you later, son,' his mother said, and went out again as fast as she had entered. A door slammed.

'What the 'ell were that in aid of?' Johnnie said.

Tina was struggling for words. She couldn't help it, she laughed. Then she felt enraged, idiotic, sick, in rapid succession. 'Go on, get out of here,' she said, and turned her back. 'Put your clothes on and hop it.' She swung round again. 'How did your mother know you were coming here? You told her, did you?'

'Yes.'

'Why did you?'

'She axed me.'

'I see. And you told her.'

'Yes.'

'You didn't stop to think she might be angry?'

'No.'

'Not after Cornwall?'

He shook his head. 'She ain't bothered about that any more.'

250

Tina stared at him in disbelief. 'Or about you being friends with me?'

'No. Why should she be?'

'Did I dream what just happened?'

'Nothin' did.'

'All right. Oh shit, shit, I'm sick of this crap! All right. Will you please,' she implored, 'put on your clothes and go home? I can't understand anything any more. I think I'm going to scream.' She brought her hand up to her mouth.

Johnnie looked frightened. He scrambled into his jeans and snatched up his anorak and left without a word.

On Saturday morning, as Tina was about to leave for her mother's to collect Jan, a stranger called. His face looked vaguely familiar. Behind him, cars swished through puddles on the blackened roadway. It had rained hard in the night.

'Good morning. Mrs Blecher?'

'Yes.'

'I beg your pardon, I should have been in touch. I'm a voluntary social worker – may I come in for a moment?' Introducing himself as Adrian Bagley, he showed her an identity card in a plastic wallet. He was a young man with an eager manner.

'Is this some mistake? I didn't ask to see anybody.'

'No, of course not.' He was affable, sincere, slightly pompous.

He stood in her living room. Suddenly her heart jumped in her chest. 'Is it about Jan?' she asked in fear. Her throat was constricted and she could hardly speak the words.

'Jan?'

'My daughter. She's not here, she's –'

'No, no. I'm sorry to alarm you. This won't take a moment. I'm acting quite irregularly, off my own bat – you see I was young John Hunslett's social worker. I'm a friend of the family.' He smiled a brief smile of good will.

'So was I.'

'Yes, so I understand. Let me see, how shall I put this?' His eyes went over the room expertly: poor, but in good taste. He expelled his breath to show appreciation. Tina Blecher was not what he had expected. He had been prepared for someone rougher, more hostile. He was quite taken with her. He appraised her swiftly, in quick snapshots, as he had done the room. He found her attractive, very.

'Is Marilyn all right?'

'That's the point – I'm afraid not. She's about to admit herself to a psychiatric hospital voluntarily. In that case we'd have to take her son and daughter back into care.'

'God, no.'

'Mrs Blecher, can I be blunt? Mrs Hunslett has been advised to proceed against you but is reluctant to take that step.'

'Proceed?'

'For indecent assault on a minor. It could be a police matter.'

Tina took this without flinching, staring back. 'I see,' she said finally. 'Whose idea is this? Hers?'

'I'm afraid I can't say. You do understand I'm here unofficially, as a friend, an intermediary as it were. I imagine you'd prefer to avoid any unpleasantness if at all possible. In my experience of these matters the court would place you on probation – assuming you have no police record – but the newspaper reports and so on would be painful for you, I'm sure. Then there's your daughter to consider. How old is she?'

Tina stood as though contemplating, her mind blank. 'Five.'

'Yes, quite.'

'Is this her word against mine?'

'Well, no. The boy confirms his mother's allegations.'

Tina glanced this way and that. For a long moment she didn't speak. 'Nobody has to worry,' she said quietly, 'if that's what you're driving at. I'm moving.'

'Oh, really?'

'Yes.'

'Are you going far?'

'Out of the county.'

He coughed. 'In that case I'll certainly let Mrs Hunslett know. I think that may be sufficient to deter her.'

'I thought it might.'

'I must go. At least I've put you in the picture about the situation as I understand it.'

'Thank you.'

'Not at all,' the young man said freshly. 'Good day – and good luck.'

That's a cool one, he thought, moving off down the street; but nothing hard about her. Not like some of his cases. One thing puzzled him – she didn't look the type. Well, he'd taken a chance, he could have been in trouble there. The sun shone. He walked briskly, in the wet brilliance of the street, smiling at nothing.

Tina sat down, furious with Johnnie and feeling wretched and helpless about him. She held on very tight to herself, afraid that if she let go and began shaking she would fall to bits, unable to stop. She refused to blame herself for the onset of Marilyn's illness, easy though that would have been at this moment. It had happened a number of times and without her involvement. She fought down an attack of hysteria that the words 'indecent assault' threatened to bring on. Hearing them in her mind, hearing the man's voice saying them, she felt sickened. One emotion after another overflowed in her.

She had told the truth – she was planning to move. In the event, she left sooner than expected. A junk dealer gave her a knock-down price for her bits and pieces of furniture. She wrote to Jan's school to withdraw her, and was gone in the space of a week. She attempted a dignified, sorrowful letter to Marilyn and then tore it up as hypocritical.

A fortnight later an envelope postmarked Bakewell came for Jenny. In the terse letter Tina said she was living with her mother for a while as a temporary arrangement. Sam had died of cancer which had spread incredibly fast, and she, Tina, was four months' pregnant. She definitely wanted to keep the child. She was going to London, and then afterwards she thought she might try living in South

Wales, where she had a cousin. She had heard that the people there liked babies, and they were left-wing, she added, for Jenny's amusement and approval. 'Let's hope I have a left-wing baby.'

The next day, knocking on the street door of Tina's old place, Johnnie noticed that there were no curtains at the front window. This was Tina's living room. He kept knocking until someone came. It was Julie from upstairs.

'What do you want?' she said.

'Is Tina in?'

'She's not here anymore. She moved out.'

'When?' he asked stupidly, not knowing what else to say.

'The other week. You're Johnnie, aren't you?'

'That's me,' he said eagerly. Suddenly he liked this solemn creepy woman. He thought she was about to give him a message, a personal word just for him. All she did was stare blankly at him.

'She's gone,' she said, and began closing the door.

'Where to?'

'She didn't say.'

The door closed in his face. He stood staring at it, then went mooching off down the street, keeping close to the wall as he always did when he was alone.

A letter came addressed to Marilyn. It had a London postmark. Inside the envelope was a letter to Marilyn and a note for Johnnie.

Dear Marilyn,

I hope you are keeping well and not letting things get on top of you. You deserve to have some luck. Well we all do. I am in London now with a friend, it's only temporary so I won't give you an address, I shall be moving soon. There is a lot of temporary work for typists which is why I came, because I need to earn some money for myself and Jan. Whether I shall save anything in this place is another matter. Another thing, I wanted to say how sorry I am if I was the cause of upsetting you about Johnnie, though it was none of my doing. He liked to come round and I liked having him. He's a good lad and he thinks the world of you. Don't let anybody tell you different. If he's a bit hard to handle sometimes it's only growing pains, he's doing the best he can in the only way he knows. I hope this all makes sense. I know how you worry about him. Well my feeling is he's going to be all right. So take care of yourself. Remember me to the girls.

Love, Tina.

To Johnnie she had written:

I feel sad Johnnie at the way I left without seeing you again, you should have had a proper goodbye from me, and I never said it, well it's too late now. That's life I suppose. Be a good boy and look after your mother. Tina.

Johnnie's mother must have been the source of the information he heard later from Eileen about Tina going off to London. He didn't get his note. In Marilyn's mind, London was an enormity into which people fled and were lost forever; and perhaps in Tina's case she wanted it to be true. Nevertheless, to Johnnie it was a real place. Didn't his own sister live there?

He was two months with foster parents, then arrived one night at Sue's address in Shepherd's Bush. It was early June.

'Johnnie, good lord! How did you get here?'

'On the coach,' he said gravely. In fact he had hitched down, lying to drivers about his age.

'Come in, then. Are you on your own? It's late, isn't it?'

'I thought you could put me up.'

'Honest, Johnnie, I can't really do with you. Look at my condition.'

'Just for the night.'

'What are you up to, eh?'

'I thought I'd come.'

'Well you have. What about our mam, does she know?'

'Not exactly,' he said, and grinned.

'You're a little devil. She'll be worried sick.'

'I left her a note.'

'Saying what?'

'I was comin' to see you.'

She was looking angry; then she smiled. How she had changed, how adult she seemed! Then she furrowed her brow. 'You haven't run off?'

'No.'

'Honest.'

'Straight up I haven't.'

The next day he wandered aimlessly in the direction of Hyde Park, staring ironically into people's faces, footloose, jingling his change. He would live here one day, he promised himself. This was where Tina, his friend, lived. He walked with a little swagger because it was a fine day, bright with chances, the sun slanting down, and he had talked his sister into letting him stay another night. On his way out she had given him a pound to spend.

He strolled along like a young cat that was purring away inside to itself for no reason. In the jammed flood of Oxford Street he saw at least three Tina-like women appear and vanish in the crowds ahead. At that distance, though, it might have been the same person coming into view and then blocked, hidden. That was possible. In this city anything was possible. Once he dodged along in and out of the gutter to catch up with one, before she turned her head and he realized his mistake.